THE RIVER
AT NIGHT

THE RIVER
AT NIGHT

ERICA FERENCIK

R A V E N BOOKS

LONDON · OXFORD · NEW YORK · NEW DELHI · SYDNEY

Raven Books
An imprint of Bloomsbury Publishing Plc

50 Bedford Square
London
WC1B 3DP
UK

1385 Broadway
New York
NY 10018
USA

First published in Great Britain 2017

British Library Cataloguing-in-Publication Data
A catalogue record for this book is available from the British Library.

ISBN: HB: 978-1-4088-8657-1
TPB: 978-1-4088-8658-8
ePub: 978-1-4088-8659-5

2   4   6   8   10   9   7   5   3   1

Printed and bound in Great Britain by CPI Group (UK) Ltd, Croydon CR0 4YY

To find out more about our authors and books visit www.bloomsbury.com.
Here you will find extracts, author interviews, details of forthcoming
events and the option to sign up for our newsletters.

For George

There was clearly felt the presence of a force not bound to be kind to man. It was a place of heathenism and superstitious rites, to be inhabited by men nearer of kin to the rocks and to wild animals than we.
—Henry David Thoreau

Before

March 20

1

Early one morning in late March, Pia forced my hand.

A slapping spring wind ushered me through the heavy doors of the YMCA lobby as the minute hand of the yellowing 1950s-era clock over the check-in desk snapped to 7:09. Head down and on task to be in my preferred lane by precisely 7:15, I rushed along the glass corridor next to the pool. The chemical stink leaked from the ancient windows, as did the muffled shrieks of children and the lifeguard's whistle. I felt cosseted by the shabby walls, by my self-righteous routine, by the fact that I'd ousted myself from my warm bed to face another tedious day head-on. Small victories.

I'd just squeezed myself into my old-lady swimsuit when the phone in my bag began to bleat. I dug it out. The screen pulsed with the image of Pia Zanderlee ski-racing down a double black diamond slope somewhere in Banff.

My choices? Answer it now or play phone tag for another week. Pia was that friend you love with a twinge of resentment. The sparkly one who never has time for you unless it's on her schedule, but you like her too much to flush her down the friendship toilet.

"Wow, a phone call—from you!" I said as I mercilessly assessed my middle-aged pudge in the greasy mirror. "To what do I owe the honor?"

Of course I knew the reason. Five unanswered texts.

Pia laughed. "Hey, Win, listen. We need to make our reservations. Like, by tomorrow."

I fished around in my swim bag for my goggles. "Yeah, I haven't—"

"I get it. Nature's not your thing, but you're going to love it once you're out there. Rachel and Sandra are chomping at the bit to go, but they have to make their travel plans. We all do."

With a shudder, I recalled my frantic Google search the night before for Winnegosset River Rafting, Maine.

No results.

"Just wondering why this place doesn't have some kind of website. I mean, is it legit?" I asked, my voice coming out all high and tinny. Already I was ashamed of my wussiness. "I'd hate to get all the way up there and find out this is some sort of shady operation—"

I could feel her roll her eyes. "Wini, just because some place or something or someone doesn't have a website doesn't mean they don't exist." She sounded windblown, breathless. I pictured her power walking through her Cambridge neighborhood, wrist weights flashing neon. "It's a big old world out there. One of the reasons this place is so awesome is because no one knows about it yet, so it's not booked solid before the snow's even melted. That's why there's space for the weekend we all want, get it? This year, it's the world's best-kept secret—next year, forget it!"

"I don't know, Pia . . ." I glanced at the time: 7:14.

She laughed, softening to me now. "Look, the guy who runs the white-water tours is a good friend of my dad—he's my dad's friend's son, I mean, so it's cool."

"Can't believe Rachel would want to—"

"Are you crazy? She's dying to go. And Sandra? Please. She'd get on a plane right now if she could."

With a wave of affection I pictured my last Skype with Sandra: kids running around screaming in the background, papers to correct stacked next to her. When I brought up the trip, she'd groaned, *Hell, yes, I'm game for anything—just get me out of Dodge!*

"Wini, listen up: Next year—I promise, we'll go to a beach somewhere. Cancún, Key West, you choose. Do nothing and just bake."

"Look, Pia, I'm at the pool and I'm going to lose my lane—"

"Okay. Swim. Then call me."

I tucked my flyaway dirty-blond bob—the compromise cut for all hopelessly shitty hair—under my bathing cap, then hustled my stuff into a locker and slammed it shut. *Do nothing and just bake.* Did she really think that was all I was interested in? Who was the one who rented the bike the last time we went to the Cape? Just me, as I recalled, while all of them sat around the rental pouring more and more tequila into the blender each day. And my God— we were all pushing forty—shouldn't *awesome* and *cool* be in the rearview mirror by now?

I crossed the slimy tiles of the dressing room and pushed open the swinging doors to the pool. The air hit me, muggy and warm, dense with chlorine that barely masked an underwhiff of urine and sweat. Children laughed and punched at the blue water in the shallow end as I padded over to my favorite lane, which was . . . occupied.

It was 7:16 and frog man had beat me to it. Fuck.

For close to a year, this nonagenarian ear, nose, and throat doctor and I had been locked in a mostly silent daily battle over the best lane—far left-hand side, under the skylights—from 7:15 to 8:00 each weekday morning. Usually I was the victor, something about which I'd felt ridiculous glee. We'd only ever exchanged the briefest of greetings; both of us getting to the Y a notch earlier each day. I imagined we both craved this mindless exercise, thoughts freed by the calming boredom of swimming and near weightlessness.

But today I'd lost the battle. I plopped down on a hard plastic seat, pouting inside but feigning serenity as I watched him slap through his slow-motion crawl. He appeared to lose steam near the end of a lap, then climbed the ladder out of the pool as only a ninety-year-old can: with careful deliberation in every step. As I watched the water drip off his flat ass and down his pencil legs, I realized that he was making his way to me, or rather to a stack of towels next to me, and in a few seconds I'd pretty much have to talk to him. He uncorked his goggles with a soft sucking sound. I noticed his eyes seemed a bit wearier than usual, even for a man his age who had just worked his daily laps.

"How are you?" I shifted in my seat, conscious of my bathing cap squeezing my head and distorting my face as I stole the odd glance at the deliciously empty lane.

"I'm well, thank you. Though very sad today."

I studied him more closely now, caught off guard by his intimate tone. "Why?"

Though his expression was grim, I wasn't prepared for what he said.

"I just lost my daughter to cancer."

"I'm sorry," I choked out. I felt socked in the soft fleshy parts; smacked off the rails of my deeply grooved routine and whipped around to face something I didn't want to see.

He took a towel and poked at his ears with it. A gold cross hung from a glimmering chain around his thin neck, the skin white and rubbery looking. "It was a long struggle. Part of me is glad it's over." He squinted at me as if seeing me for the first time. "She was about your age," he added, turning to walk away before I could utter a word of comfort. I watched him travel in his flap step the length of the pool to the men's lockers, his head held down so low I could barely see the top of it.

My hands trembled as I gripped the steel ladder and made my way down into the antiseptic blue. I pushed off. Eyes shut tight and heart pumping, I watched the words *She was about your age* hover in my brain until the letters dissolved into nothingness. The horror of his offhand observation numbed me as I turned and floated on my back, breathing heavily in the oppressive air. As I slogged joylessly through my laps, I thought of my own father rolling his eyes when I said I was afraid of sleepaway camp, of third grade, of walking on grass barefoot "because of worms." As cold as he could be to my brother and me, not a thing on earth seemed to frighten him.

I had barely toweled myself off when my phone lit up with a text from Pia. A question mark, that was it. Followed by three more. Methodically I removed my work clothes from my locker, arranging them neatly on the bench behind me. I pulled off my bathing cap, sat down, and picked up the phone.

My thumbs hovered over the keys as I shivered in the over-heated locker room. I took a deep breath—shampoo, rubber, mold, a sting of disinfectant—and slowly let it out, a sharp pain lodging in my gut. I couldn't tell which was worse, the fear of being left behind by my friends as they dashed away on some überbonding, unforgettable adventure, or the inevitable self-loathing if I stayed behind like some gutless wimp—safe, always safe—half-fucking-dead with safety. Why couldn't I just say yes to a camping trip with three of my best friends? What was I so afraid of?

Pool water dripped from my hair, beading on the phone as I commanded myself to text something.

Anything.

I watched my fingers as they typed, Okay, I'm in, and pressed send.

2

The lurch and grind of the Green Line trolley, Monday morning, inbound to Boston. Sunshine filtered through grimy windows, warming the solemn faces of nine-to-fivers dressed for the office, coffee cups in hand. My phone beeped with a new message from Pia, titled Our fearless leader! :), CC'ed to Rachel and Sandra. Attached were photos of our white-water rafting/hiking guide, twenty-year-old University of Orono student Rory Ekhart.

Shoulder-length dreadlocks, eyes the exact green of an asparagus mousse we'd featured in our March issue. And that bursting-wide smile—as if whoever took the photo caught him laughing or in a state of joy. Rangy and loose-limbed in a mud-spattered T-shirt and shorts, he stood straddling a narrow stream banked by white birches. An ax dangled from one hand. The tagline read, "Third-year SAG undergrad Rory Ekhart on the trail maintenance crew this summer at Orient Ridge."

In another shot he could have been anyone: a man in a cyan-blue parka, hood up and slightly cinched, face in shadow as he held a hiking pole up in victory or salute against a setting sun behind a snowy mountaintop. In the last photo he wore his biggest grin yet; he was beaming. In full camouflage he knelt on some treeless ridge, the butt of his rifle jammed into the dirt next to his kill: an enormous moose lying on its side, its expression even in death both ferocious and sad.

I finally got around to Pia's actual message, where I found myself scrolling through a bottomless list of camping gear needed for the trip: thirty-nine must-haves, not including optional stuff such as playing cards and a sun shower, whatever that was.

I looked up to see I'd traveled two stops past my own. I jumped to my feet, my mind a whirlwind of wicking shirts, water-purifying tablets, carabiners, Dr. Bronner's soap, and bags with hooks I imagined suspended from trees and batted about by the giant paws of nine-foot bears on their hind legs. Excusing myself through jam-packed commuters to the platform, I hoofed it hard back up toward Beacon Street and my office, regretting my choice of stacked heels and narrow skirt, which shortened my already-short stride.

I leaned into the heavy doors of our charming but drafty 1920s brick building. Yanked skirt into place, tucked wind-whipped hair behind ears, jabbed at the going-up button. Five floors later the doors sucked open on the fancy new marble-floored lobby, which had felt empty since we let our receptionist go. An antiquated concept, receptionists, we'd been advised at our last come-to-Jesus meeting. Nobody wanders in from the street, after all, and those with appointments know to expect their visitors at the agreed-upon time. With our numbers so low overall, it was time to cut the wheat from the chaff, or whatever expression was used to send this lovely and kind—if a bit scattered—single mother of twin girls packing. But in the end I didn't have much to say, considering my position as a graphic designer at *Chef's Illustrated* had been cut in half just months before, my benefits shredded, and my corner office lost to our new Web developer, a toothy, twenty-five-year-old MIT grad named Sarah.

I tossed my purse on my desk, picked up the phone, and dialed.

"Pia Zanderlee," she answered breathlessly.

"You okay?" I tapped my machine awake and inhaled the smell of hot German spice cookies and *bûche de Noël*. We'd been testing Christmas recipes from around the world the past few weeks. "You sound like you're running."

"I'm trying to make this eleven o'clock flight to Chicago."

I heard muffled airport sounds in the background: kids crying, flight announcements, snippets of conversation amid the bustle of travel; sounds from lives I imagined were immeasurably more exciting than my own. "Should I call you back?"

"No, just . . . what's up?"

"Well, I got that list and . . . what's 'wicking'?"

"It's fabric that pulls sweat away from your skin, so you don't get cold and get hypothermia."

I googled *wicking*. An athletic young woman jogged across the screen. Animated steam flowed out of her shirt and shorts. "What about coming with me to REI sometime, help me pick out some of this stuff?"

"I don't know, Win, maybe. I've got a pretty full schedule till we head out."

But you live one town away, I thought. *What's the big deal? Help me navigate this terrifying list you sent.* "You traveling a lot these days?"

"Just this one trip for work. I'm back Thursday." I heard her drop the phone, then pick it up. "Everything okay, Win?"

"Yeah, great, just . . . you know, wanted to be ready for the trip." I cleared my throat. "So . . . will there be bears, do you think?"

Pia laughed. I pictured her: tall and graceful as she stood in line for her flight, chestnut hair shining under bright airport lights. Confidence emanating from her; an utter lack of self-consciousness making heads turn. People mused, *How do I know her? From television? The movies? Somewhere . . .* "We're gonna be fine, Win. Bears don't care about us. You leave them alone, they leave you alone."

"What are water shoes?"

"Can I call you when I land?"

"Sure," I said, knowing she would forget. A few taps on my keyboard brought up *shoes, amphibious.*

"Go to REI. You'll be cool. I'll see you in a few weeks." She hung up.

Loneliness occupied the air around me, even buzzing as it was with chatter, with activity, with sounds and smells. *I thought it would be fun,* I mentally said to the dial tone, *to go to REI together. To laugh about amphibious shoes. To hang out and catch up before we go on the trip. You know, like friends do.*

Alissa, one of an endless parade of college-age interns we cycled through *Chef's,* joined me at my desk. She wore a sad black dress inexplicably off the shoulder, an odd choice for such a cold morning, her pale flesh sprayed with freckles. I tugged at my turtleneck, trying to remember the last time I'd even made a stab at such a casually sexy look.

"So," I said as I pulled up the May issue, "what brings you to graphic design? Are you a closet fine artist?"

Her eyes were bright blue but oddly sparkless. "No. I can't draw at all."

"But you want to be a pixel pusher? A Photoshop queen like me?"

"I guess," she said. "I couldn't think of anything else to do." She crossed pasty white hands in her lap and stared at my screen.

Wow, I thought, *if you're this uninspired by life at your age, you'll be a corpse by the time you're thirty.* But I held back from sharing how I mastered graphic design in the dark ages with T squares and X-Acto knives. I'd learned through experience that kids don't think it's cute or even interesting—who can blame them?—that you happen to be a dinosaur. It frankly scores you no points at all.

I also spared the poor girl my history as a fine arts major at the Massachusetts College of Art, where I met my now ex-husband, Richard Allen, a printmaking student I used to make love to in empty classrooms redolent of oil paint and turpentine. I didn't disclose to Alissa that we knew our union was forever, that we swore to be artists no matter what it took, and that we were going to change the world.

Instead, I pulled out some "before" and "after" proofs. "My job is to make the food look even better than it is—better than Suzanne can make it look, even with all her lenses and filters. See? I toned down the red in the red velvet cake here, got the frosting to glisten, sexed up the greens in the arugula, painted some dewdrops on the tomatoes . . ."

Alissa cocked her head and doled me out a real smile. "Pretty cool."

For a second I almost felt hip, pitiful as that sounds. I shuffled the proofs into piles, sat back, and regarded her. Hell, maybe she had something to teach me. "So, have you ever been white-water rafting?"

Her eyes grew wide, and for a moment I thought I detected life there. "Oh my God, no, I would never do that."

I felt validated, terrified. "Why not?"

"I just think it's stupid. It's so dangerous."

"But—you've never been?"

"No. And I don't hang glide either, or go skydiving." She recoiled a bit. "Why, you're not going, are you?"

"Actually, yes," I said. "I'm afraid I am."

I was brain-deep in an ad for oatmeal raisin cookies around three that afternoon when a rush of mortality flooded over me. I felt my face flush as a vague nausea suffused my body. It felt almost like embarrassment, as if I were caught deleting raisins as I was waiting, at age thirty-nine, for my life to begin. I'd tasted whiffs of this particular despair in the past, but never like that day. Maybe it was the swimmer and his dead daughter, maybe it was Alissa's horrid youth freshly in my face.

All I could bring myself to do was gaze out the window, marvel at how a few flakes earlier in the day had gathered forces into an early-spring blizzard of stunning beauty. I tried to recall—couldn't—the last time I'd taken up a paintbrush with any joy, or for how long I'd forced the square of my creativity into the round hole of graphic design. The day Richard left, I'd stuffed my paintings-in-progress, sketchbooks, easels—every last brush and tube of paint—in the back of my closet. I wanted no more to do with that part of myself.

So I forgot about beauty—not only what bloomed in my head and wanted to be on canvas, but the wild, flawed kind all around me. In fact I'd been whoring up the imperfect for a paycheck for so long I couldn't face the real anymore: my aging body, the crash and burn of my marriage, the unfathomable loss of my brother, Marcus.

I gathered my things, made some noises about not feeling well, and left the building.

Snow swirled around me, making magic every detail of the city. No cornice, streetlamp, awning, or tree branch had been left unadorned. Packed trains rumbled by as I trudged along Beacon Street, but I had no interest in climbing aboard—even in my office clothes and heels—to arrive at my lonely apartment sooner than absolutely necessary. Block after block, all I could think about was Marcus and how much he had loved the snow.

One winter night, when Marcus was five and I was eleven, we built a snowman together in our front yard in Lee, Massachusetts, by the light of a full moon. I picked him up in his snowsuit and held him—his face flushed with excitement—as he popped in buttons for eyes, poked in a carrot for a nose, and with profound concentration arranged pebbles in a crooked smile.

I set him down and we stood back, admiring our work. He signed, red gloves moving quick, "Is snowman alive?"

Snowflakes melted on his cheeks, stuck to his long black eyelashes. I said and signed, "No."

Brow furrowed, he signed, "Is it dead?"

"No." I shook my head slowly, wondering.

"It's alive!" he signed, then smiled and clapped and ran off into the yard. Snowsuit swishing, he pelted me with snowballs.

That night I tucked him in. It was something I did a lot since Mom slept most of the time and Dad worked constantly. Marcus signed with a hopeful smile, "No school tomorrow?"

I looked out at the driving snow and wind. "Probably not. But don't get too excited. Just go to sleep." I smoothed his hair and kissed him on the head. He was asleep in seconds.

In the morning, Marcus thundered down the stairs and leapt on the couch to look out the window. He made a small, agonized cry and sprinted to the door. Before I could stop him, he flew outside in his Bugs Bunny pajamas, barefoot. The world of white was gone and our yard had turned muddy and green again. The temperature had risen in the night as a rainstorm blew past; our snowman had melted into a gray lump, eyeless, carrot nose drooping into the dirt.

"Snowman dead!" he signed again and again, his face contorted with panic. He tore off to the far corners of the yard, frantically gathering the pitiful lumps of snow that remained. Suddenly he stopped, overwhelmed by the futility of it all.

I ran outside and caught his arm as he raised it to hit himself in the forehead, already bruised from some earlier disappointment. I wrapped my arms around him, straitjacketing in all his little-boy rage and pain, feeling his hitting energy ripple through him in cycles until he had worn himself out. Shirtless, Dad stood in the doorway, a hulking shadow. "He okay?"

"It's all right, Dad. He'll be fine in a few minutes."

Marcus smelled like warm milk and Lucky Charms. With hot, sticky fingers he signed into my chest, "Want snowman alive. Sad, sad."

I tucked his body tight into mine, my knees wedged in the cold, muddy ground. He felt like part of my body, the part that cried and laughed and let myself be silly. "It'll snow again, Marcus," I whispered. "And we'll make an even better one." I held him as long as I could, knowing that sooner than I wanted to, I'd have to let him go.

Thursday

June 21

3

I am usually the lightest of sleepers, but the night before we left for the river I sank so far down a black well of dreams that I had to claw my way to the surface to wake up. I dozed through the polite chirp of my alarm and would have gone on except for a windstorm that blew in just before dawn. Dry, cool gusts howled through my open window, shuddering the panes. I slept caged in a dream of violence with no narrative, like a scrap of old film with only a few frames still visible. On a clothesline, a torn linen dress twisted in the wind. A haggard face of a woman turned away again and again, always in shadow, an endless loop. I never got to see her eyes. I jerked awake in a sheen of sweat to the frantic clanging of a wind chime over my kitchen window, a set of bells inside an oblong pine box my mother had given me that only ferocious storms brought to life. It was as if she were trying to tell me something.

Through all this, my cat, Ziggy, snored on, all eighteen pounds of him slung across my feet like a sack of warm sand. As I slid out from under him, he gave me this look, a mix of *How dare you* and *What the hell are you doing, it's just past five and we usually sleep till at least six thirty*. When I reached down to scratch his head, he gave my hand an uncharacteristic swat of his hefty paw, claws in evidence. I snapped my hand back and sat up, regarded him. Saw the lion in him clearly.

I spoke softly to him, cooed my eternal adoration; watched the lion fade and my kitty return. He thumped to the rug and swaggered toward the bathroom, resigned now to the early hour, then leapt to the counter for his morning brushing. Feeling the same tug of routine, I followed him there, but with a silvery jolt of joy down my spine, I let it go.

I buzzed in my friends. First came Pia's laugh, big and hearty, followed by several sets of clomping footsteps up my uneven, narrow back stairs; more laughing, then a clattering sound as if something ceramic had broken. A heavy sound, full of wood. I remembered the dead ficus I'd stashed there and forgotten to take out to the garbage, and ran to open the door.

All six feet of Pia burst through the doorway and rushed to hug me with abandon—nothing ladylike—she even lifted me a little off my feet and held me there for a second, knocking the wind out of me. She smelled like Dunkin' Donuts and lavender shampoo. In jeans, a flannel shirt, and sneakers—despite her height and ropy length—she managed to look feminine and even a touch gamine. Behind her, Rachel, a blur of kinky-curly black hair and glasses and red fleece, flew up the stairs and threw her arms around the two of us. Sandra, carrying the remains of the potted plant, set the wedges of shattered clay on the kitchen counter and smiled when she saw us with our arms wrapped around each other. She joined the hug party, and we all stood screaming and laughing with a kind of joy that is simply not a daily event.

"I broke your pot!" Pia said, still jumping up and down.

"Fuck the pot!" I said, jumping with her.

Soon we loosened our clinch but stayed in a tight circle as we held hands. "It's been so long!" Rachel said.

"Forever!" Sandra said, breathless. "Wow, look at us. We're all so beautiful!"

"What's our secret?" Rachel said. "We get younger every year."

"Chardonnay," Pia said as she let go of my hand and Rachel's. "And adventure!" Face flushed, she reached back to free her auburn hair from a tangled ponytail. It tumbled down, still damp, to her shoulders. With no pretense at a style, she swooped it back, knotting it into the rubber band. As the rest of us poured ourselves coffee and chose our favorites from a box of Italian pastries I'd picked up in the North End the night before, Pia rummaged in her day pack, extracting a dog-eared map of Maine, which she flattened with her palms on my kitchen table. I loved how it looked: a tangled burst of roads, rivers, lakes, and towns and no onus on me to pretty it up or make sense of it.

I placed our coffee cups on the map's four tattered corners. Every part of it wanted to scroll up—keep the secret of where we were going—but under Pia's hands the mountains rose up, the streams flowed and became real. Lush forests rang with life, and blue rivers snaked north to Canada. I squinted at the map, blurring everything so I could picture the curvature of earth, water, and sky, conjure the creatures that crawled, swam, and flew there.

"So listen up," Pia said, quieting our chatter. "Today we drive to base camp, which is in this tiny town called Dickey, here. About nine, maybe nine and a half hours." Pia's long finger skimmed across two feet of map, stopping at a small black dot where all the red and the green lines—roads—ended, as if by agreement. Just a blip on the map surrounded by swaths of forest and wriggling blue lines. I felt some of my old terror, but—with my friends around me—drawn to these mad green places and rushing waters, I thought, *This is my world too; don't I deserve the chance to see it?*

"Excuse me while we join the twenty-first century here." Rachel flipped open her iPad and tapped at her screen. "Find out a little more about where the hell we're going . . ." Funky horn-rimmed glasses exaggerated her already large blue eyes, while the chronic worry lines between her brows deepened. She found Dickey and pulled out the detail with her thumb and forefinger. It looked like an intersection, not much more.

Rachel frowned as she scrolled up and down. An emergency-room nurse for over a decade, she possessed both an affection for detail and a mounting exhaustion with surprises. So really, who could blame her for preferring her rare time off to be trauma-free? There wasn't much, life-and-death-wise, she hadn't seen. I almost couldn't bear to listen to some of her stories about horrific wounds or accidents, or the things people did to themselves—or each other—that landed them in emergency rooms. But her sharing of these episodes was the preamble to most of our visits. Listening seemed the least I could do.

"Holy crap," I said. "Maine is freaking huge. I never realized . . ."

"Ogunquit. That's as far north as I've been. Remember?" Grimacing, Sandra pointed to a red dot only an inch of map space north of the New Hampshire border. "Ugh. That's where Jeff and I spent our honeymoon."

"So what's up with the ole Jeff-ster?" Rachel said, smirking.

"Please," Sandra said, waving her away. "Let's not go there yet."

"Just think," Pia interjected, oblivious. "Over five thousand square miles—"

"—of trees, trees, and more trees—" Rachel said, shaking her head.

"—and gorgeous wild rivers. And we're going to explore one of the least traveled ones. See places no one's ever seen before. In fact, it's possible we won't see anybody but each other for five days."

I wasn't 100 percent sold on why any of that was a good thing, but I nodded along with everybody else as we sat down at my kitchen table. Unphotoshopped maps were one thing, zero civilization another.

Rachel flipped her glasses on top of her head, folded her arms, and leaned back in her seat. At about five feet five inches she was just a touch taller than me but wiry; the stress of her job no doubt kept her slim. "Funny thing, Pia, you never mentioned Rory's little scrapes with the law."

Pia took a healthy bite of her chocolate-dipped cannoli. "He sold some pot. He's human."

Rachel swiped through a few more pages on her screen. "Disorderly conduct, trespassing, vandalism . . ."

I watched a vein throb on Rachel's forehead, imagined the blood pulsing there even as I tried not to. As per her habit, one leg bounced over a crossed knee. My stomach tightened down.

"That was years ago."

Sandra stiffened. "Like, how many years ago?"

"Ask Rachel," Pia said as she stood up and stashed her coffee mug in the sink. "She's the one with the stats." She turned, facing us. "Look, he's twenty now. He went through a bad stretch—he told me all about it—but he's cleaned himself up. Back in school, going for his degree, trying to start his own business, all that good shit. What are we, fucking angels?"

Sandra reddened and looked away. Rachel shook her head, issued a profound sigh, and leaned back over the map. "Where do we actually get in the river? Show me."

Pia pointed and we all stared at a blue line on the map, then the topographical view on Rachel's iPad, as if this blip of color told us anything.

A hollow feeling bloomed in my chest. "Where's the closest town?"

"Eagle Lake. Thirty miles east, plus or minus."

"Do cell phones work up there?" Sandra asked. I thought of her eight-year-old boy, Ethan, born with one leg shorter than the other but recently clocked at an IQ of 158. His thirteen-year-old sister, Hannah, was his fierce protector at school, where kids bullied him without mercy.

"We are venturing into the Allagash, my friends, part of the un-organized territory." Pia slipped on her day pack, squinting into the sunshine that streamed through the window. "Lots of stuff doesn't work up there. We ready to rock and roll?"

Rachel shook her head and got to her feet. "Oh, screw it, Pia. You may be one crazy bitch, but you know in the end we follow you around like a bunch of little ducklings."

The tension left the room as we all broke into laughter. Pia and Rachel gathered themselves at the door.

Pia glanced back at Sandra and me. "Ladies?"

"Go ahead," I said. "We'll be down in a second."

Sandra collected pieces of the ceramic pot into a pile, scooping up the dirt with her hands. "So"—she smiled up at me—"tell me the truth, Win. You nervous about this trip?"

"Me? Nervous about taking off to the middle of nowhere for five days? Never."

We shared a laugh as she tossed the shards of clay into the bin, slapped the dust off her hands. "There's nothing wrong with a little fear. Keeps you sharp."

"What about you?"

"I'm more afraid of not going, I think." She planted her hands on ample hips and gazed into the middle distance. A stunning mix of Japanese and Polynesian, Sandra Kato-Lewis (we called her Katy-Loo sometimes, or just Loo) had a face like a heart and shining black hair almost too thick to braid. Some mistook her dreamy quality for spaciness, but fifteen years of knowing her had taught me that nothing got by her. Speaking up for herself was another matter entirely. So was grasping her own beauty, so brutal was she to herself about carrying some extra pounds on her petite frame. "Don't you want to break away for a while, have a big adventure? With the kind of year you've had, honey, this may be just what you need."

She, of everyone, understood best the depth and breadth of my grief for Marcus. How Richard's abandonment had slapped me senseless.

"I guess I am a little nervous." My shoulders sagged. "What's my problem, Loo? Why can't I just go with the flow?"

She laughed and hugged me. "You can do this, Win, you'll see. Fresh air, the woods, nature, every second not planned to death— you'll love it! And don't worry, I'll protect you from the bears, and from everything else too. Come on, let's get out of here."

After Sandra disappeared down the back stairwell, I watched Pia and Rachel mill about as they waited for us in the grassy courtyard. I knew that no one and nothing can keep you safe; still, I let Sandra's words comfort me as I huffed my cumbersome pack up to my shoulders. Resting it on the kitchen counter, I said my goodbyes to Ziggy, who had jumped up, purring his loudest. He rubbed against me hard, falling on me with all his weight as if to say, *What are you, nuts? Stay here with me.* I kissed his head, inhaling his delicious Ziggy smell, assured him a neighbor would be by to keep his bowl brimming till I returned, took a good look at the place that had seen far too much of me lately, and left.

4

We jammed ourselves into Pia's Chevy Tahoe, which had been meticulously packed with ground sheets, extra tents, groceries, wet-weather gear, emergency rations of dried (astronaut!) food, even a fly rod. She was always fanatically prepared for any eventuality. None of us had ever lacked for sunblock, a lifesaving Chap Stick, an extra sweater, raincoat, or beach umbrella. But the obsession with preparedness was tempered by her lust for risk. At the dude ranch in Montana we visited one summer, Pia put in a bid to ride "the most crazy-ass horse on the playa," so she could, as she put it, "challenge" herself. Conversely, I couldn't bring myself to saddle up even the most ancient mare because I couldn't get over that horses weighed thousands of pounds, as well as my certainty that whichever one I chose would sense my terror and hurl me off like the cowgirl wannabe I was.

But Pia actually did it. After pestering the head cowboy at this place, threatening to never come back, hinting she'd post negative reviews, and finally agreeing to sign away all liability, she climbed up on this unbroken horse the cowboys were afraid to touch, this Appaloosa demon that snarled and bucked, in seconds tossing her up and over its gorgeous head. I watched her do a complete flip in the air, landing hard on her hands and ass. I stopped breathing as I waited for the dust to clear. She got up and walked away, though she'd sprained a few fingers and bruised her tailbone badly. That was it, she declared, "for the day." But I got this feeling, talking to her about it later over beers at the ranch's Horseshoe Saloon, that she almost wished something more dramatic had happened, something that would have somehow freed her from herself.

I hoped there wouldn't be too much bucking-bronco craziness this time around. My wish—the one I always had when we four were together—was that our energies would balance each other out. Sandra's tact and level head would temper Rachel's sharp wit and knack for speaking the truth, regardless of the consequences. As for Pia—and I could only guess about the others—being with her made me feel buoyant, more robust somehow. In shape by proxy. Because as much as she drove me to distraction, she always seemed to be vaulting toward the unknown with her own brand of wonder and a fearlessness utterly foreign to me. It took me out of myself. I was looking forward to that.

As Pia navigated the city streets, I found myself gazing from the front passenger seat at all the things I would no doubt appreciate later: telephone wires, streetlights, houses with running water, indoor toilets, and warm beds. I wondered what kind of snakes Maine had, what sorts of stinging insects. A large part of me wanted to back out, feign sickness, make my phone ring with some sort of emergency: "Wini, we can't get these carob chips out of this month's Devil's Food Vegan Brownies! Get in here now!" I forced myself to do none of the above, but still felt shivery even in the morning sun.

We crossed the Tobin Bridge, following signs to points north. Boston receded quickly behind us in a blue-gray haze.

"So, Pia," Rachel said, leaning forward from the backseat. "What are the chances we freaking croak on this river?"

Pia laughed. "Statistically? You're in more danger driving home from work than you are camping or white-water rafting. Some drunk asshole could be flying at you the wrong way and, splat, it's over! And it's only a long weekend, for crying out loud. Rachel, seriously, what are you missing by going on this trip?"

"A little weeding," Rachel answered gamely. "Was going to clean out the shed with Ryan. Maybe hit the mall on Sunday." Ryan was her third husband, a maxillofacial surgeon with a couple of teenage daughters a few years older than her two sons. She tended to marry well—divorce even better—but never seemed to truly settle into domestic peace.

"Sounds life changing!" Pia said. "Sandra?"

"Correct papers. What else? Maybe sort out the kids' school clothes for fall." Sandra taught undergraduate English and philosophy classes at her local City College of Chicago.

"Win?"

"Get some food for Ziggy. Swim. Scare up some freelance work."

Pia's hands flew up from the wheel to dismiss us before she settled her sunglasses down over her eyes. "I rest my case."

Pieces of the northern suburbs slipped by, places so familiar I failed to see them anymore, so with a kind of gladness I felt myself letting go and drifting off. Sometimes the engine's rumbling beneath us lulled me into a misty consciousness through which I watched Pia drive—one of her favorite things to do—then felt myself falling off again into a firmament of my own design. I woke as we crossed the bridge from Portsmouth, New Hampshire, where I gazed down at the sparkling blue water of the Piscataqua River and sailboats bending under a brisk wind.

"We almost there?" I mumbled, mouth sticky.

Pia laughed. "Not exactly. Two hours down, seven to go, not counting pee stops." She glanced at Rachel and Sandra, fast asleep in the backseat. "So, you've been swimming?"

I made a dismissive sound and slid back in my seat, suddenly aware of my girth. Pia worked out like a demon, CrossFitting and triathlete-ing her way through her weekends. I'd never heard of her embarking on a bike ride less than twenty miles long, or taking it easy in any way, and she dieted herself down to a slapping slimness, like she could slip into the stingiest size 8 but could also lift a Volkswagen off a small child if necessary, because she would know how to use her back and legs in such cases, and she'd be able to commandeer the proper help—I pictured stunned passersby doing her bidding—on the fly.

"I do my laps a couple times a week. For whatever good it does me. Look, Pia, I'll never be you—"

Her jaw tightened. "Just getting older stresses out your body. You need to be ready for that, get a jump on it. Besides, I want to be ready for when the shit hits the fan in this crazy-ass world."

"So you can what, outrun global warming?"

"So I can outrun what global warming will do to so-called civilization."

I pictured Pia sprinting gazellelike from tsunamis and rising ocean tides, from famine and disease. "So you're going to be one of those survivor types who lives in the woods and shoots at whatever happens by?" Don't know why I was being such a priss. Maybe part of me thought she might actually try it, and it scared me. "Live off the land?" I teased a little more gently.

"Something like that." She downshifted as roadwork narrowed the two-lane highway to one. An actor-handsome cop waved us by, his eyes resting an extra moment on Pia's face. She didn't seem to notice. "Don't make fun of me."

"I'm not, Pia, I just don't really get what you're planning here."

She looked at me with such intensity. "It's like this, Win. I'm sick of everything, you know? I'm sick of dragging my ass around the world to fucking sneaker expos, hanging around with hip-hop"—finger quotes—"'stars' and hawking the latest line of bullshit miracle insoles guaranteed to make you run faster or lose weight, some lie like that. I'm dying of boredom tweeting about ankle support and bubble soles and how the right sneaker can make your life worth living."

"I spend my day making photos of flank steak look juicy."

"So you know, then, what we're up against."

I thought I knew, but watching her face, I wasn't sure.

"That's why I go on these trips," she said with a shrug, "because what I do is meaningless."

I gave her a look. Impatience, I guess; a touch of Pia-exhaustion, already.

"Don't you get it? The world we know is dwarfed by the worlds we don't. Why not explore them all? Being out there in the wilderness, you have no idea what'll happen, really. It could be just you and this gorgeous night sky, or maybe you're surfing and some big-ass wave comes at you, and if you don't ride that sucker, it'll pull you under and have you for lunch, or you might turn a corner on a hike and there's some beautiful deer and her little fawn—now *that* has meaning, all of those things, and I need more of that and less of trying to make money so I can pay bills to live in a way I just don't care about anymore."

"But money lets you go on all these trips."

"I get it, yeah, still—I don't need half the crap I have. I don't need my fancy-ass condo. I'm never home anyway. I've saved a little money. I could quit my job tomorrow and live out somewhere on my own for a couple years"—she gestured at the passing trees, rolling farmland—"and just make it on my own. I feel good out there, by myself, not having to count on anyone or anything."

The "anyone" comment cut me. How could she think she didn't need people, didn't need her friends? The "anything" bit struck me as bullshit as well. I studied her as she drove, planning some sweet life under the moon and stars where she was magically fed, kept warm, clothed, and entertained.

"God, I want a cigarette."

I laughed and loved her again. "When did you quit last?"

"Two weeks ago." She shook her head in disgust. "Ever been in a room with thousands of high-tops? It's hell. Sneakers reek, you know. The rubber. The chemicals."

"Just quit the stupid job." I held up her fancy phone.

She finally laughed. "Let me get through this trip. Then I'll give notice. Dump the condo. Disappear. Get off the grid."

"Do you even know what that means, Pia?"

She gave me an odd look. "Of course I do, Wini." She shrugged. "You'll see."

Minutes later we pulled over at a rest stop and tourist-information area. Bored middle-aged and older women in green vests milled around with too much information to give and not enough travelers to give it to, so they loaded us down with all manner of maps and brochures. Sandra and I couldn't tear ourselves away from a floor-to-ceiling map of Maine on one wall that showed all the collisions with moose over the past year. Each red dot a crash. There were so many on our route—straight up into the Allagash—it looked as if someone had splashed blood from Portland to Canada.

Sandra stared at the red dots as she gnawed on the black licorice she'd bought at the gift shop. "This can't be real."

"Afraid it is," said one of the women in green. "My best friend's sister and her new husband died on their wedding day in 1973, right after the ceremony on their way to the reception. Boom, like that. Gone. But it was fall, you know, rutting season. Moose are crazy then." She let go a creepy laugh. "One whiff of something good, and they just tear across the road, don't look both ways!"

"Jesus Christ," Rachel said under her breath as she walked around a nine-foot monster plastic moose in the middle of the room, its antlers grazing the twelve-foot ceiling.

"You'll be fine," the woman said. "It's summer. Just keep your eyes out."

I trailed behind as Sandra, Pia, and Rachel burst out of the building, howling and wisecracking about rutting season and two-ton mammals hurtling across highways for hot moose action. As we settled back into the car, it occurred to me that we were already dressed for this new world. Rachel in her red fleece vest, multipocketed hiking shorts, and ankle-high boots; Sandra in her purple Patagonia jacket; Pia outfitted head to toe in REI's finest. Already I sensed a profound separation from the normal, even from the people we had been that very morning in my cozy apartment in Boston.

A thought came to me that I couldn't force away: *What we are wearing is how we'll be identified out in the wilderness.* This middle-aged woman in this blue jacket, these nylon pants, these Timberland boots. I noticed for the first time a small zipper on my new hiking shirt and counted three cunningly hidden pockets, one on either side of my waist and one on my sleeve, where I could put things like keys, or maybe a note telling someone what had happened to us. I imagined what I might say, if I'd be able to conjure anything profound. All I knew was that no one expected us home for five days, and no one I knew expected to hear from me at all.

5

After Portland, where the rocks in the bay at low tide looked like slumped-over bodies, the miles seemed to fall away more quickly behind us. Green became the rule, man-made structures the exception. Trees shot up taller somehow, sprouted thickly even in the median strip, creating a forest there just as lush as the one rushing by on our right. Trucks roared past us groaning with the incomprehensible weight of hundreds of massive logs. I thought longingly of the outlets in Kittery we'd blown by, all the charming B&Bs in the Yorks and Ogunquit. Rachel googled "northernmost Starbucks in Maine," mumbling something about stopping there for "one last latte." Sandra did her best to hold on to NPR, but we lost even that around Lewiston.

Pia drove with her steady intensity, refusing all offers to pitch in behind the wheel. We drove through tiny, eerie towns, each with its own weather-beaten church. Bradley, Old Town, Olamon, LaGrange. Hand-scrawled signs said things like CONNECT TO GOD ANYTIME, NO BROADBAND NEEDED. Five- or six-headstone cemeteries, sometimes oblong or even triangle-shaped, perched on the crests of hills or overlooked rushing streams, providing for the dead some of the best real estate around. We passed trailer parks with no name: just half a dozen metal lumps clustered together as if for warmth or safety. Snowplows, firewood, and boats lay scattered on front lawns, apparently for sale. Real estate signs announced 30,000 ACRES AVAILABLE NOW—with no phone number—while immense barns imploded slowly on abandoned lots. One house we approached looked kempt and tidy, as though some happy person lived there and enjoyed the upkeep, but as we passed and looked back, we saw a nightmare of rotted frame and plastic sheeting, hastily duct-taped and flapping in the breeze. A woman in a house-coat and backless slippers stood on a weed-sprung driveway and stared at us, arms crossed hard.

For miles we found ourselves stuck, cursing, behind a guy driving a rust-bucket flatbed stacked high with unnamable farm machinery, tools that threshed and cut and hoed, and what looked like an exploded washing machine dangling over one side. Each time we tried to pass, he'd swerve to the left and cut us off, dis-gorging a clanging engine part or length of pipe that Pia master-fully navigated around. Finally he hooked a crazy fast right onto an unpaved road, fishtailing in a cloud of red dirt. The last we saw of him was his fist waving out the window before he disappeared into deep woods.

The wind picked up as the day cooled from T-shirt to long-sleeve weather. It seemed intent on muscling our car into the other lane, whipping big clouds full of personality across a bright blue sky. A wooden cross and withered roses marked a death at the side of the road. I wondered who had died there, and if anyone still thought of them.

Surrounded by the comforting presence of my friends, I let myself think about Richard; how he still haunted the apartment. Half-awake each morning I would reach for him across the bed, only to find a terrible emptiness. As I gazed out the window at all the green rushing past, I tried to picture what he might be doing at that moment. Perhaps locking up after office hours at school; he'd done his time and gotten tenure, had been able to stomach academia where I could not. Or maybe he was busy trying to get the new grad-school girlfriend pregnant. After three miscarriages, I'd given up on trying to save our marriage with kids. It seemed as if anything made of Richard and me could not take hold in my barren body. When does hope turn into masochism? We ended up getting dogs, big ones that died in a decade, less, then turned to cats, which broke our hearts only slightly less often.

Fairly early on, I went from the one he loved to the one he'd married. I felt it at holiday parties, at art openings for his students, when his faculty meetings stretched into dinner, then later and later arrivals back home. From the beginning I never felt attractive or hip enough for him, always slightly amazed he'd picked me. After a while I figured it out: not only did I put my creative goals second to his—I'll never know why—but I was a great audience for him. Problem was, ever-lovelier fans in the form of female graduate students cycled in yearly, until he finally chose one. All I had to do was open my eyes. But it's my Scottish stock. We're stubborn, and when we say yes, by God, we mean it. We hold on forever, choking the life out of the thing we must have. My terror of being alone had one result: I was alone.

After Millinocket, we left the speed and efficiency of the interstate and took Route 11, the road that would take us all the way to Dickey and the lodge. English radio stations turned French. We spun the dial, fascinated. French rock and roll, French talk shows, the news in French, French easy listening. Signs welcomed us to Aroostook County, while evidence of civilization—including houses—became rare. The ones we saw looked abandoned; creepers veined across walls and nosed into windows. Bushes muscled over rooftops, joining others in a living canopy, all with the intent of digesting the structure beneath.

We drove mostly in silence, as one does when entering another world, through Grindstone, Stacyville, Knowles Corner. Here, signs of initial excitement about a new business venture appeared to be followed by the marks of a much-longer-lasting and enduring despair. A colorful placard announcing DADDY'O'S LOBSTER ROLLS! sported a grinning cartoon lobster, but the arrow pointed to a darkened trailer that tilted helter-skelter in a swampy field. Five dollars bought you a rain-soaked mattress propped up by chairs in a front yard.

By the time we reached Patten, it seemed people had even given up on naming things. A sign outside a rotted motel said MOTEL. The word GUNS painted in twenty-foot letters covered one side of a barn. On a hand-painted shingle, a restaurant announced that FOOD was available within.

But soon, even those sad enterprises faded away. The woods on either side grew dense, impenetrable, alive with their own logic and intelligence. Mile upon mile unspooled before us with nothing man-made in view, no shotgun shacks, no stores, nothing. The world of the forest dwarfed our strip of holed-out road. I sensed green-sprung life anxious to swallow it; imagined trees and plants breaking up the road as they burst through, erasing it as if it had never existed. It was beautiful and frightening to see how nature didn't give two shits about houses, buildings, and bridges, that it would shrug us off the first chance it got. I opened the window a few inches. Afternoon blew in on a fresh, clean breeze—full of chlorophyll and wood and cold mountain water—it shocked me fully awake and almost made me high.

"I hate to say this," I said, "but I have to pee."

Pia tapped the brakes, heeding signs that signaled sharp turns ahead. "We all do, I think. Want to practice going in the woods?" She glanced over at me with a smile.

I shivered. "There has to be something around here."

More green flew past, broken only by vast unnamed lakes bordered by tall pines standing sentry. Ignoring the double no-pass lines in the road, a truck loaded with Porta-Johns roared by. Pia's hands whitened on the wheel.

We drove another half hour, then forty-five minutes, everyone's bladder bursting by then, as we bumped along on pitted tar dead level with the earth. I had the sense that anything could come brawling out of the woods, snarl across our path, then disappear into the forest on the other side.

Down a short dirt drive, a log cabin butted up into a hillside, a satellite dish stuck to its flank like a wart. A wooden sign that read SUNDRIES/GUNS/TACKLE/BAIT hung askew over the door. A smaller sign underneath—an afterthought—read CARHARTT QUALITY BOOTS. A yellow light burned behind glaucous windows. Heavy pine branches clawed at the car as Pia crawled along the shoulder. I was struck by the sameness of the view in all directions, the sheer density of growth, and how easy it would be to lose our way just steps from where we sat. I felt watched, though I couldn't remember feeling farther from civilization.

Pia turned to us. "Ladies? Your thoughts?"

"Perfect setting for the next *Saw* movie," Sandra said.

Pia rolled her eyes. "*That's* the spirit, Katy-Loo."

"I'd like to say I don't have to go that bad, but . . ." I shifted in my seat as I watched Rachel's jaw work at her gum.

She cursed under her breath as she reached for the door handle. "When in Maine . . ."

The rest of us got out of the car in thick silence, shaking out our stiff limbs and brushing ourselves off. Daylight lingered, a peach-colored glow through blackened trees. Pia did some kind of runner's stretch, groaning a bit. We waited until she was done, then followed her down the dirt path to the entrance of the store.

A muscular metal spring slammed the torn screen door behind us as we stood awkwardly in front of a vast candy display. Necco wafers, Rolos, giant Hershey's bars, Bonanza taffy, Now & Laters, licorice pipes, all coated with a gray film of dust. Behind the counter in the receding darkness a lightbulb ticked and swayed over a display case of sausages coiled like snakes in a white metal pan. Flies buzzed behind the glass or turned quietly on yellow strips that curled from the ceiling.

Claws scratched across a wooden floor. A filthy dog, a mix of pit bull and something hairless and bigger, scrambled out from behind the display case and galloped at us, tongue flapping. It licked our hands as if frantic for our love, wagging hard its half-a-tail, which looked lopped off for no particular reason.

Pia and Rachel cooed at it. They lifted its pig-pink muzzle up to their faces and accepted every kiss, while Sandra and I more or less backed away after a quick pat or two. We wandered past wooden bins overflowing with potatoes, carrots, and radishes still wearing their sooty coats of earth. Jars of homemade bread-and-butter pickles, pots of "Marge's Blubarb Jam" cinched with cloth checkerboard hats, knitted dolls staring through button eyes, and moose-themed ashtrays crowded the shelves. Coffee burned in a crusty pot on a glowing hot plate.

"You get offa them ladies, Corky." A squeak, followed by a whiff of acrid body odor mixed with a sweetish onion smell.

We all turned to the source of the voice, the smell. Another squeak, more shrill this time, like rusted metal parts grinding together. A circle of light cast by a banker's lamp on a glass counter illuminated a massive pair of hands spread open on a magazine.

We followed the light up to a gelatinous mountain of a man, maybe five or six hundred pounds, wearing overalls and no shirt, sitting in what looked like a mattress folded in half and fitted into an armchair of sorts. Uplit, his tufted red eyebrows grew untended. His features nestled close together, a face meant for a smaller man but tucked in between rolls of flesh and jowls. A neat, oddly fussy mustache had been waxed into two perfect tips. I doubted he could get out of the chair contraption on his own.

"That's okay," Pia said, trying to shed Corky, who had begun to hump her leg, its age-spot-stained back curved and straining. "I love dogs."

As we approached, he flipped his magazine shut and slipped it somewhere under the counter, a practiced move. Underneath the glass shelving all manner of bullets glowed copper and silver in rows of cardboard boxes. A crossbow hung from the ceiling. Girlie magazines, scratch tickets, chewing tobacco, and more candy and gum filled the racks and displays behind him, disappearing into the gloom.

The man looked at all of us but especially Pia. The old up and down. "What can I do for you ladies?" His voice was surprisingly high and soft.

"Actually," Pia said with her blinding Pia smile, "we've been driving since Millinocket and could really use a bathroom right now, if that's okay."

The mustache twitched. The man took a pen, tapped it twice on the counter, then pointed with it at a sign behind his right shoulder without turning his head. It read, BATHROOMS FOR CUS-TOMERS ONLY.

"Oh!" Pia said. "Of course." She glanced at the girlie mags, the bullets, the crossbow, and stepped back to the candy aisle, returning with a Snickers bar.

He rang up her purchase and, expressionless, head-gestured to a door in the shadows behind him. "Light's outside on the right."

Pia thanked him with embarrassing intensity as the rest of us pretended to be fascinated by rolls of duct tape and fishing tackle. She emerged a few moments later and nodded at Rachel, who visibly braced herself before heading to the bathroom.

"Excuse me?" the man said, staring at a point somewhere toward the top right corner of the ceiling, one pupil drifting skyward independently of the other.

Rachel halted in her tracks. Like a statue, arm out for the bathroom light.

"What did I just say?" he said flatly, curling a meaty thumb at the sign. "Customers only."

"Oh . . . oh." Rachel reached out for one of the magazines, her hand jumping back as if burned when she saw what kind they were.

Gravel crunched under tires outside. The muffled sound of men's voices, citizens band radio, switched off. A truck door slammed. Through the greasy windows of the store, the dead eyes of a doe regarded us, its body roped to the bed of the truck, slender front legs crossed daintily. Its velvet black nose still glistened with moisture. Heavy footsteps and the creak and bang of the screen door.

A big young man in a John Deere cap blustered in, still full of the rush of killing. Head down, he muttered, "Hey, Vincent," wrenched open the glass door of the case that held the sodas, and tipped back a bottle of Fresca, almost finishing it in one go. He wiped his mouth, heard the silence. Turned to look at us, his face long and wolfish. "Whoa, Vince, got yourself a party."

Rachel's hand still hovered near the magazines. She moved it a bit to the right. "I'll have a . . . couple of scratch tickets."

"What kind?" the fat man said.

"Whatever's lucky."

He rolled his eyes and swiveled in his mattress chair, its metal innards shrieking, then reached an arm as thick around as my waist up into the darkness and snapped off a couple of tickets. He tossed them on the counter as Rachel slipped into the bathroom. "Looks like you got yourself a real beaut out there, Graham. Need anything to dress 'er?"

The hunter took us in one by one, as if we were words in a sentence he was trying to understand. Greasy black hair stuck out crazily from under his cap. Blood clotted his fingernails and stained the ragged hem of the long underwear that poked out from under his shirt. His eyes came to rest on me and stayed there. "Tried to cut her, but my knife is for shit. Mind if I use your—"

"Kit's out back. Knock yourself out. Where'd you bag 'er?" The fat man popped a caramel in his mouth from an open bag of candy.

"Up by the ridge. Got up in my lucky tree, looked down, and there she was. Like it was meant to be."

Rachel, head down, emerged from the bathroom while I grabbed a couple of mealy apples from a bin and a miniature Mr. Goodbar and set them on the counter. The bathroom held its own horrors, but I wouldn't let myself look at them. At that point I would have peed on a pile of body parts.

Old hands at this now, Sandra threw some Wrigley's spearmint on the counter and sped by me as I headed out of the john. Laughing at something the hunter said, the fat man rang up our purchases and tossed them in a paper bag. Pia was bent over the case of bullets.

The hunter sidled up to her, puffing himself out in his red lumberjack vest.

"You hunt?"

She turned and folded her arms. "No. I don't murder beautiful helpless animals."

My stomach churned. *Good God, Pia, don't be an idiot.*

The hunter smiled and took in her height, shape, and heft in a glance. "But I bet you go ahead and knock back a big juicy burger, right?"

"Actually, no. I'm a vegetarian."

Such a lie.

Sandra skittered out of the bathroom. The hunter narrowed his eyes, reached into the soda case, and pulled out a can of Genesee cream ale. He snapped off the tab and mouthed off the foam. "So, where're you muff munchers headed?"

"Ease up, Gray," the fat man said, handing Pia the paper bag. "That'll be $8.98."

Pia paid, her hands shaking.

"Let's go," Sandra said, as if we needed encouragement. We stumbled over each other in our rush to the door, where the hunter had placed himself, blocking our exit.

"I didn't hear an answer," he said.

Standing inches from his sweaty armpit, I inhaled the hoppy burp of beer, his unwashed hair; watched the veins pop on his forearm as he drank. Half of his ring finger was missing, the end purplish and bruised looking. No one moved.

"We're rafting the Winnegosset," I said so softly I almost couldn't hear myself. Even as I said it I wanted to slap myself.

He shifted his weight. The boards groaned under his feet. "Some asshole named Rory?" He said *Rory* like he suddenly had shit in his mouth.

"Yes, he's—"

"Don't tell me, you're paying for the privilege?"

"We—"

He stared into me, his eyes rheumy and rimmed with red. "That Ekhart bastard's got no right to the Winnegosset, no more'n me or you or anybody else. That's God's river, just like the Penobscot and the Dead." His voice was even. "Rich pricks like him and his dad should be shot and hung up to bleed out—"

"Gray, what did I just tell you?" the proprietor said in his signature monotone. He finally looked at us. "Have a nice evening, ladies."

With a lusty "Fucking bitches," the hunter dropped his arm heavily to his side and stepped away from the door, just enough for us to pass through.

6

We were still howling with laughter when we turned onto Round the Pond Road, which—according to our directions—led to the lodge. After ten hours of driving, I couldn't imagine anything more wonderful. Outside our windows, mountain lakes mirrored what light remained, ghost clouds in a denim sky. Night was upon us. Only our headlights and the dotted yellow line helped us navigate the way to a warm dinner and bed.

"Hey, Pia, you old muff muncher," Rachel blurted. "Are we almost there?"

We all guffawed. "You know, the thing is," Pia said, tapping her brakes as the road narrowed and hugged the banks of a pond where bullfrogs croaked and plopped, "you fucking bitches need some patience, okay? We're about a minute away, I think."

"'I'm a vegetarian,'" Rachel singsonged. "Yeah, right, Pia! You're half bacon, for crying out loud."

"Don't talk about food," I chimed in from the back. "I'm freaking starving."

"For some muff!" Sandra tossed in, and we all cracked up again, helpless.

We arrived at a cleared patch of land and something like

civilization. Industrial lights glowed greenish in the windows of a long, low building, while a few spotlights near the roofline attempted to breach a profound darkness. Half a dozen cars huddled in the lot. Smoke, caught by an evening breeze, twisted up to the sky.

"So, Pia," Rachel said, "who else is staying in this place?"

"Day hikers mostly. School groups, lots of Scouts. But the river's a good fifteen miles from here, which is why Rory's driving us most of the way before we hike."

Stiff and sore, we tumbled out of the car into night air at least twenty degrees colder than Boston's balmy high seventies we'd enjoyed that morning. Pia and the others gamely hefted their packs and headed to the lodge while I tried to hustle mine to my shoulders. Not happening. Finally I cradled it in my arms like an enormous baby and carried it up the stairs into the warm light of the building.

A ragtag collection of comfortable-looking couches and beat-up La-Z-Boy chairs crowded the lobby. The place smelled of cedar and turkey and mashed potatoes, a touch of pot. Beyond the couches stretched two rows of cafeteria tables, benches on either side. A crowd of eighteen or twenty people, a mix of college- and middle-aged along with a couple of families with kids, had already sat down with their meals. Latecomers stood among various chafing dishes, chatting as they piled food on metal plates. Talk and laughter animated the place, made even noisier by the clatter of a wide-open kitchen area where young people stirred giant pots of stew and pulled bread from an oven that seemed to take up the better part of one wall. Such a pleasure to heap all that unpixelated homey chow on my plate and dig into its sloppy, steamy deliciousness.

Just as we tucked ourselves in at the far end of one of the tables, a dreadlocked young man, fit and strapping, fairly exploded through the doorway. Though he was well over six feet, his backpack made him appear even taller. He carried a cooler under one arm and a sleeping bag and pad under the other. With an exuberant sigh, he dropped his gear on one of the couches—just in time to receive enthusiastic hugs and high fives from most of the kitchen staff.

Pia still held on to the tray she'd set down a full minute ago. She could not take her eyes off him.

I, on the other hand, was already halfway through my plate of food.

Rachel sipped her iced tea as she watched the scene impassively. "Do you think I should take her vitals?"

Rory glanced around the room until his eyes fell on us or, I should say, on Pia. He bounded over to our table and held out his hand to her. She extricated herself from the bench, stood up to her full six feet, and trotted out that thousand-watt smile, coppery hair shining under the naked bulb that dangled over our table.

"It's so good to finally meet you," she said, glowing like I'd never seen before. They shook hands until he pulled her into a quick but bearish hug.

"You're tall." He folded his arms, considering her. "Couldn't tell that over Skype." He nodded, appearing lost as to what to say after that. She stared at him. We all did. Everyone enjoys beauty, after all. Fitted out in a T-shirt that said U. ORONO AGGIE: DOWN AND DIRTY EVERY DAY, ripstop nylon shorts, a bear-claw necklace, and several rope and leather cuffs around his wrists, Rory made the rounds, introducing himself to each of us with a charming politeness tinged with condescension. Male energy vibrated off him.

His hand was a surprise: big and soft, a student's hand. "Welcome to the Mooseprint Lodge. Are you psyched about our trip? It's going to be kick-ass!"

Pia uncorked a bottle of red wine and filled four plastic cups, skipping Rachel, who hadn't had a drink in years.

"So, Rory," Rachel said, an eyebrow arched, "are you certified to do this sort of thing?"

He nodded his thanks as he accepted the wine. "Absolutely. I grew up white-water rafting. Do it every second I'm not in class. I'm in the aggie program, as you can see," he said with a smile and a nod to his shirt. "Someday I want to run my own sustainable farm with livestock. Make cheese, stuff like that. Live communally. I'm pumped about it."

"That sounds fantastic," Pia said. "I've always wanted to do something like that."

"For real?" Rory said, echoing all our thoughts. Of all the hot items on Pia's bucket-list blog, none of them involved cheese. "I'm just not cut out for some office gig. I'd want to die in, like, two days." He glanced behind us at the steam tables piled with food. "I'm going to grab some chow before they close up. Be right back."

We watched as he heaped his plate with dinner, including two slices of vanilla sheet cake and two glasses of milk from a metal dispenser, before balancing it all on a tray.

"So," he said, threading his long legs between the table and the bench, "how do you ladies know each other?"

We looked at each other and smiled. "Pia and I grew up on the same street," Rachel said. "But we met Wini and Sandra here when we all worked at the same cheesy clothing store, probably fifteen years ago?"

"Everything fell apart the second you washed it," I said. "The stuff was so cheap!"

"Especially with our employee discount of—what was it, fifteen percent off? Remember?" Rachel fell back in her seat, laughing. "We were so excited about that, a whole dollar off some crappy dress!"

"Anyway," I said, "we had so much fun together that we started hanging out and doing things after work."

"Drinking, mainly," Pia said.

"True." Rachel shrugged.

"One year we pooled all our money and took this pathetic little vacation together—"

"—where was it, Rockport? Something like that . . ." Sandra said.

"Gloucester," Pia said. "One-star hotel on a postage-stamp beach—"

"—but we loved it, didn't we?" I said.

Pia dug into her mashed potatoes. "We felt like movie stars. Going out for dinner, sleeping late, not lifting a finger for a whole week. Fifteen years later, here we are."

Even though the stories we were telling were true enough, they couldn't express what all those years meant. Husbands, kids, jobs; then divorces, unemployment, and for some of us new husbands and even more kids. But there had always been us, bound by invisible golden thread the fifty-one weeks a year we were apart. Tied in a golden bow the week we spent together. On the surface it might have been about fun or feeling glamorous or exploring someplace new, but when the world, including our own families, got us down or turned its back on us, we were our own family. Dysfunctional in our own female-friendship way; but our bonds were unbreakable.

"Very cool," Rory said, looking vastly entertained but possibly just humoring us. "But I have to say—hands down—this is going to be your most exciting vacation yet. You ladies realize we're going to raft a river that no one besides me and my dad has had access to before?"

"We were wondering about that," Sandra said. "Nobody owns a river, right?"

He studied her briefly before answering, "It's about access, really. People can get to the river if they hike to it, like we're going to do tomorrow, but it's impossible to get a raft up there without a vehicle. My dad owns a couple thousand acres. He built a private road to the river for our rafting business." Rory poured himself the last of the wine. "Just think, this is the most remote and probably the best white-water rafting anywhere in Maine, and you're going to be able to go home and say you were the first group to hit that water. How's that for the watercooler Monday morning?"

"Fantastic," Pia said. "I love being in the middle of nowhere."

"You are in the *middle* of the middle of nowhere."

"Even better!" Pia turned to him, tucking her knees up under her baggy sweater like a college girl. "I rafted on the Dead once and it was great, but I felt like I was being spoon-fed the entire time, know what I mean? Really coddled. Plus the guide was awful. He made us feel like we were just one more raftload of tourists to shuttle down the river." She rattled on about how she hated being with strangers and how glad she was to be with us this time.

A young woman, red haired and full figured, slid in next to Rory and slipped her arm around him. She plopped a greasy paper bag down on the table. "I saved these for you in case you got in too late. So you owe me."

Rory opened the bag and looked inside. "Awesome, brownies. Thanks, Annabeth."

The woman pushed out her lower lip in a faux-pouty way. Popped back to her feet. She winked at us, then eyed him as she flirtily untied her apron and retied it more snugly around her waist. "Aren't you glad to see me?"

A look of melancholy passed swiftly over Pia's face; I'm not even sure she was aware of it.

"Kinda busy right now, kiddo."

"Ookay." Annabeth twirled away from us. "Be that way. You know where to find me."

He watched her walk away, then turned back to us. "Look, for now, the river is ours."

Pia watched Rory hoover up his dessert. It was gone in three bites. "Well, *I* think it sounds amazing."

"I don't know about that," I heard myself say.

"You're in great hands with me, Wini," Rory said. "I bagged it last weekend with my dad, third weekend in a row. Piece of cake."

My face grew hot as I stared down at the wide planks of the floor.

Rory shrugged. "It's white-water rafting. It's got risks. You can't have a piece of the wild and not go out in the wild. You can watch it on TV from your cozy chair, you can hear about it from your friends, but there's nothing like actually being on a river and showing it who's boss. Are you with me?"

I folded my arms. Felt my friends' eyes burning into me. *My God,* I thought—*how old do you have to be to listen to your gut?* Could I really be the only one not buying into this showing-nature-who's-boss crap? The brave, smart thing would have been to back out, gather my shit, and grab a bus home. Instead I sat all deer-in-the-headlights as my friends waited for me to say something, afraid to stay and afraid to go. I simply couldn't open my mouth to speak.

7

"Come on, guys, let's hit the bathroom." Pia struck out into the night without a moment's hesitation. We followed along behind her, as if she would keep us safe.

The lights in the latrine were kept on all night, and I made a note to myself to be grateful for these small comforts. I was about to step over the lip of cement into the horrid little building when I noticed a beetle of stunning proportions crawling along the concrete floor. It must have been a couple of inches long and an inch or more wide. Rachel bumped into my back as I halted in my tracks.

"What's up—whoa," she said.

Pia was already washing her hands. She turned around and saw what had stopped me. "Come on, Win, don't be a weenie. You'd better get used to stuff like that. It's just a beetle. They don't bite."

Rachel laughed and stepped around me, giving the insect a wide berth. Sandra emerged from one of the bathroom stalls and started to brush her teeth, turning to discover me still outside. She rinsed out her mouth. Armed with a glass she found on the counter, she tiptoed behind the beetle and placed it over the insect. It lifted its enormous black wings and beat at the glass with a *thwapping* sound, its body hitting the sides with such force that it actually moved the glass a couple of inches across the floor.

I washed my face quickly and ran out of there to join the others as they traipsed down a grassy slope to the bunkerlike building at the bottom of the hill. Inside, a group of women in their twenties had taken over one side of the place, filling it up with their gear. Many had already snuggled themselves inside sleeping bags on the top, middle, and bottom bunks, reading books by flashlight or headlamp.

The corrugated-metal ceiling vaulted into darkness over our heads. A canvas tarp suspended from a metal bar separated the men's from the women's quarters. We claimed our bunks: lengths of hard rubber stretched between four poles, barely wide enough to lie down on without fear of falling out. Sheet-metal walls did nothing to keep cold air out; it blew in freely through the three-inch gap between them and the damp cement floor.

With a clatter of boots and gear, Pia banged her way into the building and heaved her pack onto the bunk above mine. She turned in a circle, taking it in. "This is the freaking Bellagio compared to the rest of our weekend," she said with a laugh. At that moment, the lights were cut with a thump. I only realized how loudly they had been humming when the silence rushed in.

Hours later I lay sleepless in the room full of women, some snoring softly, but many—like me—still in search of, if not a comfortable position, at least one where they could somehow fall asleep. Above me, Pia slept in her usual fashion: immediately and deeply. One long arm hung down just a foot from my face. Rachel and Sandra, to my left and to my right, both read by tiny book lights.

I stared up into the shadows remembering the only other time I'd gone camping.

I was twelve years old. My dad, determined to cure his phobic daughter and his mute, strange son with the wonders of nature, drove me and six-year-old Marcus to a lake in New Hampshire one summer weekend. My mother stayed home, no doubt in a paroxysm of joy to be free of us for three whole days.

After helping set up our saggy tent, I wandered down to the beach and waded into murky water up to my knees. Marcus bulleted past and threw himself in, doggie paddling in a circle around me before slipping under the surface like a seal. I felt his small hand grab my ankle. He burst up and out of the water smiling ear to ear.

"Swim with me," he signed.

I scanned the dark water, small waves tipped golden by fading sunlight through gathering clouds. Behind us, Dad washed dinner dishes in the lake. "Tomorrow," I said and signed. "I don't feel like swimming right now."

"Wini is a dummy," Marcus signed, still grinning, before he splashed me hard and dove in again. Wrapped in a blanket at the end of the dock, I sat and watched him swim. Dad called to us about getting ready for bed, but I knew I could ignore his first attempts at gathering us, so I lingered. To the east, diagonal lines of rain connected cloud to water, pitting the surface.

Marcus floated around in a swampy section before he stood up in waist-deep water and began signing to me. I couldn't see his hands very well, so I didn't answer. Pouting, he smacked at the water, clapped his hands, and finally jammed his fists on his little hips.

"Come back here, Marcus, I can't see what you're saying." The first drops of rain cooled my forehead, the backs of my hands. I got to my feet.

He doggie paddled closer to me, blinking as the rain came down harder, then stood up, shoulder deep.

"I saw frog," he signed. He dropped his head back and opened his mouth to catch some raindrops, then repeated himself with exaggerated movements: "I SAW FROG."

A smudge of darkness curled on his forehead, just above his right eye. I squinted through the pelting rain.

Dad called from the beach, "Get outta that water! *Now!*"

"Come on, Marcus. Don't piss off Dad." Neither of us wanted to deal with our father in a rage, and his tone of voice told me he was headed there fast.

Marcus swam closer and stood up. A few yards away now. The paisley shape on his forehead had swung a little to the left. As I watched, it curled up even farther, like the letter *C*.

He reached the dock, climbed the ladder. Stood shivering in the rain. The thing on his forehead multiplied at least a dozen more times across his body. Leeches, their heads buried in his tender boy flesh, hung from his forehead, chest, belly, the insides of his legs.

"Look at me," I said and signed quickly. "Don't look down."

But he did. He gaped at the liver-colored thing writhing near his belly button. A high-pitched scream tore from his throat; tiny fists locked at his sides. I threw my blanket around him and wrapped his stiff body tight, scooped him up, and ran to the beach, where Dad sprinted toward us.

Dad's eyes were wild. His white undershirt, stained pink with fish guts, was plastered to his muscular torso. "What happened?"

"I don't know, I—"

"Give him to me!" He wrenched Marcus from me and set him down. The blanket fell to the sand. Dad looked to me and Marcus and back as if I had put the leeches there. "What the motherfuck-ing hell . . ."

Marcus looked down at himself, then at me, and started flapping his hands like he wanted to fly away, all the time wailing at the top of his lungs. Dad lunged at him and carried him, running full tilt back to the campsite. I ran after them, stumbling in the soft, wet sand.

Dad dropped to his knees outside the tent and crawled in with Marcus, who was completely hysterical, slapping at his head and face. I tumbled in after them.

"Hold him down." Dad scrambled in his knapsack. Hands trembling, he freed a Camel nonfilter from its pack and lit it. Marcus ran around and around the tent in his little madras bathing trunks, arms outstretched to either side, screaming.

I sprang at him, caught his legs, and pulled him into my lap, roping him in with my arms.

Dad held the lit cigarette against the biggest one; it hung down long, twisting and writhing, from Marcus's chest. I could almost see his little heart hammering underneath his pale skin. The thing sizzled and thickened under the glowing cigarette, retreating into its meatiness, blackened, then dropped to the canvas floor.

We all watched it coil and loop, smoldering, as the rain pelted the tent until, with a steady hand, Dad lit the next cigarette.

Two hours later, the three of us pulled into a McDonald's. Dad let us order anything we wanted, as much as we wanted. Marcus got two of everything: two cheeseburgers, two chocolate milk shakes, two orders of french fries. We sat in the red plastic booth mostly in silence, the rain slashing at the gray highway, Marcus cramming himself with food and signing "Good" and "More" every now and then.

I was starving too and busy stuffing myself with all my favorite things—chicken sandwiches, shakes, and fries—but I noticed Dad hadn't eaten much at all. He sat back in his seat, arms folded, alternately staring into space and looking at us like he was disappointed we were still ourselves.

One by one, the book lights switched off and total darkness entered, like another presence. I listened to the trees bluster and fill with wind, creaking and rustling. A few raindrops tapped at the roof here and there before a gust of much colder air blew in through the gap between the walls and the floor as if it wanted in, was looking for us. Soon the rain gathered all its strength and came pounding down.

I wanted to wake Pia and ask what the plan was for hiking and white-water rafting in a storm, if there even was one. Shivering in my sleeping bag, forming and re-forming my makeshift sweater-as-pillow, I couldn't imagine a more miserable thing to do. I lay there ruing the day I said yes to this thing, thinking: *I came on this trip out of loneliness and fear of being left behind by my friends. What good can come of that?*

Lightning flashed, illuminating the narrow slice of ground between the walls and the floor, followed by booms of thunder. With a wave of nausea, I felt in my jaw the shame of how it would feel to stay back, alone in the lodge, forever remembered as the one who—immobilized by cowardice—could only watch as her braver, stronger friends hiked up and over the hill and out of sight.

Friday

June 22

8

Like so many mornings after a torrential rainstorm, the day broke awash with brilliant sunshine and fresh air. Though the sun had warmed the tin room to the point where I'd grown hot in my sleeping bag, the wretched position in which I'd finally fallen asleep had morphed into borderline comfortable.

I gazed at the cot above me expecting to see the impression of Pia still sleeping there, but it was flat. To my left, Rachel's bed was empty too, her bedroll neatly tied. I was relieved to see Sandra still bundled in her red sleeping bag, head tucked down. Like Pia, she was a natural-born sleeper.

Led by aromas of French toast and coffee, I climbed up the hill across grass flattened by the night's downpour. In the distance, our destination: smoke-blue mountains obscured and then revealed by morning fog. I felt equally pulled and repelled. What did the mountains care about our plan to climb them, rafting the waters that divided them? They had eternity before us, and eternity after us. We were nothing to them.

• • •

We swung out onto the main road—Sandra, Rachel, and me crammed in the backseat—and drove about twenty minutes or so before Rory turned sharply onto an unmarked dirt road not much wider than his truck. Up in front, he and Pia kept up a lively conversation the rest of us weren't privy to with the radio blaring and the roar of the engine. I watched her demonstrate some point with her long, elegant hands, then laugh. His white teeth flashed as he smiled at her, his strong arm resting on the open window.

We three sat in silence, bumping along so hard my teeth were chattering, feeling the main road recede as the forest came at us fast. Branches reached out and scraped across the windshield, snapping back behind us. The road decayed into two muddy grooves with grass down the middle, and the truck bounced so violently in deep ruts I thought the engine would fall out.

"You ladies all in one piece back there?" Rory called to us.

Rachel said we were, barely, just as a long green branch popped into my open window, dragged itself across my chest, and disappeared behind us. I didn't think the road could get any narrower, but it did, until I didn't see any difference between what we were doing and driving through the woods. Rory drove fearlessly and too fast.

We came to a break in the trees where the sky could breathe in, then rolled into a field of wildflowers, waist-deep heather, and clover. Rory barreled through the tall grasses, freeing a knot of blue butterflies that swirled up in a purple twist. Wild rhododendron and laurel bushes crunched under the wheels and clawed at the undercarriage. He never slowed down.

The land dipped down farther and there was the sensation of falling forward into something we shouldn't. I smelled mud and water. Cattails taller than the truck hammered at us. The wheels caught in some kind of suction and the engine ground louder than it should have for how fast we were going until we dropped down hard on the back left wheel and stuck there, me piled up on top of Rachel and Sandra. We were scared but couldn't help laughing as we disentangled ourselves.

"Shit," Rory said, smacking the wheel. "This wasn't a swamp two weeks ago."

The truck groaned and sank a bit more. Wedged in my seat, I watched a dragonfly maybe four inches long hang in the air a foot from my face, a masterpiece of color and construction. It examined me with thousands of black eyes before it helicoptered away.

Rory manhandled the wheel and lead-footed the gas. The wheels whined as they turned, digging us deeper. He turned to Pia. "Can you drive a stick?"

"Sure."

We laughed. Pia could pilot a plane. Rory jumped out of the truck with the grace of a much smaller man, pushed his way through the weeds, and disappeared behind the truck. "On three!" he yelled.

Pia installed herself in the driver's seat and took over. Several unsuccessful attempts to free us later, Rory made his way to where we sat clumped in the backseat. He draped his heavy forearms over the window, face, hair, and clothes more mud than anything else. "Hate to ask, but I could really use some muscle back here."

Rachel opened her door, the corner of which wedged into the muck and high swords of grass because of the way we were pitched. Her hiking boots sank into a foot of mud; it flowed up over the tops of them, flooding them with carbon-black ooze. Sandra tumbled out after her, laughing and cursing, then turned back to me with a questioning look.

"Let me know if you need me," I said with a weak smile, picturing snakes and other evil creatures that lived in muck.

I felt them heave into the back of the truck as Pia revved the engine, cursing and slapping at the dashboard. We surged half a foot, maybe, far from what we needed to get out of that hole. I sat in a ball of shame, loathing my fearful nature, a sudden headache pounding behind my eyes. More groaning and pushing, some heated discussion, then Sandra's face in my window, coated in black mud. She smiled, her teeth and the whites of her eyes gleaming.

"Wini, hon, I think this might be an all-hands-on-deck sort of deal."

The mud was up past her knees, almost up to her shorts. Shuddering, I pushed open the door and lowered my legs into it, never losing eye contact with her. She grabbed my hand and together we Frankenstein-stepped to the back of the truck, the hum of insects constant around our ears.

"On three!" Rory grunted, and Pia gunned the engine as we all leaned into the cold, immobile bumper. Sheets of slime shot back, covering every square inch of us; I tasted it in my mouth, felt it clogging my ears. I stood with the others, spitting, coughing, and laughing at the sight of each other. Baptized in primal ooze, a weird joy flooded me; the inception of a new kind of freedom. It was only earth, water, decayed plants and animals. We came from it and we were all headed back someday.

Rory rested his hands on his narrow hips. "Sorry about this, but, you know, shit happens."

"Let's keep going!" Pia yelled from the front, and we put our shoulders back into it. Each time more mud slammed back at us, but nothing was budging and the truck only sank deeper.

Pia sprang from the cab. "We need to put something under the wheel."

She began to gather reeds and long grasses; we all did, Rory helping with a knife he carried. We put together a mat of stalks and branches and wedged it under the tire. The wheel turned once, then caught, and the truck leapt forward and up, as if flying into the morning sky.

We drove a few minutes more after the swamp, passing a hillock of twisted apple trees and the blackened carcass of an abandoned truck. Ancient stone walls crisscrossed the fields, at places in stunning shape and in others more piles of rocks than anything else. Once I thought I saw something dark and lumbering dissolve into the forest, but I couldn't be sure; at the time I chalked it up to a play of shadows from passing clouds or simply my skittish imagination.

Rory eased the truck up and over a crest of shale and loose rocks, nosed it into a stand of white birch that skirted the forest, and killed the engine. Silence had its moment before woodland sounds started up again, a whir of insects and the rustle of unseen creatures among trees and undergrowth.

"I never felt so disgusting in my life," Sandra said, shifting in her seat in her filthy clothes. We laughed, and dried mud cracked and fell in chips off our faces and onto the backseat.

Like a lost tribe of mud people, we followed Rory to a stream just outside the truck, really only a trickle of water that slipped over mossy stones before disappearing under a mess of tree limbs. It was so meager we had to take turns cleaning ourselves, which we did politely. All we could do was splash the worst of it off our faces and arms and legs, not anything like a real soak that would have done the job.

Rory tossed our gear out of the truck bed as if it weighed nothing, leaned our packs up against the birch trees, and locked the doors of the cab. This was it. We were into it now, the wild green world—about to shed even the truck and vanish into the forest.

The sun lingered at its apex, warming the tops of our heads. I could feel it beating into the part of my hair. Pia sprayed herself with Off! and we all copied her.

"We'll get to the river tonight," Rory said as he rummaged in his pack and pulled out a rag. He soaked it in the stream and wiped his face. "We can really get washed up there."

Something metal glinted from the side pocket of the pack where he'd gotten the rag. I hadn't seen too many in my life but knew it was the handle of a gun. I looked away but felt Rory's eyes burning into me as he stuffed the rag back over it.

Pia hoisted her pack over her shoulders, clipped the belt, and laughed. "We're going to be so beautiful by the time we get this mud off."

"Impossible," Rory said. "You ladies couldn't get any more beautiful." The rest of us chuckled politely, but Pia actually perked up at this comment. Rachel gave Rory a long, hard look as she downed a few swigs of water. Sandra grimaced, cursing softly as she worked a wide-toothed comb through mud-hardened hair.

"You know what," Rory said, "I really like how you all handled our situation back there. You jumped right in, no hesitation. Well, most of you." He winked at me, and I felt myself redden. "That's a survival skill." He knifed a piece of apple and slid it in his mouth.

Rachel wandered over to the entrance of the trail, a subtle opening in dense green forest. "So does anyone, I don't know, live out here?"

"I doubt it. Bear, moose, that's another story. If you see a bear, don't run, whatever you do. Especially a cub. Speak in a low voice and back off slow and gentle."

Rachel plunked her hands on her hips, her kinky curls in a muddy topknot on her head. "Seriously, Rory, how many bears have you seen out here?"

"None. But I know what their scat looks like, and I've seen plenty of it."

Rachel snorted. "Bear poop? Come on, how do you know it's—"

"Last year an older couple came out here to camp—a mile away, maybe, near the river—and spotted a cub on the ridge. They got real close. Theory was they wanted to take a selfie with the thing, or that's what their last Facebook update said, anyway. Too bad mama was watching; you know, just biding her time."

Sandra put her comb down, eyes wide. "What happened to them?"

Rory snapped his shoulder straps together across his broad chest, yanked them taut. "Nothing good."

My jaw tightened so hard I got light-headed and had to lean against my backpack for a moment. Rachel took a step toward the trailhead and peered into it as if she could find the answer there. "So come on, *what*?" she said breathily, her forehead shining with sweat.

"Pieces of them were found, that's it. So the moral of the story is, don't do stupid shit, and listen to what I say. Are we good? Ready to roll, ladies?"

We all nodded as we gathered our gear, the only sound soft grunts as we heaved our packs onto our shoulders.

9

We set off. Rory in the lead, followed by Pia, then Rachel, Sandra, and me. The order felt profound in a way I didn't quite like, but I let it go because right away I had other worries. Just keeping my balance with a pack on my back—which Rory and Pia had winnowed down to "a very doable" thirty-five pounds or so—and walking in high, stiff hiking boots took up most of my brain. To keep from falling backward I leaned forward, using muscles I didn't know I had. What were they, stomach muscles? Core? Back? I gritted my teeth as I watched my chubby white knees pump up and down, negotiating my shoes into crevices between rocks and tree roots. The straps of my pack dug wedges into my shoulders. Already I was thinking about food.

In minutes, I was coated with sweat and breathing hard, noting somewhere in my brain that the path hadn't even started going uphill yet. My ankles turned in my boots if I misjudged a step. I realized I'd better concentrate on every footfall; my mind wandered anyway. A grueling argument I'd had with Richard just a year ago flooded back to me. I'd asked him if Marcus, then in his early thirties, could move in with us. Insisted on it, since he had nowhere to go after the death of our mother. The fight had been one of the most vicious we'd ever had, and, to my surprise, I ended up "winning." Marcus moved in the following week. One Sunday soon after, Marcus and I returned from a day of shopping to find all of Richard's belongings gone from the apartment. Apparently this change of scene had pushed Richard into the arms of his girlfriend, someone he'd insisted up until that day didn't exist.

A root shot up out of nowhere, trapped my boot, and I went flying, whiplashed from my memories. I can still conjure the fright of being airborne, all that greenery shooting by and rocks and earth zooming up to meet me. I lay in a fetal pile waiting for the world to stop moving, panting and cursing and crying a little until I could bring myself to examine my bloody palms and test my fingers. They all seemed to work. "Don't be such a fucking baby," I said aloud. "You fell, now get up."

Something called to its mate high above me, a mournful coo followed by a shrill peep-peep-peep. I felt watched by insensate green. Underbrush crowded the path, yearning to erase it. I remembered something a friend who once lived near a cornfield had said to me: after a spring rain you could hear the stalks growing; they made an eerie, creaking sound.

I closed my eyes. Opened them. I was still in the middle of nowhere, alone.

"Rachel! Sandra! Rory! Pia!" I hated the sound of my voice. It sounded weak, thin, useless.

Only forest noises answered. I reached in one of my countless zippered pockets for my cell phone. No coverage.

I began to wonder if I was on the right trail. Yes, blue flashes of paint still marked the occasional tree on the path, but was there for some sick reason *more than one blue trail*? Had I taken a wrong turn and not noticed? A wave of love for civilization and its myriad comforts washed over me as I turned in my cathedral of tree and stone. It all looked the same to me. Nature was a language I simply didn't speak.

I tightened my pack, retied my shoes, and began to climb. To summarize: I never knew there was so much up. The first time I clambered up a cascade of rocks, huffing and drenched with sweat, it didn't occur to me that this would be only one of many messy encounters with gravity. I'd make it up one steep rise of earth and stone, congratulate myself—even get a bit smug on a level stretch—only to face the next heartbreaking climb.

A dull ache had fired up in both feet, mainly my heels and both little toes. Figured I'd ignore it, let it hang out with the pain in my shoulders, thighs, calves, and hands. I had no concept of how far I'd walked. A mile? Three miles? Five? I knew how it felt to walk a mile in the city in sneakers on a nice day, how it felt to swim my tidy ten laps at the Y, but this was different. I only knew that a couple of hours had passed, and I'd seen no sign of anyone. Everything in my life became the dumb brute act of moving forward, as animals must—food, sex, and shelter leading them on.

I heard water before I saw it. A delicious hush off to my right. I couldn't quench a desire to see it, to rest my eyes on something other than green trees and gray stone. Thorns and brambles caught at my clothes and bare flesh as I bushwhacked toward the sound. The land fell away sharply under my feet.

Something moved down below, a black blur. A thick branch snapped back, young leaves glistening. I stopped breathing.

Something pink dappled through the leaves. I squinted, sorting out the layers of green from the objects below. A white arm, a pair of hiking boots placed side by side on black slate, socks draped over them. In silence, I drew aside a branch and saw Sandra's shining hair and curved back as she sat on a rock, arms wrapped around her knees.

She turned and waved when she heard me call her name. I fumbled my way down the steep bank. Following her lead, I unbuckled my pack and let it drop to the earth. Crazy to think mine was a "pared down" version. Nothing ever felt so good. I nearly skipped over the rocks to join her in the sunshine at the base of a waterfall just taller than a man.

Grimacing, I took off my shoes and peeled off my bloodstained socks; blisters on my heels and toes had already broken.

"Shit, Wini, what are you doing?" she said with concern as she looked at my feet. She unzipped a side pocket in her pack, dug around in it. "How can you even walk?" She laid out a sheet of moleskin, a little packet of disinfectant, a Swiss Army knife. Using the tiny pair of scissors on the knife, she snipped off a small patch of moleskin. "God, I hope I have enough of this stuff. You poor thing!"

I wanted to cry a little, I was so relieved to find her and that she knew what to do, but instead I let her ease my feet into the icy stream while I nearly fainted from the pain-pleasure of the rushing water.

"Let's see what we've got here," she said as I extracted one foot and rested it on the warm stone. She glanced up at me with red-rimmed eyes. "Here, hand me that little towel from my bag."

"Oh, Loo, what's the matter?"

She shook her head and wiped her eyes with the backs of her hands, bending back down to her task. "Oh, you know, same old thing."

Which meant Jeff. None of us could stand him, this husband who had for fourteen years been treating her like a possession. *Better be home by ten, who are you going with, better not be lying, I might just drive by and make sure you're really there at your so-called girls' night out . . .* All sweetness and smiles in front of Pia and Rachel and me; roaring like an animal with Sandra in the privacy of their home and smashing his fist through the wall next to her head if she arrived back only a few minutes late. Just standing next to him gave me a whiff of violence.

I sat close to her and put my arm around her.

"He said don't bother coming home."

"Come on, Sandra—"

"I talked to him back at the lodge. He said he never gave me permission to go on this trip. He's crazy, but you knew that," she said with a sad little laugh.

"It's been a long time, you know, with this man."

She nodded, face deep in shadow, thick black hair sweeping forward.

"Every year you say you're going to give him another year and then—"

Fresh tears flowed out of her. "I know, my God, I know! I just wanted to be with my friends, especially you. I mean, how often do we get to see each other?"

"Never enough."

"But I couldn't let him destroy this weekend. It's too important to me."

We hugged, and it struck me—as it always did—how small she felt. I thought about her words. Rachel and Pia had been best friends since grade school, but Sandra and I had each other's back, an unshakable trust and understanding. She was the one who had carried me through the first days of horror after Marcus's death— was still carrying me. She understood my heart, and all our hearts; she saw the truth behind Pia's manic trekking, Rachel's rigidity, my chronic inertia; forgave it all and loved us anyway.

Without looking up from her work, Sandra said softly, "He was my rebound relationship after Joe, you know. How stupid is it to actually *marry* your rebound guy?"

"Yes, but—"

She waved me away with a little laugh. "I guess that's not news to anybody, but look, Win, I am done with Jeff. I made my decision back at the lodge. All this time I've been staying in this for Ethan and Hannah, but if I were being honest with myself, those kids are exactly the reason I have to get away from him! They're getting older, they're picking up on things. Ethan's started having these nightmares . . . kids are just sponges, you know? But I'm telling you, something about being with all of you guys again, it inspired me. . . ." She wiped her eyes and looked at me. "Anyway, I wanted you to be the first to know."

"Loo, that's great to hear—" I touched her forearm, and she seemed to tear up again, so I withdrew my hand.

"That's all I can say right now. I don't want to talk about it. It'll take me back there. I want to be here, on this trip, with my friends." She looked up, blinking. "In this sunlight, by this stream. Okay?"

"I hear you." I winced as she cleaned my other foot, dried it. "How much farther to the campsite, do you think?"

"A mile or so."

"Don't you think it's a little weird that they've left us behind like this?"

"You know they're going to do what they're going to do." She put the knife and moleskin back in her pack, sat back on her haunches. "Let's just enjoy the ride, okay? I mean, *look* at this place." She laughed and threw up her arms. "This is soooo not my marriage, not my bills, my PTO conferences, my job. It's our adventure, Win."

"But you won't leave me behind, will you?"

She looked at me. "Of course not."

"Rory has a gun. I saw it—"

"How did—"

"It looked like he was keeping it hidden."

She shrugged and reached for her socks and boots. "We're in Maine, Win. In the woods. It's not a bad thing to have."

Back on the trail, we fell into a rhythm of walking together, me several yards behind but always keeping Sandra in view. I think we were both too tired to talk. We tramped through a marshy area, then across a series of wooden boards laid down over stretches of mud. I spotted cloven footprints deep in the black ooze and showed them to Sandra. We agreed they were deer, or maybe moose, but neither of us had any real idea.

The swamp gave way to old-growth groves of hardwood and birch trees. Orange and yellow mushrooms popped up in the rich decay of fallen trees, while chipmunks crisscrossed the trail at every turn.

As we climbed higher, the hardwoods thinned out, and we wandered among shoulder-high fir and spruce. Soon, even the conifers fell away. Above the tree line now, we walked on bedrock, scree kicking back behind us. Fairy-green lichen jeweled stone outcroppings. The air freshened on the ridge. To all sides, undulant mountains in heartbreaking shades of blue rolled off into soft clouds. The view stunned me, and I gasped. I don't know why I was surprised to find such beauty. We followed the cairns that marked the trail—Pia had told us this curious name for these little piles of rocks—pausing to put on our fleeces as a cold wind whipped across bare stone.

Sandra and I stood side by side and looked down. A few hundred feet below us, a river, swollen and churning and alive, rounded a bend and plunged into pine forest. Even from our elevation we could see whitecaps. My stomach tightened. Through a break in the canopy of green just below us, smoke drifted up into the late-afternoon sky. As much as my feet screamed from inside my shoes as we descended the ridge to the campfire, I relished a small, private flame of pride that I had made it this far into this strange new world.

10

I thrashed my way along the last of the trail, which angled steeply down, following glimpses of Sandra as if she were my talisman. The thought that we would find food and shelter in any form gave me renewed energy. With every step the sound of the river grew louder until it inhabited the air around us.

In minutes Sandra and I stumbled into a clearing. An explosion of colorful gear took up much of the open space, except for a fire that burned cheerfully in the center of a circle of rocks. Six o'clock sun painted long shadows across the confusion of tents, back-packs, and sleeping bags. An orange-and-yellow raft with bright blue handles leaned up against a stand of trees. Five oars rested on the ground next to it. Rachel, cursing, knelt on one of two tents spread flat on the ground. She glanced up at us. "Wow, finally. I was about to start back and look for you guys."

Sandra laughed as she let her pack slide off her shoulders onto a nearby rock. "Nice to see you too, Rachel."

"Where's Pia and Rory?" I asked.

Rachel looked up at me from her hands-and-knees position, her glasses slightly cockeyed on her still-mud-streaked nose and forehead. It occurred to me that here was a woman who might not age well, especially in the face. Too many of her emotions already lived there in ever-deepening lines around her eyes and mouth—even at age thirty-seven. But I loved her scrappy toughness; in fact, we all made fun of her for injecting her own Botox, and most of the time she took our ribbing with surprising good nature.

She sat back on her haunches. "Rory's 'showing Pia the river,'" she said with heavy use of finger quotes. She rolled her eyes and got back to work on the tent.

I listened to the river, a constant but not unpleasant roar through the woods beyond us. Sandra pulled out a bag of raisins from her pack and offered me some. I couldn't believe how hungry I was. The curved spine of Rachel's tent sprang up with a snap.

"Would I be interrupting anything if I went down there to check it out?"

Rachel shrugged as an answer before disappearing into the tent. After a moment she crawled out, grabbed her sleeping bag, scuttled back in, and zipped the screen shut.

"Okay, we'll be right back," I said to the tent.

Though there was no trail I could detect, Sandra followed me through a short stretch of dense growth toward an opening where leaves glimmered, catching and holding what daylight remained. I had a vision of forest creatures watching us as we blundered toward their watering hole, fleeing back into the woods or standing, unblinking, one soft paw raised in wait.

I burst through the opening, landing on a narrow strip of sandy mud that gave under my shoes, so I launched myself onto one of hundreds of smooth stones scattered across the shallows. Silvery water trilled over rocks, never more than a couple feet deep as far as I could see, but the river was so much wider than I had imagined! Broad enough to surround a twenty-foot island shaggy with young cottonwoods, roots exposed in shallow soil eroded by the current. Basking in the sun's last rays, Pia lay stretched out on a slab of shale in the middle of the river, one knee bent and one arm flung over her eyes. Perhaps asleep, perhaps not. A metal bucket sat next to her bare feet.

Nearby, a glinting line of light jerked across the water tautly, then crisscrossed the surface. I followed the filament up to a fishing pole to Rory, who stood several yards upriver from Pia, the current rushing around his knees. Shirtless, he let out on the line and leaned back, the pole bending until I thought it would snap as he drew back still farther and pulled, then dropped forward and reeled in hard. The sun found the gold in the dark strands of his twined hair, limned his silhouette in orange. A fish sprang from the water, a foot long at least, speckled yellow and green. It twisted and flailed in the air, fantastically alive in these, its last moments, the hook clear through one side of its rubbery face, before it splashed back down and Rory reeled it in fast.

Pia sat up, gazing at Rory as he picked his way through the shallows with his wriggling catch and dropped it in the bucket. She got to her feet, said something I couldn't hear, and he laughed and touched her arm. They hadn't seen us yet.

Pia passed me the wine and wiped her mouth with the back of her hand. Firelight played on our faces as we sipped at metal cups of the boxed merlot Rory had stashed at the campsite along with the raft. The remains of dinner lay scattered about—baked-potato skins wrapped in foil, fish bones, scraps of bread, orange peels, abandoned Ziploc bags of nuts and dried fruit. Behind us, the tents rose up, two dark cutouts against the sky—our four-person tent, and Rory's pup tent. Evening deepened around us, and always the river, its never-ending hush beyond the green and black.

Pia poked at the fire with a stick, then tossed it in the flames. "It's our fault, you know," she said with a sideways glance at Rory. By firelight she looked ten years younger; sparkling eyes, all grace and smooth, tawny skin. "We did it to your generation." She stood up, impassioned. "We poisoned the earth and the air and the water for you to inherit. I just don't know what else to say, except I'm sorry."

She was so serious and full of conviction I wanted to laugh, but I kept my face passive and unreadable. The first flush of wine percolated into my tired bones, distancing me from the aches in my muscles, joints, and feet. I shifted in my seat—my rolled-up sleeping bag under my butt on the ground—and watched Rory as he squared his shoulders and gazed into the flames. Cross-legged on a log, he wore shorts and a sweatshirt with some sports logo along one sleeve, while Sandra and Rachel sat close to the fire wrapped in their sleeping bags.

"I don't know, Pia," he said. "I think it's all of us. Not enough people of any age are doing enough. We all suck, basically."

"As long as the almighty dollar is on the line, that's what's going to win out," Rachel said.

"I guess." Pia sighed. "I still think we owe your generation an apology." She stretched out her bare long legs closer to the fire, flexed and pointed her feet in their bright red socks.

Rory laughed. "Not sure you owe me anything, but would anyone like to take a dip?"

"Now?" Sandra said, the first words from her in quite some time. We all looked at each other, then back at Rory, who shrugged.

"There's this incredible pool in the middle of the island. It's so much warmer than the river. I'll show you. It's awesome. And if the moon is as full as it was last night, we'll be able to see like it was daytime. Don't you want to really wash off?"

Everyone looked at pied piper Pia. We truly were wimps.
"Lead the way," she said.

Though we had all brought bathing suits, not one of us paused
to grab ours for this escapade. Interesting. But Rory and Pia had
jumped up and gone galumphing into the forest so fast you could
say that none of the rest of us had the chance to rifle through our
backpacks and scare them up. For my part, I had no intention of
swimming, but I had to wonder about everybody else, especially
Sandra, who I thought wouldn't skinny-dip in a million years. I
loved my friends but wasn't eager for them to see me naked or,
frankly, to see them in the buff.

The beam from Rory's flashlight danced around us as we barreled through thickets and brush on our way back to the river,
sharing the merlot that at this point we drank straight from the
box. In came my usual terror of everything—night creatures! Insects! Murderers!—but I found myself loving the sweet taste of
the air, all the wildlife I couldn't see, furred ears turned in our
direction, and the approaching nearness of the living water. I
followed the sounds of laughter and whooping up ahead until I
stepped out onto a slender bank of sand, free from the clutch of
trees.

Because the river was so wide, we could see a great expanse of
sky, and though the sun had set some time ago behind shadowy
mountains, the underbellies of clouds blushed pink. To the north,
a jagged scrim of geese squawked across the glowing horizon. I
wondered how the sky could feel so vast at times, so alive with the
complex narrative of clouds and sun, moon, and stars; at others,
so nothing, so commonplace and unremarkable. Was it because of
where we were, or because I so seldom looked up?

Rory and Pia had already disappeared into a crop of young swamp maples on the island that bisected the river. The saplings yearned skyward, their roots clutching river rocks as they drank from the sandy soil beneath. A thought bubble concerning Pia and Rory drifted by in my half-buzzed brain—*Maybe they want to be alone*—but I continued to hop from rock to rock across shimmering strands of water, emboldened by wine and the insane beauty all around me. I was starting to enjoy the idea of doing whatever came next because it seemed like fun. My God, when was the last time I'd spent even an afternoon with that as my mantra?

The pool opened before us like a granite ice-cream scoop buried in the center of the stand of trees, a perfectly round hole three yards across and deep enough for Rory to cannonball, naked, from its slippery edges. All of us watched, stunned silent, as his compact bullet of a body displaced enough water to soak us through.

Pia went first, of course. She whipped off her T-shirt like a guy, grabbing the hem and pulling it over her head without regard for hair or makeup. Next came the hiking shoes. Stumbling this way and that, she kicked them off, barely untying the laces; then socks, belt-shorts-and-panties in one sweep; last, her bra—the center clasp of which she flipped open—then flung the thing from herself as though it had been burning her flesh. For a moment she reached her arms out skyward, as if acknowledging some sort of award, then, giggling but without an ounce of self-consciousness, she dropped her arms and began to pick her way along the mossy banks to the edge of the pool, grabbing at branches to steady herself.

Rory watched, bobbing and smiling from the center of the oasis.

Pia, naked. She was as beautiful as we had imagined her, the kind of athletic woman's body that becomes nearly impossible after a certain age: toned arms; flat, nearly concave belly; not an ounce of back fat or bounce at the hips, instead just taut, curved muscle defining thighs and the backs of her legs. She found a toehold at the lip of the bowl and jumped, laughing, hair flying up and set ablaze by the vestiges of light, pale limbs flashing. In moments she popped out of the water and flipped her hair back, dog-paddling toward us.

"Come on, guys, get in here! It's perfect!"

"It's okay," Rory said, watching us. He turned onto his back and began to float. "I have five sisters. I'm harmless."

Rachel held her hands in tight fists, jammed into her hips. In her face I read disapproval, rage, maybe disappointment? She was another who surprised me sometimes . . . then she said, "Oh, what the fuck," and began to unbutton her shirt.

11

As Rachel tried the slow-and-painful method of entry into the dark water, lowering herself in bit by bit, I heard the thump of shoes on rocks and several unzippings. Sandra stood shivering as she faced the forest, wearing only her high-waisted panties and a beige bra, her hair a shining black shroud.

"Hey, Loo," I said, sipping wine from the plastic box. "Seriously, you don't have to do this, you know." I might have belched right then. "I'm not going to do it."

Pia paddled over to us. "That's just crap, Win. She should do this. You have to do this. It's freaking paradise. It's why we're here."

Sandra finished undressing, arranging her clothes in a neat pile. She turned, at first covering herself with her hands, but then let them drop. One full breast glowed in the moonlight, the nipple a dark halo; where the other had been, a pale pink scar crossed her chest. Another horizontal scar, from the cesarean she'd had with her son, Ethan, glowed faintly whitish in the moonlight just above her pubic bone. Though she was shorter and smaller than the rest of us, her body was full and soft, a stranger to diets or the gym. To me there was something wonderful about that. She stared straight ahead, as if obeying some far-off command, then calmly stepped into the water and disappeared with the smallest splash imaginable. In seconds she burst forth gasping and cursing.

Well, I had to go in now. Just as Rory had predicted, the moon had risen full and huge and shone down on us with papery blue light. The black water reflected it back in pieces.

"Hey, Rory?" I asked. "Do you think there are leeches in here?"

The women squealed until he answered, "No way! They're only in still water. This is fed by the river. You're fine."

Rachel rubbed at the caked-on mud that still covered her neck and arms. Birds cooed and chittered above us, making sleepy night sounds. I dipped my hand in the cool, soft water, swirled it around, then started to take off my clothes. I turned away to do it, thought of everyone looking at my fat ass, then laughed out loud because I realized I didn't care.

I've known several kinds of nakedness: moments of pride for whatever allure youth had granted my body, or—later—blushing mortification at my imperfections, but never the sort where I was outside in the Maine woods in early summer, with my friends and one strange man, at night, in a glacial pothole in a river . . . and I have to say it was a sensual-yet-easy nudity. There was the wild beauty of where we were, but we all looked how we looked and so what; the water so delicious you could have bottled and sold it as an elixir of health and happiness; the temperature on the shivery side but perfect to erase the shellac from a sweaty day of hiking in humid heat. I wondered, why did I ever doubt this trip would be the best thing I ever did?

"I want to hike the Appalachian Trail, maybe next year," I heard Pia say to Rory as I came up from a rinse.

"Me too," he said. "After I graduate, maybe. I hear it really changes you, being alone like that for months and months."

Pia rested in the water at the rim of the pool near him, her small breasts half in, half out of the water. "But don't you run into people on the trail, maybe end up hiking with them?"

He shrugged. Beads of water fell off his tight coils of hair, rolled down his beautiful shoulders as he launched himself from the perimeter of the bowl, a slow breast stroke, his leonine head high out of the water. "It happens. But unless you plan to do the trip with someone, you're on your own."

"Well, I want to do it," Pia said. "As soon as I quit my stupid job."

I smiled as I swam. Pia had been talking about hiking the Appalachian Trail as long as I'd known her, nearly fifteen years.

I pushed myself up and out of the water, dried off with my T-shirt and slipped on my clothes, then stretched out on the bank, a bit tipsy, half listening to chatter about plans for the next several days. My mind slipped back to a recent discussion with Sarah, our new Web developer, about coding. I'd said yes, of course, I get that coding is what makes everything we see online possible, but what is behind the coding? Who codes the code? And so on . . . Isn't it magic? I'd asked, only half joking. She'd looked at me as if I were an idiot, or worse: boring.

She'd said, "Look, there is no magic. For everything you see, there's an explanation. You just have to look behind things to see how they work. Open a watch. Take apart a car. There is always a man behind the curtain, pulling the levers; there are no mysteries left."

I had agreed with her to keep the peace and finish our awkward conversation, but I still wondered. Once one mystery is solved, isn't there always another lying just beneath?

•   •   •

"Wini . . ." A wet hand shook my arm. "Wake up!"

A spray of night stars. The moon in a caul of cloud.

"We're heading back." Rachel's wet hair hung in tangled ropes, her glasses glinting silver in the moonlight. She stood up and tucked in her shirt, the fabric sticking to her slim torso. A back-to-business feeling coming from her. Nearby, Sandra floated, toes up like a corpse.

I sat up shivering, bits of gravelly rock embedded in my T-shirt. How had I ever fallen asleep this way . . . but the acrid taste of vinegary wine reminded me. I got to my feet, trying to hold on to the enjoyable stage of drunkenness as long as possible.

"Come on, Sandra, let's go," Rachel said.

Obediently, Sandra turned and swam the short distance to the edge of the bowl.

"Where's Pia and Rory?" I asked.

"Not really sure," Rachel said impatiently. "Rory was going on and on about showing us some sacred Native American place. A little bit upriver. Something about some dog star aligning with Orion's belt or some crap like that. Pia was all over it." Rachel hugged herself, the two sharp worry lines between her eyebrows in evidence even in the shadowy dark. "We said whatever, go for it. We're staying here. I just don't want to get lost."

I squinted through the trees. Smoke from our campfire marked the sky, coiling up toward diamond-hard stars. Sandra faced away from us, drying herself with care before stepping into her clothes.

The river glistened black and oily under the moon, frisking over the pebbly bottom with its endless hush. Our way across was lit perfectly by the night sky, less so in the woods where we kept our eyes on the flickering campfire.

We stumbled into the small circle of light. Sparks exploded from the fire's orange heart and swirled up into blackness. I remembered the box of wine I'd left behind at the oasis, missed it.

Beams from our three flashlights crisscrossed the campsite. Rachel's lingered on one tent, then the other, before she stepped over and peered inside both of them, lifting the triangular flaps, then dropping them in disgust.

"Pia!" Rachel called into the night forest. "Rory!" The names echoed from the mountains.

Nothing. Just a momentary hush before the chirring of insects surrounded us again.

"Okay, so where are they?" Rachel ran her flashlight across the sky, as if she might find them there.

"Maybe still at the magic place, or could be they went back for another swim," I said, kneeling by the fire.

"That is not funny, Win."

I looked up at her. "I wasn't trying to be."

Sandra picked up a few sticks of kindling from the meager stash we'd gathered earlier and tossed them on the fire. A whoosh of flame as the dry sticks caught and burned; soft white ashes floated up. "We should get more wood if we want to keep this going all night."

"Wait," Rachel said, her face lit red by the new flames. "We're not going to look for them?"

"He's a guide," Sandra said. "He knows the woods."

Rachel stomped on a glowing piece of bark that had leapt from the circle of stones around the fire. "This is so not cool."

"They'll be back any minute, Rache," I said as if I had any idea.

She jammed her fists through the sleeves of her fleece jacket and zipped it up all the way. "Look, Win, it's this guy's job to keep us safe. All of us. All the time."

I thought about Rory, his ear-to-ear smile in the pool as he looked up at Pia, her arms opening to embrace the night sky before she jumped in to join him.

"We're safe," I said. "Let's get some wood."

Sandra had already ventured out into the darkness. I pulled on a sweatshirt, shivered, and stepped out of the circle of light. Cool night air lifted up from the earth and mingled with the vapors of water and river stone. Rachel joined me, and we thrashed about in the underbrush, cursing as we gathered what we could.

Which wasn't much. No one could root out decent wood in the dark, even using our headlamps, so we gathered by our dying fire and huddled in our sleeping bags.

"I need a drink so bad right now." Rachel quickly raised her hand. "But don't worry. I've been good. Just got my three-year medallion."

"Congratulations," Sandra said, meaning it.

"Good for you," I said through my pleasant haze of grape. Each of us at one point or another had picked Rachel up from the depths of her addiction, from tearful interventions to bringing her to rehab to just buddying up with her at a meeting, but it had been nearly ten years since any of us had lived close enough to her to be meaningful in those ways once she'd moved to Philly from Boston. That said, I confess that hearing about the last day, hour, or minute she'd had a drink was one up close part of our friendship I didn't miss. Addictions to me felt adolescent at our stage in life, as harsh and unfeeling as that sounds; it was profound loneliness that haunted me; obsolescence in my profession; midlife existential dread. Now that the dying parents had arrived, the divorces, the snotty teenagers, who had time for addiction?

Rachel combed her still-wet hair with her fingers, sighed a big but somehow fragile sigh. I thought of her growing up as the youngest of nine in rural poverty, all the stories of hardship she'd shared over the years, and felt a surge of tenderness for her that washed away my petty lack of understanding. Perhaps her attraction to nursing was a way of healing her traumatic past. Naturally she overcompensated in the control department. Who wouldn't?

Sandra shivered.

"You warm enough, Loo?" I asked.

"Never," she said with a little smile, edging closer to the fire and rubbing her hands together.

Rachel rocked back and forth on her haunches. "This is so fucked."

"Maybe we should just go to bed," Sandra said. She gave Rachel a little pat on the shoulder, got up, then dropped down to crawl inside our tent. Rachel and I sat in silence a few minutes, watching the fire die down to smoke and embers, until the moon took over and we could see more clearly than ever.

12

Figuring she'd come crashing in when she came crashing in and no sooner, Sandra and I made up Pia's place in the center of our tent: sleeping bag rolled out, makeshift pillow next to ours. The three of us got oriented in the tight quarters by flashlight, tucking supplies where we could, then stashing our lights close at hand, until we all lay staring at the deep blue nylon of the tent, feeling the night breathing all around us.

"Do we even know this kid, really?" Rachel said, tossing in her bag. "What if he's a maniac?"

I thought of the gun hidden in his pack and zipped my bag up tight to my chin. "He's not a maniac. He's a normal twenty-year-old kid."

Rachel smacked at her pile-of-clothes-as-pillow. "My point exactly."

"Rachel," Sandra said sleepily, "they're doing whatever they're doing. There's nothing we can do about it. Try and relax and get some sleep, okay?"

"I don't get it. We go away together to be together and catch up as friends, and then Pia goes and does this—this—acting like a fifteen-year-old." A rustling came from outside the tent, a fussy, scrabbling sound. Rachel jerked upright, snapped on her flash-light, and covered it with her hand, which glowed red with her living blood. "What the fuck is that?"

Sandra stayed motionless in her bag, her thick black hair spilling out, the sparks of her eyes shining. Her eyelashes cast freakishly long shadows against the tent from the odd angle of Rachel's flashlight. "The food. We left it out."

"Fuck, we're such idiots." I lunged for the zipper of our netted door.

"Wini, don't!" Rachel yanked me back by my T-shirt. "Anything could be out there!"

We all sat up now, listening to our ragged breathing and the sound of a can hitting a tree, rolling, rattling. Claws scraped on metal. I thought of the can of baked beans Rory had opened earlier and eaten without heating them, how he'd offered some to us and no one had taken him up on it. Cellophane rustled; I pictured the energy-bar wrappers by the fire. The pile of fish bones stuck to sheets of foil.

"We need to scare it away!" I whispered.

"Why?" Rachel breathed.

"Because Pia and Rory are out there."

"What if it's a bear?" Rachel's eyes were huge, dark circles underneath.

"I have a knife." Sandra scrambled through her pack, flashlight bouncing. She pulled out her Swiss Army knife. We all stared at the ridiculous thing.

"Just let it eat the food and go away, whatever it is," Rachel whispered hoarsely. "Do we have food in the tent? Anybody?"

I thought hard. "An apple, that's it."

"Nothing," Sandra said.

"Turn off all your flashlights," I said.

They clicked off. The sounds continued, from all over the camp now. Whatever was out there, there were more than one of them. Our eyes adjusted to the new darkness. Tree shadows fell starkly across the nylon ceiling; I pictured the heavy limbs looming over us. Getting down on my elbows and worming my way to the front of the tent, I unzipped the mesh a few inches and lifted the flap.

Six pairs of eyes glowed silver in the blackness. A family of raccoons, midchew, gaped at me from different sections of the camp. A well-fed one sat up on its haunches. It clutched a piece of granola bar with its eerily human claws, peered at me through bandit eyes.

"Get away!" I cried, scrabbling out of the tent. But even when I'd gotten to my feet, they didn't budge; they just kept eating and scavenging, some not even bothering to acknowledge me. I took a step toward the biggest one, hesitated. Felt the cool, wet earth soak up through my socks as a new equation occurred to me. Whose habitat was being invaded here? The big papa one dropped down to all fours, took a few steps toward me, its big ass waggling. Behind me, Sandra stumbled out of the tent, then Rachel.

Yelling, "Get out," Rachel snatched up a stone from the fire circle and hurled it at the thing, smacking it square in the face. It let out a squeal of pain and indignation, then turned and ran into the forest, the others scuttling after it.

Without speaking we fell upon the scattered garbage and gathered it up. We triple-bagged it and lashed the sack of trash high up on a tree limb several yards from the camp. The rest of the food we tied in baggies that we stowed in the cooler and stuffed that under the raft for lack of any better ideas.

We'd just reinstalled ourselves in the tent when we heard Pia's laugh and Rory's low voice, soft footsteps in the camp, whispers.

We tensed in our bags, waiting for Pia to lift the flap and crawl in next to us.

But she didn't.

Rory's front screen unzipped; we heard the thump of bodies on canvas over hard dirt, more zipping. Pia giggled, the sound ringing up into the night like bells until she clamped down on it, but soon it was unloosed again and morphed into her signature cackle. We three lay there listening, helplessly, to a symphony we couldn't escape. Pia's laughter was cut by the low rumble of Rory talking, and I found myself straining to hear what he said, or any part of it. I caught something idiotic like his opinion on the best kind of boots to wear for stomping around in shit on the farms in aggie school, followed by something lower I didn't catch that prompted another squeal from Pia.

Things got quiet and for a few seconds I thought we might be spared, but no. We had, without question, front-row seats at the opera of love. Just before the main event, I found myself straining to remember the last time I'd had sex, and it came to me as foreign and ancient as if it were someone else's memory. Who: Richard (of course); when: summer, two years ago; where: a cheap hotel in Chatham after a wine-soaked afternoon on the beach; how: not very well—even then he'd felt far away from me, barely present in the room. Followed by a pinot grigio hangover like no other and not even sunset.

I slapped a mosquito on my forearm, shattering a momentary quiet in both tents. Sandra had curled herself into the corner of our tent, her arm flung over her ear. Rachel lay on her side, staring at Sandra's spine. I stretched out on my back, watching the top of the tent as if it were a movie screen. On it played Pia and Rory getting it on. A sudden urge to laugh bubbled up in my chest, passed, then turned into a cough that ricocheted among the trees.

Soft moaning and more rolling and zipping followed the few quiet moments. My God, they might as well have been in the tent with us. We could hear them climbing the mountain, deep breaths followed by short bites of air, then back to slow. The night in its emptiness only amplified their sounds of lovemaking. What better way to fill it? Though keenly self-conscious and embarrassed (later I thought, *Why? Was I the one screwing a twenty-year-old three feet away from my best girlfriends?*), I also felt alive; that way of being in the moment that doesn't waste time on reflection, and it was great to feel it, even though—hell!—I wasn't the one being radically, inappropriately, wrongly, wonderfully fucked.

Rachel flipped over and got up to her elbows, glasses flashing in the darkness. "Doesn't she know we can hear them?" she hissed.

Sandra said nothing. She had cocooned herself, feigning sleep.

The sounds stopped next door, but beneath the silence was a sense of gathering, and I could feel that old train climbing that old hill, just as the orchestra started up again in earnest, with much panting and shuffling. Pia cried out, evidently having herself a fine orgasm, one of those beauties launched from the darkest planet in the deep space of your spine, the kind that leave you hoarse and dizzy, that make your legs fall off and float away and that's just fine with you.

Rachel dropped her head in her hands. Took off her glasses and rubbed her eyes. Some stray hair, black curls shot through with silver threads, popped loose from her ponytail. "Jesus H. fucking Christ," she said loud enough for all the forest to hear. "This is ridiculous. I did *not* sign up for this."

I smiled into my hands.

Whether or not Rachel had signed up for anything, after a brief pause the lovers started up their engines once again. I felt as if he were touching me, and part of me wished that were the case. And why not? I would have loved to fuck Rory too, to fuck the star-pinned sky, the shining moon, the trees full of birds, all of it. Instead I lay there in awe of their stamina and capacity for simply getting it on, again and again, as if this was what they'd come here for, as if they were the only two people on earth, as if this was the last time they'd ever get the chance.

Saturday

June 23

13

How, when, and in what order we all lost consciousness I'll never know, but I do know I was the first to emerge from either tent in the morning, leaving everyone else sleeping still and silent.

It felt like seven, maybe earlier. The ground under my feet squelched with rain that I'd evidently slept through. Now the sun glowed with a peach-colored light behind the mountains as I made my way to the river, dew soaking my long pants. As I walked, I recalled recent weekday mornings back home: the waking up full of dread, the shower that felt like violence, the dirge of what to wear and how much face to paint on, the subway ride with the rest of the undead.

Not so that morning. Photoshop emergency at the magazine? Sorry, can't possibly get to it. I'm three hundred miles away in the wilderness of northern Maine . . . let the magazine go bust and my job blow away, there's not a damned thing I can do about it.

Looking back, I equate this stage of enjoying the wilderness with the second glass of wine. Everything is lighter; you can see the funny side of disaster. But things rarely improve with the third, they get dangerous with the fourth, and you better pray to God someone is around to scoop you off the floor after that. It was our second day in the woods, and we were days away from home.

I stood on the bank of the river and watched it move. Near our camp it rushed clear over tumbled-smooth stones, turning a deep blue in mysterious places downriver. Behind me mountains rose up black, still in shadow. I made my way across wobbly river rocks to a sun-warmed slab of granite and sat, splashing my face with water so cold I wanted to laugh or scream, couldn't tell which.

Rachel charged out of the trees by the bank. She glanced around, steaming with impatience. I waved at her, shelving my lovely isolation for the moment. Sandra appeared behind her, looking bedraggled.

Rachel kicked off her sandals and splashed over to me, Sandra in her wake.

"What are you doing out here?" Rachel said brusquely.

I swatted at a legion of blackflies, mean little biters who stuck to me as if I were viscous.

"Hi," I said, suddenly weary as I made room for my friends to join me on my oasis.

"Did you sleep okay?" Sandra said. We looked at each other, acknowledging the smiles invading both our faces before we burst out laughing.

Rachel did not laugh. She sat with her knees tight to her chest, stabbing at our island of rock with a stick she'd found. A crazy, knotted curtain of hair fell across her face. She flung the stick in the river, jerked her head back, and wiped her tearstained face with her hands.

"I just want to know one thing. Why are we all out here?"

We were silent.

"Somebody please tell me."

My head began to ache behind my eyes. Needed coffee. "Look, Rachel, it's not the end of the world—"

Rachel jabbed at the air with her finger. "You know, Win, that does not answer my question. Sandra, come on, help me out here."

Sandra gazed at the rising sun, squinted. "To be together. To be kind to each other. To catch up with—"

"Okay, so how is *fucking the guide* going to help that goal along, d'ya think?"

Sandra and I burped out little laughs, which we quickly contained. Rachel cast a dagger-filled glance at Sandra.

I said, "Sorry, Rache, sorry. I agree. It doesn't help the cause. But you have Sandra and me, don't forget."

Rachel shook her head, muttering something I didn't catch. As I'd uttered my consolation, I pictured how the loss of Pia really would go down for the rest of the weekend. The three of us gelled and could be mellow together, but Pia was our glue, that martini we shouldn't have, our say-anything girl, our life of the party. Somehow she sparked all of us to be our least reasonable, our best, most adventurous selves.

"Think about it, you guys," Rachel continued. "Will the rest of this trip be spent listening to those two get it on every night?"

"I think we should let it go," Sandra said, dipping her fingers in the water. "Pia is Pia, I mean—"

Suddenly there she was, picking her way along the bank, her reddish brown, fiery mess of hair glinting like a halo around her head, a baggy sweatshirt hanging down almost to the bottom of her frayed shorts. Barefoot, she stepped gingerly into the river facing away from us and toward the low sun. She stopped and stretched elaborately before she dropped her arms, turned, and saw us.

Her face lit up. Waving and smiling as if she hadn't seen us in weeks, she splashed over to where we sat, the sun outlining her form in gold.

"Hey, guys, what's up? I got up and you were all gone, it was kind of weird!"

I scooched over to make room for her on the rock, but it was already pretty crowded, so she stood a few yards away with the water flowing all around her calves, looking gorgeous and young, which is what great sex does for everyone on the planet.

"What a day, huh? I can't wait to get on this river," she continued to our dull, exhausted, angry faces.

"You know, Pia," Rachel said, "I am not going to fuck around with you. We're super pissed off."

I shifted on my rock, suddenly sore-assed. Sandra stared at the current washing over brown river rocks, as it had for millennia.

Pia's smile stayed but her eyes got sad. The years returned; as much as a decade, maybe more. Her shoulders sagged. "Lighten up, you guys, I just—"

"So did you think you were alone with your little friend last night, in some dreamy five-star hotel? Is that what you thought?" Rachel hammered away.

"I—"

"Because we were right there with you guys, Pia. We didn't miss a fucking thing, thank you very much."

A darkness passed over Pia's face as she looked at us, one by one. I felt strangely muted, as if Rachel had this one by the eyeteeth and to jump in would bloody us all even more. Sandra wrapped her arms around her knees and buried her face there.

Finally Pia shrugged, held up the palms of her hands. "Look, guys, it happened. I'm sorry. It's over."

"Is it?" Rachel said.

Pia crossed her arms hard across her chest. "Well, that's *my* fucking business, don't you think? Last time I looked, I was a grown woman and could sleep with whoever I please, when I please."

Rachel's body recoiled into itself, but her face did not soften. I had a flash of Rachel's promiscuous teen years, and for a second I thought Pia would knock her down with a few choice memories, but she didn't go there.

"Maybe this is crazy, but I thought you might be happy for me," Pia said. "He's a nice guy." She looked off and away, her manner momentarily regaining its former sex-stunned dreaminess.

"He's twenty, Pia! You're almost thirty-six!"

"So who are you, the sex police?" The cords in Pia's neck stood out as she spoke. "Just because you don't get any—"

"Come on you guys, stop it," Sandra said from under her curtain of hair.

"—doesn't mean I have to walk around with it zipped up the rest of my life—"

"That's not what we're saying," I said.

"Then what the hell *are* you saying?" Pia held herself as a friend might. Looked at me. She began to cry. My chest tightened to hear it. I thought, *My God, sometimes we are closer than lovers, we female friends.* And sure that scares men, but sometimes it scares us even more. "I'm telling you, this is so fucked. . . ."

"What was your plan, Pia, for this trip?" Rachel said, her voice a touch more gentle.

"Plan?" Pia said sarcastically. "I was *planning* on having a wonderful time in nature with my friends. Evidently that won't be the case. Evidently, I'm going to be demonized for—"

"We were planning the same thing, Pia," I said. "As girlfriends. No guy drama."

She looked at me like I had cut her, then at Sandra. Tears rolled down her cheeks. I couldn't tell if I wanted to slap her or hug her. "Loo?" she said. "Do you fucking hate me too?"

Sandra lifted her head as if it weighed a thousand pounds. She didn't look at any of us. "We came on this trip to be together, Pia. It took a lot for us all to be here. Emotionally, financially, logistically . . . I mean, Jeff is totally pissed at me. Ethan's got a project in the science fair and I'm missing that—"

"Not to mention the grand I dropped at REI," I loathed myself for saying, even as I did so.

Pia shook her head, wiping her eyes with her long sleeves. "Shit, this is—"

"And to tell you the truth, Pia," Sandra added, finally focusing on her, "it always just seems easier for you to take what you want. Like with Joe."

Pia gulped, whitened. Even Rachel looked stricken. Fourteen years ago, Pia had slept with Joe, Sandra's ex, a little too soon after their breakup. Like, the next day. As far as I knew, the subject had never before been broached; in fact, I couldn't remember hearing either of them say his name in years.

"You were done with him."

Sandra sat up, her spine straightening. "You made sure of that, I guess."

"Come on, Sandra, you guys were always breaking up—"

"And getting back together." Sandra turned to Pia, fixing her with a hard stare. "Who knows what could have happened?"

The air thickened, grew still.

"So I made a mistake." Pia hugged herself. "That was freaking forever ago. I don't see what that has to do with now."

"Whatever, Pia, you wanted to get laid," Rachel said. "You could have held off till we were done with this trip."

"Yeah, yeah, I get it. Someone gets some action around here and nobody else can handle it," Pia said without conviction. She surveyed our hardened faces. "Jesus Christ, you guys are tough." With a trace of fear she added, "This isn't fair."

We looked at each other, at the sparkling river, as if we were the saddest people in the world.

"Fine, so I screwed up! I can't *unfuck* the guy!" Agitation colored her voice. "What do you want me to do?"

"We wanted this trip to be about us," I said. "About our friendship."

"We wanted you to be here with us," Rachel said. "Not off with some—"

"So we're here!" Pia shrieked. "*I'm* here!" She plunged both arms into the water, lifted a heavy stone up over her head, and heaved it back into the river. "What else do you want?" She turned and sprinted to the shore, where she grabbed her sandals and disappeared into the forest, not stopping long enough to put them on.

14

The smell of pancakes reached us at the banks of the river and seemed to pull us bodily back to the camp. I couldn't remember ever being so hungry.

Rory was bent over the fire, which he'd somehow gotten started and roaring even though everything was wet. He had on a soft gray T-shirt that said U. OF ORONO—GO BLACK BEARS! in red letters and the same bright orange nylon shorts he'd worn the day before. Whistling to himself, he expertly flipped the cakes and stacked them on a beat-up metal pan that he'd balanced on a rock next to a squeeze bottle of maple syrup. Another pan, full of black coffee, steamed next to a container of dried milk. Pia stood a few yards away in a sun-dappled glade, brushing her hair with quick, sharp strokes.

"How's it going?" Rory flashed us a smile as we filed into camp. "Anybody hungry?"

"I could use some coffee," I said. "Breakfast smells great."

He handed me a tin plate and gestured at the pile of cakes and coffee. "Dig in. We've got a long day ahead of us."

Sandra hesitated, then took a plate and served herself. Rachel did the same in silence. Rory stood with his hands on his hips, watching us. "Everybody sleep okay?"

I looked up from my food to see if he was kidding or being sarcastic or just what was going on, and his face did hold a question, but it was something more along the lines of *How about it, ladies, are we going to make a big deal of this thing, or are we going to let it drop?*

"Fine," I said, my mouth sticky with syrup. "I slept great. Like a rock."

"Sandra, how about you?"

"Good." She nodded to her food. "This is delicious. Thank you."

Pia wordlessly served herself breakfast, then sat near the fire, away from all of us. The sun had begun to take on altitude and strength, even under our canopy of leaves, and I stood up to take off my fleece.

"Rachel?" he asked.

Rachel tested a few bites of the pancakes but set them aside. She sat on a rock and peeled an orange. "Can't put my finger on why, but I didn't sleep a wink."

"Sorry to hear that," Rory said. "But tonight's gonna be a different story. The river will wear you out, and you'll all sleep like babies."

By eight or so we'd dragged our gear out of the tents and rolled up the sleeping bags and pads. Rory had gone down to the river to wash the dishes and pack those up too. We took down our tents, which were still wet and covered with leaves and pieces of bark, and rolled them as tightly as we could, sitting on them like luggage, per Rory's instruction. Everything had to fit on the raft from now on, including us.

We all lifted the raft, which was so much heavier than I'd imagined, and carried it sideways, awkwardly, from the campsite through the woods to the river and the put-in place, an inlet even farther upriver than our little island, so by the time we got there we were all sweaty and fly-bitten and hot. Then of course we had to double back, collect all our gear, and lug it to the raft, with Rory making an extra trip for the food and the second tent, leaving us alone to not talk to each other, or to sit by the river with a paperback, or to do nothing but watch all that water rush by, our silence like a wall I couldn't muster a strategy to burst through, dig under, or climb over.

Exchanging only the information necessary to get the job done, our faces drawn and solemn, we arranged our gear, separating out what needed to be stored in dry bags from what didn't, and strapped everything down across the center beam of the raft. We wore our white-water rafting getup: wicking fabrics, water shoes, and life jackets. Sandra in her hot-pink top and black shorts, Rachel sporting a black tank and dark purple shorts, me in a yellow T and aqua hiking shorts, and Pia in a bright white T and red cutoffs—we were already starting to look out of place next to the muted palette all around us. Our helmets and paddles rested by our sides.

Rory spent an hour or so teaching us about the best way to throw a rescue rope and other safety techniques, about chicken lines and carabiners; we learned about eddies and the different kinds of water we were going to hit; how to read the water, our positions in the boat, and how to paddle. During the drills, Sandra, Rachel, and I sat in a semicircle on the ground while Pia stood away from us and closer to him, finding every opportunity to not look at us. I tried not to think about how much fun we weren't having.

Shirtless, Rory climbed into the raft and demonstrated the best way to sit and hold our oars. He straddled the lip of the raft, its thick rubber barely denting at his weight, then leaned back with bent knees. We watched his perfect abdomen tense flat as a board.

"This is the lawn-chair position. Remember it, okay? If we bail in some big water, you want your feet up, toes up and together like this, and keep your arms high." He demonstrated. "If you fall in, first of all, don't panic. You'll be okay. You all know how to swim. Flip onto your belly when you can, but don't try to stand up until you're in shallow water. Or still water. And the key thing," he said to the four of us, looking at Pia for an extra couple of seconds, "is to listen to me. Not just some of the time, but all of the time. And do what I say. Got it?"

We all nodded like children.

"And to remember that we are a team. I can't emphasize that enough."

We stared at him as if to look at each other would break some sort of spell.

"Last thing. We steer *into* the rapids, not away from them, and that's going to feel weird, but that's how we get through them. Any questions?"

Rachel eyed a bracelet Rory wore: braided strands of dull black hair strung with a few bright beads. "What's that on your wrist? Is that your girlfriend's hair or something?"

He looked hard at her, turning it a few times with his other hand. "It's from my sheepdog, Lally. She died last year in a car accident."

Pia made an "Oh" sound and took a step toward him as if to look at the bracelet, but he ignored her. "Anything else, about the trip?" Visibly hurt, she shrank back.

"I was wondering," Sandra said, strapping on her helmet. She already looked younger than any of us, but with her face framed by headgear she could almost pass as a teenager. "You talked about 'big water' earlier. What would you call this water, then?"

He looked across the vast, humming river and laughed. "A bathtub! This is called riffle, if you need to call it something. It's just fast, shallow water."

Rachel picked up her oar, hefted it. "What about all this rain we've been having?"

"It'll affect things, definitely. We'll have to keep our heads up."

She shaded her eyes with her hands as she looked at him. Stray coils of hair popped loose from her short ponytail, framing her face. "How many times did you say you've been down this river?"

"This'll be my fifth run. I know it inside out." He took a swig of Gatorade. "Anybody besides me know CPR, have first-aid experience?"

"I'm an ER RN," Rachel said, fastening an elastic strap over the temples of her glasses. "Remember?"

"Right. Good to know."

The sun beat down on us. My life jacket felt heavy and hot, and I started to get a little queasy. I could taste the processed pancake flavor in my mouth.

Rory dug around in one of the dry bags, pulled out a map, and laid it on the ground. We all gathered and knelt by it, studying it. It looked homemade, just a legal-size piece of paper, something printed off Google Maps and laminated. The river burst out of the top right corner, a fat blue line that narrowed as it turned and twisted diagonally across the paper, widening just before it continued off the page and forever, as far as I could tell. Squiggly green lines marked off elevations surrounding the river. No towns were marked.

Places along the river had been inked in with a steady hand.

The Tooth marked a point where the river narrowed the first time; a few turns later a red X indicated *The Hungry Mother* (someone had crossed out the word *fucker* after *Mother*), followed by *The Royal Flush*, *Satan's Staircase*, and—where the river grew wide— *The Willows*.

Rory snapped his head back and grinned, a signature cocky move that was beginning to wear on me. "Came up with those names myself. What do you ladies think?"

Pia laughed. "They're awesome," she said, her shoulder now grazing his. Perhaps he only moved in an effort to keep the map flattened on the ground, but he pulled away from her and dropped his finger on the top right corner of it, where the river was the fattest.

"We're here. Today we travel . . ." His finger traced the blue line around the first narrowing, the Tooth; the second, the Hungry Mother; and third and twistiest of all, the Royal Flush. "Fifteen miles altogether. The Tooth and the Mother will be tricky but okay. I'm not sure about the Flush. We'll scout it first, then we'll either run it or portage. We take out around here tonight." He jabbed at a place a third of the way across the map. "We set up there, camp. In the morning it starts out easy. There's a long, calm five or six miles. It'll feel like the Mississippi, but then it'll narrow and get fast again around here." He pointed at Satan's Staircase.

"I don't like the sound of that," Sandra said.

"It's a series of drops. Not bad. You guys'll be old pros by then. In fact the extra water might help us in this case. Smooth it out."

Personally, I was having trouble with the Hungry Motherfucker and the Tooth, but I kept my mouth shut.

"After the Staircase, there's a lot of smaller rapids I didn't bother to name, three, four miles. Some shallows, some swamp, some rime, like where we are now. We take out and camp at this place I call the Willows because there's this grove of them. Really beautiful. On Monday we glide on down to our takeout, a mile or so, which is here." He pointed toward the bottom left corner where a smiley face was drawn in. "My dad'll be waiting for us with plenty of cold beers and tons of food."

"I have one more question," Rachel said as she got to her feet and brushed the dirt off her clothes. "Why are you hiding your gun from us?"

"Rachel, he's not—" Sandra started.

Rachel held out her hand for silence. "Let him talk."

Rory's puppyish mood vanished. He ripped at the Velcro on one of the corner pockets of the dry box, pulled out a hard leather case, and opened it up. A pistol was strapped to one side while rows of handgun magazines filled the other.

Rachel frowned. "Still doesn't seem necessary—"

He shut the case, slipped it back into the dry box. "It would be pretty fucking stupid to be out in these woods without a weapon."

"All we've seen are raccoons and chipmunks."

He snapped his life jacket closed, tugged hard on the straps to adjust it. "Just because you can't see animals doesn't mean they aren't out there, watching. Smelling you. Moose? Bear? Wolves? They know we're here. They're watching us now."

I felt my breakfast ripple up my throat. I barely made it up the bank and into the woods before it all came out of me, the bits of orange, blobs of pancake, all awash in syrupy-coffee bile. It was pure terror, I knew it. The sun baked the back of my neck as I heaved again, till nothing was left.

I felt a soft hand on my back.

"Are you okay?" Sandra handed me her water bottle. I took a swig, swirled out my disgusting mouth; spat.

I stared into the wall of trees, at the hidden creatures watching us. "I can't do this. We're not even talking to each other. It's not safe."

"We'll be fine. We have to get Rachel to chill out. I'll get her alone at lunch or—"

"She okay?" came a voice a few yards away. Rachel appeared, knee-deep in ferns, her serious, fine-boned face framed by cleaving shadow.

"I'm fine," I said, my voice thin and weak.

"Then we'd better get going. Those guys are already in the raft."

15

In seconds the power of the river moving beneath me silenced every thought in my mind. The bank receded quickly behind us. At only a couple of feet deep and around forty feet across, the river rested like a giant in its rough bed of granite and slate, murmuring and turning, dreaming its big-water dreams of endless falling and flowing, gathering its strength for horrors none of us could imagine. Reeds that had stood tall near the banks were now flattened by the current.

I know we all felt it—even then, while the titan was sleeping—that there was a force larger and terribly powerful in charge that we'd better heed above all our petty infighting. The impression of riding something sensate was unmistakable; even when we steered the raft with our oars and Rory's terse direction, the river had its own idea of where we would go and what would happen to us. Still, I did my best to master the stance Rory had demonstrated in his lesson: arms straight out, paddle flat and dug in deep, then pull. We did what he said, exactly.

The water deepened, turned bluer, brown river stones vanishing in the depths. Whitecaps foamed at the crests of small finlike waves. Rory rode high in the stern behind me, Sandra in front and on the right, Pia to my left, Rachel in front of her. We were bottom-heavy in the center with all the gear; Rory called to us to sit higher on our seats. For a few minutes, we seemed in balance, paddling easily together, but then Sandra abruptly stopped rowing.

"Forward right, dig!" Rory called to Sandra, who sat with her paddle over her knees just long enough for the back of the raft to swing in a sickening arc to the left, turning us. "Sandra, wake up! Come on, *pull it*! Dig hard, Pia, now!"

But Sandra sat craning backward in her seat, peering into a patch of forest that retreated swiftly behind us, until the raft spun around and we found ourselves racing backward, rolling over small boulders we couldn't brace ourselves for because we faced the wrong way, whipped along by the vigorous current.

Rory yelled over the water, "Wini, pull back! Backpaddle *now*!"

I did it but it felt wrong, as if I was just going with the river and what was the point of that? Pia and Rachel dug forward with everything they had while Sandra backpaddled with me. Our strokes felt uncoordinated and mindless, like we were all steering different rafts and Rory's commands were gibberish. We found ourselves turning again until we raced sideways to the current, which began to push my side of the raft up and out of the water. Out of instinct I stood and heaved my body weight down on the hard rubber lip of the raft and watched Sandra do the same. Waves of cold water smacked our faces, washing over us, soaking us through.

We all cried out because what else could we do? We screamed out of fright but also a keen excitement—these were roller-coaster screams, zip-lining screams, taming-the-wild-Appaloosa screams; as out of control as we felt, we still had faith in Rory and his ability to harness the surging waters beneath us.

And then—*bang!*—we stopped, jammed sideways into a fallen tree, its long, heavy limbs combing the blue water that pulsed over them and muscled underneath, the raft shuddering and rippling as the river strong-armed us in place.

Rory leaned into the tree, one hand on a bright blue D ring. "Everybody all right?"

Stupefied, we all nodded. He vaulted out of the raft on the side closest to the bank and stood up. I was shocked to see the water was only waist-deep. Behind him the root system of the fallen tree loomed above us like a colossal black claw.

"Ladies," he called to us over the noise of the river, "I'm not sure what happened here, but whatever it was, it can't happen again, okay?"

We looked at him as if he were God.

"Actually, that's not true. I know what happened. Sandra, what the hell were you doing back there?"

"I'm sorry," she said, shivering. "I think I saw something."

We all waited for her to elaborate. She didn't.

"Like what?" he asked.

"A person or something."

"Really." Fear registered briefly on his face, followed by a look of impatience. "Nobody lives out here, trust me. Maybe it was a deer, or a juvenile moose, something like that?"

She gave her head a quick shake. "I don't know. It was so fast. I could have been wrong, I guess."

"How do you know nobody lives out here?" Rachel squinted in the glare, water beading on her lenses.

"We're twenty-five, thirty-five miles from anything. We've got animals for company, that's it."

Pia looked at him, still visibly crushing. I started to wonder, *Maybe she really does like the kid, in some kind of a real way, and vice versa.* Hell, they both loved the outdoors; even beyond the sex there seemed to be a kind of sparkly repartee. Why was it so impossible for any of us to grant them the possibility that they might have something good going after all?

"I'm going to free us up from here," Rory said. "Push us out. But you have to be ready. We're about ten minutes from the Tooth. It's our first white water, Class III, mostly, some II. It's not our hardest today, but it's not our easiest, because, guess what, I can't arrange things in order of difficulty, 'cause this is nature. So I don't care what you see, hear, feel, or whatever happens, you do what I say, when I say it, exactly how I say it. Are you with me? Are we good?"

We nodded, big-eyed.

"Now, I need someone to get in the water and help get us out of here."

"I'll do it," I said, shocking myself.

My hands shook as I wedged my oar under the seat and dropped into the water, gasping at the cold as I found my footing and faced a slope of alluvial wash that had built up against the fallen trunk. Gravel, sand, and silt glittered pink in the sun. I stood behind Rory, placing my body between the raft and the tree as he painstakingly freed us. The river pulled and tugged at various parts of me, interested yet unconcerned with me, full of wild intent and various unknowable plans. I stood in it, enthralled, my flesh reveling in its thousand-year-old journeys and calls, wondering—if I stayed in long enough and listened hard enough—could I understand its river language, decipher the meaning of colder here and warmer there? Part of me never wanted to get out.

Rory and I turned the raft, maneuvering it to where, with one last push, it would be freed from the tree's grip. He lifted himself back in, all grace and ease, before I tried to climb back over the side, cursing my weak upper body as I deadlifted myself to a certain pitiful point and hung there. Pia, Rachel, and Sandra leaned over to give me a hand and we shared a laugh—a momentary truce—before we took our places and were moving again.

16

In minutes, the river narrowed by nearly a third of its width.
Dense spruce replaced alder and ash; enormous walls of trees
on both banks cut off the sunlight as impenetrably as if we were
coursing down building-lined city streets. The corridor of light
shone brilliantly down along the ribbon of the water, which had
turned an eerie yellowish green as it rocketed over a garden of
boulders as big as cars.

Rory's words had hit their mark. Now when he called to
us—which he did endlessly—we acted as one organism. A thrill-
ing kind of grace. We passed rock formations that would have
caused us to stop and stare in wonder if we weren't hurtling by.
Again and again, Rory steered us clear—barely—of stone carved
into person-size bowls by waves that had curled up and licked
back against themselves for untold millennia. As if cued by the
water, the wind picked up and the river took to sharper turns.
We'd no sooner fly around a bend than Rory would scream at us
to row the opposite way. In fact, all of us were screaming pretty
much all the time.

Immense stones sprang up in the uneven riverbed, forcing us
to ride churning water that crashed through a series of chutes,

each more terrifying than the last. The water changed constantly but was always the same. My senses flamed with readiness for any insanity that came at us next, *fear* a meaningless word I had no time for. We rode high up on a rock as big and long as a truck bed, stayed up there—balanced!—for several seconds until we slid sideways down into water so furious it created its own weather—a fine, stinging mist. We emerged from it. I had all my limbs. I believed in God. Time flew and it stopped, and I had no thoughts. Rory's shouting was constant and nearly drowned out by the roar of the river, but the one time I turned back to look at him he was wild-eyed and laughing, his long, soaked dreads flying out behind him from under his helmet, his oar held up in the sky as in victory.

The boulders racing toward us grew fewer and smaller, but still the water moved with such urgency that relaxing one nerve was unthinkable. We rounded a curve and with no command from Rory—there was no time—we all ducked flat into the raft as we slipped under a fallen giant of a tree suspended only a few feet above the water. Our silence together felt more intimate than anything we'd said to each other thus far.

"Now that," Rory said, resting his oar across his knees, "was fucking beautiful."

We shared some genuine smiles and high fives, then quieted, watching. I was soaked to the skin—we all were—but the sun baked us dry where it hit us—mostly on our chests and arms. My feet stayed soaked in my gummy water shoes, and I could feel my helmet gluing my hair to my head, the strap chafing at my neck.

The river turned again, one bank suddenly bare of trees, just a field of stumps blackened as if by fire, and the water spread out into a pond that seemed to drop off in the distance. A few yards away, a ghostly gray heron, with one long leg disappeared in the muck and one bent backward, turned to look at us. Its reflection shimmered silver in the shallows. With heartbreaking grace, it lifted its prehistoric wings once and flapped, then twice; on the third flap it floated up and through sooty trees, long legs hanging down. The sky opened wide above us, a great blue eye.

"Everybody okay?" Rory said. We nodded, stunned and speechless. "Just so you know, you conquered the Tooth!" He looked at Pia. "Are you ready for more?"

"Bring it on!" She rowed steadily, eyes front.

"Everybody forward, let's dig!" Rory whooped and stood up on the back of the raft, holding up his oar like a weapon. "Here we come, Hungry Motherfucker! Woohoo!"

Even the brief respite on the pond was enough to make me aware of the stiffness in my back, shoulders, and legs from holding on so hard in the rapids we'd just run. I tried to stretch a bit even as I paddled, watching as the narrow section of the pond that seemed to drop off to nothingness came closer and closer. As much as I'd been staring at it, I hadn't yet realized that no bank was visible because there was no bank. Just a complete and total drop.

I think all of us—save Rory—would have pushed the stop button if we could have at the mouth of that thing. My breath left my body as I peered down at where the pond ended. A magnificent skull of rock appeared before us, so vast that all the volume of water in the pond thinned out to only a couple of inches deep. The forehead of the rock skull sloped steeply down, vanishing in a girdle of foam and a murky black pool.

Rory yelled, "Backpaddle!" We gladly did—for a blissful second, I thought we were going to bag this one—then he called out, "Oars up! Lean back!" We dropped down onto the smooth pate of stone with a flapping sound, my heels hitting hard even through the rubber. We skimmed over the thing for what felt like a full minute, headed straight down.

Just before the front of the raft slammed into the pool, Rory shouted, "Everybody lean right! *Now!*" He lurched forward, grabbed the line, and leaned, pulling right with all his weight. Commanded to do the same, so did we.

And then I was drowning.

17

It was almost peaceful, those first few seconds under the water. Certainly quieter than above. Stunned by the cold, I couldn't comprehend where I was. I watched my dead-white hands grope in front of my face as bubbles escaped my mouth and floated upward to a sun that shimmered yellow and wavy through the water. That's what I saw, but my mind's eye held the picture of Rory riding the side of the raft, cowboy-style, hooting and waving his oar until he and the four of us came tumbling down into black water.

I realized where I was. Punched my fists upward, opened them, and hauled the water back, aiming toward the squiggle of golden light, but it was cut by shadow, as if a storm cloud had drifted over the sun. Still I shot up through dark water, lungs screaming for air. I bulleted up and out and smacked the top of my head on something hard, coughing up river water that tasted of iron and moss and fish. I took a breath. Treaded water that lapped at my neck. A stink of wet canvas, rubber. Panicking, I whipped around in my tiny space trying to figure out why our tent was bobbing in front of me, soaked but still strapped onto other gear that hung at odd angles in the water.

I had come up underneath our upside-down raft.

The dry box came at me fast, and I realized the raft was moving, pushed by the current, so I filled my lungs and dunked down, feeling my way along its undersides to the rim, where I pulled myself up and into daylight.

Coughing and sputtering, Pia, Sandra, and Rachel bobbed in the eddy that scythed the bank. Yards away, the skull rock rose up white and round, as though the moon had sunk itself halfway into the river. Rope in hand, Rory side-stroked to a slice of shore where the beards of ancient cedars hung down in tangled knots. He pulled himself out by a drowned branch, tied up the raft, then slipped off his helmet and shook his head like a dog.

"Whoa, ladies! Great job!"

Rachel dragged herself up the bank and sat, breathing heavily. Soaking wet, she looked scrappy and capable. Pia stayed treading water in the relatively calm portion of the eddy, while Sandra and I swam past her.

"Why did we do that?" Rachel's voice was laced with disgust. "Why did we lean right?"

Rory un-Velcro-ed a vest pocket and pulled out a 3 Musketeers bar stashed in a Ziploc bag. Offered it to her. She shook her head and waved him away.

"So we could flip," he said through a mouthful of nougat.

Sandra pulled herself up onto the bank, hacking and shivering. She took off her helmet and emptied it of river water, her hair oddly wedge-shaped on one side, flat to her skull on the other.

"You've got to be fucking kidding me." Rachel examined her miraculously unbroken glasses before strapping them back on. "What the hell is wrong with you? We could have all drowned!"

Rory straightened, puffed out a bit. "Hey, man, chill. We're all still here."

"This is nuts," I said as I hauled myself up onto the shore, feet squelching in my thin rubber shoes. "I came up under the raft! *Under* it!"

"And you got out, right? Just like we talked about in training? Remember, we went over a bunch of different scenarios."

Pia pulled herself handily up and onto the bank, removed her helmet, and wrung out her hair, accepting the half a candy bar he offered her. Smiling, she lifted a wet dread out of his eye and tucked it behind one ear. He moved closer to her.

Rachel took a step toward him and raised her hand. I thought she was going to hit him, but she jabbed at his chest with her finger. "You are an irresponsible child, and I am going to report you when we get back, do you hear me?"

He calmly finished the chocolate and crushed the wrapper in his hand. "Listen, this isn't Disney World—"

"Yeah, we get that," Rachel spat back.

"I just made you more safe, not less safe, get it?"

"No, I don't." She turned to Sandra, who was trying to unwedge her hair with her hands. "Do you get it, Loo?"

She shook her head and feigned interest in the sky and the trees as if this was a battle she had zero interest in taking on. "Nope. Not at all."

"This raft—any raft—flips, and when it does, you have to be prepared. You get no warning. You need to always be ready to be upside down and in that water. So you just had a little practice, okay? Some awesome real-life experience, not some bullshit talk."

"You know what's bullshit talk?" Rachel said as she took another step toward him. Fury steamed off her. Rory fell back a step in surprise. "You, saying you're going to take care of every detail of this trip. What about leaving us three alone last night, garbage all over the camp, while you and Pia did your thing? You said we have to watch for bears—"

"—and some raccoons came to visit," Rory said with a shrug.

"So we were lucky!" Rachel said, furious. *"That time we were lucky!"*

"And you did what I said to do. You showed me you could think on your own. Follow directions. Good for you. Now listen." He took off his vest. "Tell me. Are you cold? Hungry? Thirsty?"

Except for Pia, we all nodded, swore under our breath, articulated our own versions of rage and discomfort.

"Then help me flip the raft back over. We'll get you warm, have lunch, and get back out there. It's three miles to the Flush, then we're home free. For the night, anyway."

It took all of us and all our strength to right the raft by pulling on a nylon rope threaded through the D rings on the sides of the boat, each braced and hauling from our places on the bank while Rory pushed the thing up from the water. We were scratched and bruised by the end of it, but everything in the dry bags had stayed dry, and a lunch of tuna sandwiches, oranges, and reconstituted tomato soup wasn't half-bad. Faces toward the sun, we drank frosty cans of Miller Lite in almost one swallow. Rachel, Sandra, and I roasted ourselves dry on flat outcroppings of sandstone and shale we found, too tired or frustrated or freaked out to say a word to each other, while Rory and Pia unpacked and repacked the gear on the raft, all the while bantering and laughing like old friends.

18

Just as Rory said, the river widened again. It took turn after graceful turn, white water replaced by a dark, fast-moving current that pulled us forward in a businesslike manner, its playful sparkle gone. The light was changing as the afternoon came on; colors deepened, became richer. Still, Rory called out commands that we followed to the letter, the sound of his voice translating seamlessly into actions as if this were something we had always done, would always do.

Once in a while my friends splashed me with the exuberance of their rowing, but at this point we were all getting good at not caring about being wet; in fact, I couldn't recall the last time I'd been completely dry. At calmer points when the air was still and the sun settled on us—more at our backs now than in front—I could smell myself, and it hit me that my last shower had been a couple of days ago. We all had helmet hair now, even Rory. My inner arms stung where they had chafed from rowing, the soft skin rubbing constantly against the rough canvas of my life vest, my hands stiff as claws from clutching the oar. A fresh layer of sweat covered me as we paddled harder, searching for deeper areas since the river continued to flatten and broaden.

In places my oar made contact with the riverbed and vibrated there, thrumming up my arm with an odd communion. Finally we scraped on stones, so we all got out and walked the raft, Rory towing it, until the water ran deep enough to lift us up again.

We settled into a good rhythm together at the next stretch, a couple of miles where the riverbed became sandy and the water turned impish again, each part of the river busy with some task. On our right, sprightly bubblings danced over a set of shallow, step-down rapids; to our left, water fluted and turned, scouring out a series of glacial potholes. But once again, and quickly, the banks closed in on us, and the water, now muddy with churned silt, took on a deep-throated rumbling, as if all this time we had been listening to contralto and suddenly we heard the water in baritone. For the first time, I had the sensation of going downhill.

"Heads up, ladies," Rory yelled. "Get ready for the Flush!"

We whipsawed around a bend, and everything changed again. The front of the raft dipped and my stomach with it as the regular river disappeared and some maniacal thing took over. Sandra glanced back at me and yelled something I couldn't hear. I looked ahead and saw what she was trying to show me. A meringue of white water for what seemed like miles. Water quickened, leapt, broke, and foamed again. And always we kept falling, the river dropping out from under us again and again. Blinded by white waves that broke over our heads, we banged down and down, my knees and spine stunned and throbbing with pain.

Again Sandra turned and screamed something back at me—at Rory too—I wasn't sure. This time she pointed behind us with her oar. I looked up and behind the raft, and for a glimmer of a second, I saw it. A section of log as long as the raft and nearly a foot thick bobbed and churned behind us. Black and oily looking, it rolled and tossed in the waves but followed the raft as if intent on us.

"Face front!" Rory bellowed at Sandra and me before barking out fresh commands to Pia and Rachel as we all scrambled just to keep the raft facing forward. Dark spruce leaned in from the banks as water rose all around us. Deadly rocks multiplied to either side, squeezing us into a V of white-green water that raced over what looked like a six-foot drop only seconds away.

We shot over the precipice of rock. Sandra spun around and screamed. Her face had contorted with so much terror I feared I might turn to stone if I saw whatever she saw, but I forced myself to look behind us. Rory stood on the lip of the raft, oar raised up with both hands, caterwauling his own brand of fearless ecstasy in his heaven of mortal danger. Behind him the log launched up in the air just after we did, blocking the sun, still turning as if it were alive, like it had some score to settle with him; rolling and falling, it smacked full force into the middle of his back with a meaty thud. His face stayed beatific as the oar soared skyward; both arms flew up and his shoulders bent back hideously over the log.

His body hurtled up and over us, propelled by the log, as we all fell or jumped into the swirling whiteness.

19

I burst out of the water screaming. A waterfall hammered the top of my head, forcing me back under, but I bent my knees and launched myself away from the rock face. Freed from the falling water, I was at the mercy of the current. It yanked me side to side, hurled me at rocks, and sucked me down. Gasping and sputtering, blinded by my wet hair plastered over my face, I somehow remembered the lawn-chair pose: I lay back and lifted my feet and kept my hands high.

As I hurtled toward a mess of fallen trees and boulders, I caught a flash of bright orange—Rory's shorts. In horror I realized what I was approaching. The bottom half of his body floated up, his shorts pillowing with air, his head and shoulders pinned under the log, which was wedged solid in a jumble of branches and unforgiving stone. His forearm floated to the surface from a confusion of waterlogged tree roots. Bent limply from the wrist, his hand and fingers hung down, delicately moving in the rushing water as if he were testing its temperature.

I was tossed almost on top of him, though mercifully just to the left of his bobbing shorts, where I held out my arms to brace myself against the branches. Even in my terror the pain of my skin scraping raw against the bark and stones knocked the wind out of me. Torrents of water pounded at me in an attempt to sift my body through the strainer of branches and stone. River water foamed into my mouth until I gagged and lifted myself up high enough to breathe.

The log lay solidly across Rory's back, an unbearable truth. The river roared like a freight train in my ears. I screamed something, maybe his name, maybe Pia's, maybe Sandra's, Rachel's, God's, I don't remember. I took a breath and pushed myself down into the churning depths.

I've heard time slows down in situations like this. For me it did. I recall every detail, against my own will sometimes, help-lessly.

Again the almost peaceful quiet underwater. Small sticks and leaves tornadoed by in the greenish murk. Rory's white helmet glowed silver underwater, caught between the log and a puzzle of branches and roots, his dreads jerking crazily in the flow. His right shoulder was jammed at some terrible angle under the log; his arm lost under a tumult of stone. By clear effort of will, he turned his face toward me, half-obscured by the helmet. The one eye I could see was open wide, alive and pleading, his lips lifted off his gums and moving horribly, comically, by the relentless pull of the water.

I heard dull screams from above so I pushed myself up and away from him, a train of bubbles escaping my nose and mouth. Water smacked my face as I took a breath, punishing me; I gulped down more river. Above me, Pia and Rachel, sodden, squatted on the pile of fallen limbs, desperately reaching down to get a grip on the monster log that imprisoned Rory. But it was too big and their angle wrong.

"Where's Sandra?" I coughed out.

"We don't know!" Pia howled over the roar of the water, her bloodshot eyes full of horror.

Rachel reached down for me. "We looked but we can't—"

"Get in the water!" I screamed. "Help me push it off him!"

Rachel scrambled past Pia, who sat momentarily frozen with one arm wrapped uselessly around the log, and let herself down next to me in the slamming water, eyes huge behind water-beaded lenses. Pia took one step—sickeningly—on the log that trapped Rory and slipped in. Without speaking, we took a breath and dropped down underwater.

We jammed our knees and feet into whatever crevices or breaks in rock or wood we could find to gain purchase and force our shoulders under the log, lifting with every muscle in our bodies. Straining, running out of air, we pushed. I felt as if we had submerged under a mountain and were trying to lift it. I could feel Rachel kicking at me as she fought to keep herself wedged in for balance. My face was now inches from his, close enough to see his one eye watch me with rapidly fading hope.

The log moved—in the wrong direction. It rolled farther down into the vise of branches and rock and forced him deeper under the debris. We fitted our shoulders and arms and hands under that fucking thing and screamed and cried underwater, bubbles streaming by as we heaved up with every last bit of strength we had.

Rachel and Pia burst up for air and thrust themselves back down, again and again, but I was able to hold my breath the longest. The third time they surfaced something passed between Rory and me. His eye gazed at me as I strained and pushed. There was a kind of love in it, or gratefulness. Something in him that believed in my power to lift that hellish log, a look of trust that stayed even after the eye clouded and most of the life drained away. And I couldn't tell if it was the last conscious thing he did in his life or if it was the current, but his free arm moved toward me and his fingers swept across my cheek, gently and just once, then floated ahead of him and under the log, fluttering and waving at the water's bidding.

20

When I finally exploded out of the water, gulping at the air, Pia and Rachel bobbed at the surface on either side of me.

"I think he's dead!" I screamed at their stricken faces. Rachel's glasses bent diagonally across her face, Pia's helmet was dented and cracked. A cut above her eyebrow bled steadily. She blinked the blood away.

"Let's get to shore and try from there!" Pia yelled over the river's fury.

I reached up and seized a tree limb to hoist myself onto a rock but had no strength left. We all tried. It was impossible. Even Pia couldn't deadlift herself up and out. We had no way to get to the bank except to go under Rory. I gestured to the others what we had to do; they nodded. I took the kind of breath I had trained myself to take before a dive—slow, deep, deliberate—and thrust myself down into the swirling depths and reached under him. My hand found a branch just under his chest and I pulled myself down into darkness, eyes squeezed shut this time, and muscled my way through the current and to the other side of him, his vest grazing the back of my neck.

Something grabbed my sleeve, yanked at me.

Rachel popped up like a cork to my right; Pia next to her. "Let's try from here," Rachel said breathlessly. "Maybe it's better."

It looked like a worse angle to me, but we three dropped down and under. This time we could touch bottom and that made all the difference. We all came up hard under the log and with our footing leveraged it high enough so the water worked with us now, helping us force it up just a few inches, enough to roll it onto a slab of rock that sloped down in the opposite direction.

We looked on in horror as Rory's orange shorts stayed bobbing up and down exactly as they had been, head and shoulders still submerged under the cascade of water.

I am a swimmer, I thought, *so now is when I swim.*

Against all instinct I dove back in; let the mad current take me. In seconds it thrust me on top of him, pasted me against the snarl of river detritus. His helmet glimmered in the water beneath me, his arms floating in a T shape to his sides as if he were flying underwater. I sucked in a lungful of air. Dropped down and hauled myself toward him, hand over hand, by the odd root and branch. *Don't think,* I told myself. *Just do.* One step after the next. My body held fast against the wood and stone, I reached under his chin and unbuckled his helmet.

Nothing happened. Of course he didn't float up! The helmet still encircled much of his head, and two fat stones gripped the helmet while another imprisoned his shoulder. Pounding water held his body in place.

Other hands touched my back. Someone swam over me. Was I being held down? White stars danced in front of me. Panic tasted like blood in my mouth; I forced it away. Blinked, surfaced, dove down again.

Rachel swam beneath me, treading by Rory. The water exploded to my right, and I saw Pia, her long form swimming down to us. She hauled his right shoulder from under the rock as Rachel grabbed his left, their white cheeks bulging with air, their eyes huge as they strained. Together they pushed his body down and away from the helmet, which remained wedged between the stones.

He floated up so fast I didn't have a second to think—suddenly his body was under mine, arms and legs spread. We soared up together to the surface, where the water turned us, forcing us once more against the wreckage of trees and rocks.

His head was inches from my own, slumped onto his chest but out of the water, his big body sandwiching me there, so terribly cold where his flesh touched mine. Pia and Rachel grappled with him, manhandling him off me, and—all the while kicking and fighting the relentless current—drove him toward the bank. As soon as we could touch bottom, we put our bodies under him. Wore him like a heavy coat. We dragged him to the narrow shore, his feet in their purple-and-green Tevas scoring the dirt behind us. As we did so, I turned my head and glimpsed out of the corner of my eye the bright blues and yellows of the raft, caught on a jutting peninsula of tree stumps and rock a hundred yards downriver. No hot-pink T-shirt flashed in the woods—no sign of Sandra.

"Hurry, let's get him up here!" Laden with his shoulders and upper body, Rachel nodded at a flat section of beach edged by tall ferns. I clambered to the spot, cradling his head as we awkwardly turned him and laid him down.

Pia stumbled backward into the ferns, hands clasped over her mouth. Staring down at Rory, she whispered, "Oh God, oh God, oh God, help us," as Rachel fell to her knees. Water bubbled out of his mouth and she shouted at us, "Help me turn him—Pia, go by his feet, Wini, come by me!"

Pia and I dropped down to the ground and rolled him on his

side. He felt so big, solid, immovable—how had we been able to lift him out of the water? With a muffled cry, Rachel drove her shoulder into the backs of his knees, bending them toward his chest. River water pulsed out along with something stringy, bits of tuna and chocolate—bile, vomit. She reached in his mouth with her fingers and wiped it away. Grabbed his wrist and held it for one, three, five seconds—screamed, "Fuck!"—and dropped it. "Get him on his back. Now!"

We obeyed. She held her ear over his open mouth, cursed again. Seizing his jaw with one hand, she slid his forehead back with the other, then pinched his nose shut. She clamped her mouth over his, and we heard the rush of her living breath into his chest that looked still as clay. Athletically, she repositioned herself, glasses dangling down by their elastic cord as she hovered over him with straight, stiffened arms, palms aimed at his heart. She thrust down hard and fast on his river-logged body, then hopped back to his mouth, then his chest and mouth again, over and over for countless ungodly minutes until I heard a wet cracking sound. Still she did not stop.

"Can we do something?" I took a step forward.

"Just stay away from me!" Rachel said hoarsely, wretchedly, her matted wet hair hanging down over her face. Tears coursing down her cheeks, she placed both hands by the sides of his neck, then checked his wrists again. She fell forward with a wrenching cry and pounded the earth with her fist, just once.

All the time Rory gazed upward into a dense canopy of birch and alder, waiting to be brought back to life.

21

We stood in a circle, gazing down at Rory in his hush of death. Expectant. As if at any moment he would sit up and tell us what it was like in that other place or wink and smile at Pia and pull her down with him on his soft bed of ferns under his sky of leaves and afternoon light.

Pia dropped to her knees. With a strangled cry she buried her head in her hands and began to sob from the depth of her guts. The grief of the lover left behind, pure shock, genuine loss, fear of what terrors lay ahead, or some combination, there was no way of knowing. I only knew I had never seen her so devastated. Rachel and I just let her cry. The shimmering terror of Sandra's absence hovered between us; still, we stood riveted, unable to move. Just above us, trilling over Pia's guttural moans, a songbird chose now to sing its prettiest tune.

Rory lay in speckled sunlight, his moss-green eyes open, mouth slightly parted, so that he seemed about to speak. I stared at him until it felt wrong doing so, and still I looked; we all did. His Michelangelo's *David* build, his handsome face; a beautiful boy who would always be twenty, who would never be this beautiful again. He looked even younger dead, his skin moist and dewy, his well-defined muscles seeming somehow tensed and about to move.

I thought of Marcus. I couldn't help it. The only other dead person I had ever seen. A month after we signed him into the group home, he'd broken into the meds—there was only a shitty lock a child could break—and swallowed everything he could find. He thought they were candy. At least that was my hope; it's still what I tell myself when I'm trying to fall asleep at night. Clearly Richard and I were in decay, but Marcus was the one I thought I would never have to live without.

The dread before they pulled back the sheet was like nothing I had ever felt, but when they did, when I forced myself to look, it was just his face, my dear sweet brother lying there, thirty-three years old and gone forever. He looked asleep, as if he were dreaming. And I thought, *Now I'll never know for sure.* I knew him better than anyone else; still he was locked inside, still there were unseen dimensions, unopened rooms, chapters of him in languages I couldn't decipher. No one had a clue what was inside his head. No one understood, when he was young, that it paid to look a little deeper into people like him. On most days he was like a seven-year-old boy in a grown man's body; on others he signed complex sentences to me. He'd invent his own signs for things, cracking ridiculous jokes that would make us both double over in laughter. The next day it was as if he'd traveled to the other side of the world in his mind. He'd look at me with blank eyes when I signed him his silly made-up signs, and I couldn't reach him at all.

A crashing sound in the woods behind us. We turned, trembling. Sandra, bedraggled, her face bloody and scratched, stumbled toward our strangely intimate circle.

"Thank God!" she cried, hysteria in her voice. "I couldn't find you! I didn't know where you were. . . ." Dazed, she turned in a half circle, staring up into the menacing green, the cruel blue sky. "I washed downriver, I don't even know how far. . . . I couldn't get out! But then I did and I called for you, didn't you hear me?"

Rachel and I moved toward her to comfort her, but her eyes fell on Rory and she covered her mouth, gasped, and fell a few steps toward him. I tried to put my arms around her, but she wasn't having it. She pushed us both away.

"What's wrong with him?"

"He's gone," Rachel said softly.

Sandra ran over to the body and fell to her knees. "Are you sure? Have you done everything—"

Pia nodded through her tears. She placed a badly shaking hand on Rory's belly, then pulled it away.

"He was gone back in the river, I'm pretty sure," Rachel said. She walked over to him. Kneeling, she reached down with trembling fingers—purplish with cold—and closed his eyes, one at a time. "Good-bye, Rory," I thought I heard her say before she got to her feet.

I took a look at all of us. We were a pretty sad-looking crew. As if she were trying to fit under a desk, Pia knelt doubled over on the ground, legs folded under her, forehead pressed to the earth, fingers laced behind the back of her neck. She'd stopped crying, but her back would spasm now and then. Sandra stood looking haggard, wet, and small. Two long, bloody cuts swept diagonally across her cheek as if something clawed had attacked her. Under her helmet and mop of wet hair, Rachel's glasses—still strapped to her head by the elastic strap—zigzagged crazily from eyebrow to lip. One lens was completely missing. I'm sure I looked just as hellish.

"Is everyone okay?" My voice sounded strange to me, as if it came from some doppelgänger speaking in a dark room. Sandra and Rachel nodded. They held out and examined their intact limbs, marveling at them as if they'd never seen them before. Pia remained folded over in her small-as-possible position.

Rachel took off her glasses, wiped the remaining lens with her shirt, turned, and started walking toward the river. "I'll be right back."

Pia looked up. "Where are you going?"

Rachel spun around. "We have to go get the raft while it's still light."

"We can't just leave him here!"

A fat black fly landed on Rory's nose, ambled down to his cheek.

"You can stay with him if you want. We'll find the raft and come back."

Pia dropped her head again, crying silently.

My legs felt thick and leaden as I followed Sandra and Rachel to the bank, where the river had begun to darken. A velvety evening feel had crept into it. We stood and watched it move; in my mind's eye I saw Rory, crucified by the log and hurtling forward into his tomb of water and wood and stone, but now the log was just another piece of flotsam, jammed up and lying with its brothers, to be beaten and worn down to nothingness by the infinite water.

Sandra scrambled onto a ledge that jutted out over the river like the beseeching hand of God. She pointed toward the clot of fallen trees and stone a few hundred yards downriver on the opposite bank, where the raft had been stranded less than an hour ago. "It was right there." Her voice trailed off into the hush of moving water.

We stared and stared, but the river answered us with nothing. No Disney-bright raft with cheerful yellow ropes and not-found-in-nature-blue D rings, just its own earth colors of water, tree, rock, and darkening sky. Everything was wild and involved with itself, I could see that now. It hit me full force, bodily. A breeze with the lush taste of night lifted up from the river as a deep trepidation like some thick, furred beast turned in my bowel. Nothing cared that we were here. The spruce that hulked and swayed over the river had no thought of the latest movie or book, of the lights of Boston at night, of the cheerful cafés filled with laughing students. The water in all its forms forever falling dismissed Pia's bucket list; Rachel's fierceness and sobriety; Sandra's momentous marital exit plan; my dead brother and loneliness, my wish for the bravery to change my own life. It just didn't give a rat's ass.

Sandra turned and looked down at us where we cowered on the bank. "I can't believe this. It was there ten minutes ago. Up against those rocks."

"I saw it too," I said, a silvery chill snaking down my spine.

"It probably washed down and got caught on something else." Rachel climbed up onto the ledge and stood next to Sandra. "Let's go find it."

"What about Pia?"

"We'll take ten minutes and look for it. Bring it back or tie it up somewhere. She'll be fine."

22

The forest that lined the river was impenetrable, so we had to make our way along the bank. Snarled root systems and tangled brush forced us down into the river itself. Clinging to or hanging from the odd root or branch, up to our waists in surging water, our pace turned pitifully slow. All we had was what we wore: nylon shorts, polyester wicking T-shirts, life vests, our helmets, and water shoes, which felt like thin rubber slippers. Every nugget of root, stick, or sharp stone hobbled me, and always the cold, cold water. Branches slapped back at us at every turn. It felt like someone was slowly, continuously beating us up.

Fifteen, twenty minutes passed, and we'd barely rounded the next bend. I was freezing and starving and ashamed to be hungry when someone had just died. More than anything else, I couldn't let myself think about what would happen if we couldn't find the raft.

"Sandra!" Rachel called from behind me. "Stop a second!"

I turned, nursing the dear thought that Rachel had seen something like the raft.

She clung to a sapling rooted in the mossy bank, squinting through her one good lens.

"We have to go back. We're losing our daylight."

Pia's lanky silhouette blocked a piece of the lowering sun where she stood on the ledge. We had maybe an hour of light, tops. The three of us fought our way to the narrow strip of beach near the accident.

Pia jumped down from the rock and joined us there.

"What do you mean you didn't find it?" She crossed her arms hard over her vest.

"It's a total bitch going downriver." Rachel took off her shoes with a squelch and drained the water from them. "It's probably around the next bend, but we had to get back before dark."

Mosquitoes swarmed our bodies as if they'd eat us to the bone.

"Well, thanks for coming back to get me," Pia said possibly sarcastically.

"My God," I said. "What are we going to do?"

Sandra squatted on the sand and held her head in her hands, crying softly into them.

"We're not going to panic," Rachel said, a barely detectable quiver in her voice. "That's not going to get us anywhere."

Pia gazed at the water. "The raft has everything we need."

"Food," Sandra mumbled from under her helmet. "Water, tents, cell phones, GPS, maps—"

"Rory's gun—" I said.

"Jesus Christ, I know, okay?" Rachel undid the strap on her helmet and threw it on the wet sand. "Let's just think."

"What are we going to do about Rory?" Pia said.

Rachel glared at her and whispered hotly, "Rory is in a better place than we are right now."

Tears ran fast down Pia's face but she didn't seem conscious of them. "We fucked, okay? When are you going to get over it?"

Sandra started to rock in place.

Rachel visibly rearranged her face into a semblance of calm. "Maybe I didn't say it very nicely, Pia, but think about it for a sec, okay? Finding the raft is our first priority."

Pia looked down, then met Rachel's eye. "We're going to take him with us."

"You mean what, *carry* him somewhere? Where?" Rachel turned a half circle in the tumbling green. "We don't even know where we are!"

"I think the raft is close by," I said stupidly. "Chances are we'll find it in the morning, no problem."

"And when we do, we'll take him with us," Pia said. Behind her, a gaunt cormorant on a dead branch fluffed out its sooty wings to dry.

"You're not thinking straight, Pia," Rachel said. I had a flash of Rachel singing and stumbling down Cambridge streets in her days of margaritas and Harvey Wallbangers, protesting loudly as Pia wrestled the car keys from her while simultaneously deflecting Rachel's often vicious *in vino veritas* verbal attacks. Rachel's sobriety intervened, but I couldn't help wondering if Pia's hurt ever really went away. "We can't strap two hundred pounds of dead guy to an overloaded raft we don't even know how to steer ourselves down thirty more miles of rapids or whatever the hell is in front of us."

"Yes, we can."

I couldn't help recalling a remark Rory had made earlier in the day as he was loading up the raft, something like *You can carry a lot in a raft if you're smart about it.* I had a feeling this wasn't what he meant.

"I'm getting really cold," Sandra said. We all turned to look at her. Her lips were purplish, and she was white as paper against the gravelly beach. Of all of us, she was the most sensitive to cold, wrapped in a sweater even on the warmest days. We gathered around her. Rachel and I knelt on either side, massaging her arms and shoulders. Pia sat at her feet and rubbed and slapped at Sandra's legs, then helped her take off her water shoes and nestled her feet in her armpits.

"This can't happen," I said. "We have to stay warm."

Sandra nodded, teeth chattering. Rachel took off her own vest and covered her with it.

"Is that better, Loo?" I asked.

She nodded. "I'm okay."

"All right," Rachel said. "Let's go take care of Rory. Then we have to find a way to live through the night."

23

I'll never know why I was assigned this position, but it was me who supported Rory's head as we dragged his body up the bank from the beach. His rough braids, heavy with river water, draped across my forearms as I cradled his head in my hands. The weight of it stunned me. Pia, her emotions passed or suppressed or just saved for later, grimaced with her load, her long arms encircling his wide chest. Rachel and Sandra each grappled with a leg, but no matter how much we heaved and maneuvered, reassigning body parts and weight loads every couple of yards, one of his arms dragged through the ferns behind us.

We laid him down at the crest of the bank, on a shaded, flattish area where we guessed the ground to be a bit softer. The fact that we now overlooked the spot where he died was lost on none of us, I believe, but at least he was above it, on dry land.

"So now what?" I said, placing his head as gently as I could on the dirt. Picking it up again was beyond imagining.

"Now we dig," Rachel said.

"With what?" Sandra said softly.

The act of moving him had worked down the orange shorts a bit at his groin, where under the fabric his penis arced and pointed toward his right leg, now bent as if he were leaping over something. We all stared at a fresh-looking tattoo of a winged, arrow-pierced heart with R&A etched in baroque letters just above the first few curls of pubic hair.

"This isn't right," Pia said. "We can't bury him here."

"He's dead, Pia. It was an accident." Rachel gingerly straightened both his legs. "We bury him here. For now."

"There's no way I'm going to—"

"We have to put him where the animals can't get him."

Pia covered her mouth and blinked. Sandra reached up and patted her shoulder. I'm not sure Pia felt it.

"We'll mark it with rocks or something, leave something tied to a tree by the river so we can find this place again."

"Pia," I said as gently as I could. It came out as a whisper. "It makes sense."

She didn't answer, but we made our hands into claws and scratched into the earth next to him, which got us only an inch or two down before roots and small stones made it impossible to continue. I took off my helmet and used the edge to scrape a deeper hole—we all tried—and made a bit more progress. Pia slipped her belt out of her shorts and scraped at the ground with the buckle. In the end we had a Rory-length and -width depression in the dirt, serving-platter-deep, and maneuvered him into it, painstakingly keeping him faceup per Pia's insistence.

"Hold on," Rachel said. "We should take his vest."

"No," Pia said.

"We need everything we have to keep warm."

"This is fucked," Pia said under her breath, but helped us roll him side to side to free the vest from one arm, then the other, before we settled him back down, arranging his arms by his sides. His skin felt chilled now, like the river. Nothing we wanted to touch. His fingers had started to curl, as if in a death-slow attempt to hold on.

We split up to gather rocks and pine boughs, whatever we could find to cover him. Thorn-studded brush lacerated our shins, but moving helped us keep warm. Sandra, now wearing Rory's life vest over her own, found a couple of logs that she dragged up the bank and arranged alongside him. Rachel assigned me to build a cairn on the river to mark the spot.

As I stepped from rock to rock lugging stones to pile far enough out in the river to be seen, something tan and white twitched in the leaves near the bank. A young buck stepped delicately into a shallow eddy, glanced at me as if I were nothing, then dropped its velvet-antlered head to drink. The rocks shifted in my arms; I dropped one. Before I took another breath, the buck had turned to run, hooves clattering on river stones, before it crashed into the brush with a flash of its white tail.

As I balanced the last rock on top of the cairn, I remembered with a swoon the chocolate I'd bought at the store and stashed in one of the zippered compartments of my life vest. I took it out. Examined my prize. A froggy miniature Mr. Goodbar, half out of its wrapper. I ate it quickly, facing away from the bank, as if someone were watching me. A profound thirst followed. Head down, I hurried back to the shore.

Rory looked like a forest mummy under his encasement of tumbled stone and pine boughs. Pia and Rachel stood over him, arguing.

"Of course I know his last name. It's Ekhart. Rory Ekhart."

"We have to cover his face, Pia, for the same reason we had to cover his body."

"Then let me do it." She wiped the sweat and mud and tears off her face with the backs of her hands. She knelt near his head, gazing down at him the way a mother might over her dead child. Ants had found him. They mapped the poreless skin of his forehead and cheeks. She did her best to brush them off, then arranged leaves like puzzle pieces over his face, finally covering those with smaller flattish stones she'd collected by the river.

"I'd like to say some words," she said as she got to her feet. "In case we don't get back here."

Rachel looked away, in exhaustion or impatience or disgust I couldn't tell, as Pia tilted her head at the forest grave.

"Rest in peace, Rory Ekhart. Who knows what kind of man you would have grown into. I'm sure you would have been a good man, and the world is less without you in it."

Then we left him. Quietly, in soldierly order, we filed down to the river to make our plan.

24

No one has *anything*? Are you sure? Check all your pockets," Rachel said.

Guiltily I rooted around in all the zippered and Velcro-ed compartments in my vest and shirt, turned my shorts pockets inside out. I shrugged. Sandra extricated a mint-flavored Chap Stick used down to a nub, Pia a travel-size foldout brush and waterlogged hair band. Rachel had exactly nothing. We gazed at our depressing stash arranged on the flat rock we stood on, then returned everything to our respective pockets.

"Rory's map," Pia said. "If we just had that. I'm trying so hard to remember it."

"Well, we're at the Royal Flush, we know that. So we're fifteen miles from where we started, with thirty more to go on the river. You know," Rachel said, "we should just hike back upriver to our first camp."

"I don't know," Sandra said, sitting down on the ledge we stood on. She pulled her arms and legs in, tucking herself under the two vests like a turtle. "Going downriver was ridiculous just now. Why would going upriver be any different? Either way, it'll take us forever to get anywhere."

"But at least we know where we put the raft in the river this morning." Rachel squinted into the last rays of sunlight. "Think about it, wouldn't you recognize that place?"

We nodded dully.

Rachel continued excitedly, "We get there and then look for that logging road right near the camp. We find that fucker and we're out of here."

I watched the river rushing by and tried to conjure that very morning, so many eons ago, when we pushed off from a narrow, sandy bank that looked like hundreds of sandy banks we'd passed on our way to the one yards from where we stood. Just a blur of forest and water and terror and death.

"I'm so thirsty," Sandra said. "I can't think I'm so thirsty."

"Everybody's thirsty." Rachel put her hands on her hips. "We don't have the purification pills."

"I know." Sandra pushed herself stiffly to her feet and made her way down to the water that surged beneath the rocks we stood on.

"What are you doing?" Rachel said, following her. "Don't drink that. Get back up here."

"Don't talk to her like that." Pia slipped her a sharp look. "Besides, for crying out loud, how bad can it be?"

"You could get sick! *Really* sick. You never know what took a crap upstream or what died. Some animal could be lying in the water decomposing. . . ."

Pia jumped down a set of natural stone steps to a place with enough room to kneel. Sandra lay on her belly, splashing her face and scooping water up into her mouth.

I got up.

"This is nuts," Rachel said hoarsely. "You're all going to shit yourselves to death."

"So what? At least we won't be thirsty." I practically ran down to join the others. The water tasted like slate, algae, sunlight. I couldn't get enough of it. I gobbled it up; drank to the point of nausea before I lifted my head, dizzy, my vision blurring for a moment before my thirst headache began to dissipate. The forest looked monstrously heavy in the lowering light, seeming to sprout more green before my eyes. I felt it waiting to engulf us, ingest us. One water shoe badly torn, Rachel limped down to join us on the lower rock stair but did not take a sip of water.

"It's crazy to go back the way we came," Pia said between gulps of river water. "Plus, we'd be climbing uphill. The raft has to be close by."

"We don't know that," Rachel said. "What if it's washed another twenty miles downstream? Then we're fucked!"

Pia came up to her elbows, seemed to think it over. "We're more fucked if we try to go back and we can't get to where we started. Look"—she got to her feet—"whatever decision we make, it has to be the right one, do you know what I mean? There's no time to make the wrong decision. It could kill us." A few horrible moments for that to sink in. "And come on, Rachel, really, do you remember it that well? Where we put in? Would you recognize it?"

"Wouldn't you? I guess you were a little distracted."

Pia flipped a hand in the air, dismissing the remark. "Sandra, would you know it if you saw it?"

"I think so," she said from under her battered helmet. "I remember the little island."

"Wini?"

I squinted at the trees and rocks and bruised-looking sky upriver. "It all looks the same to me. We've seen so many of those little islands, haven't we? I think we need to go after the raft."

"Then it's decided," Rachel said. "Me and Loo head upstream to try to get help. You and Pia try for the raft."

We looked at each other. A tiny, pitiful nation of four about to be made smaller and weaker still.

"Are you nuts?" Pia said, reading my mind. "It'll be dark in no time and you guys'll be somewhere in the middle of freaking nowhere, and we'll be in another part of nowhere, equally screwed. We stay together, that's it. End of story."

Rachel paced in a tight circle, hugging herself. "I don't know. I don't want to die in this place. This is . . ." She ground her fists into her forehead. "This was *not* my idea, this—this disaster, just so Pia could have her big fucking adventure." She threw her hands up toward the sky. "Couldn't do it. Couldn't just go someplace safe and comfortable where we could all relax and hang out and maybe even live through it." Her voice clogged with tears. "No, that wouldn't have worked at all. Anything fun or sane like that."

Pia gazed down at the silvery water, hands stuffed in vest pockets, statue-still. Exhaustion and shock beginning to show on all of us; the pallor of our skin, even our ability to argue.

But we couldn't all be down for the count. Not now.

I gritted my teeth and forced myself to say something, even though the words felt bizarrely gung ho coming out of my mouth. "Well, sorry, kids, we're not in Aruba. We're not sitting on the deck by the ocean drinking cosmos and watching the sun set. So let's get our shit together."

"Maybe go have some water," Sandra said. "It helps a lot."

But Rachel had caved in to her tears now, though none of us seemed moved to comfort her.

"We go downstream and look for the raft," Pia said. "All of us."

•   •   •

I think Rachel had the worst time of it. She scrambled along the bank close behind me, barely able to see through her one lens and still refusing to drink. Pia took the lead, sometimes so far up ahead and out of sight I was worried and pissed off at the same time. Ahead of me Sandra moved doggedly along, making small moaning sounds as she pulled herself from place to place. At times we had to detour into the woods, never daring to go out of earshot of the river.

The sky turned gunmetal gray. I could taste the rain coming on the air. After a wretchedly cold hour-long slog, we half stumbled onto Pia, who had come upon an inlet of sorts. A brief stretch of beach walled off by forest on three sides. Above us, a hawk circled in the dying light of the sky, threaded through the tops of the trees, and disappeared.

"We better stop here for the night," Pia said. We couldn't have gone more than half a mile from where Rory lay, but she was right. We could barely make out our hands in front of our faces. "Let's gather whatever we can to cover ourselves."

Like Rory, she didn't need to say—I thought it anyway. We cleared brush and the stones we could lift from our tiny camp so we could all stretch out a bit or at least sit next to each other, then arranged a few branches and sticks into the crudest of lean-tos. Behind us the land and forest rose steeply up, blacker than any night I had ever seen.

25

We sat huddled together, quaking and whimpering, arms around each other, legs pressed together, like one four-headed creature. As if the river at night possessed the answers, we were quiet, listening to its pulse and hush. It gleamed with remnants of the day until it mirrored the moon in glittering shards. Then that too disappeared, as if the river had swallowed it, and the current folded into its nighttime self, braiding and turning like liquid metal in the green and gloom.

Full on darkness, and all its terrors. I suddenly understood cultures that believed in demons and chimeras, werewolves and gollums. With no walls around us, no light or source of warmth, what besides the monstrous makes sense? Every sound was a beast. Behind us, all around us, the forest throbbed with the call and response of insects. Rain pattered on the leaves and dirt, dimpling the water, tapping on our heads and shoulders through our silly pine-bough ceiling, taking its sweet time to steadily soak us through and make our misery complete.

"They won't even be looking for us until Monday," Sandra said.

"Try Tuesday," Rachel said. "If we're lucky."

Pia's stomach growled. "I'm so freaking starving."

"I'm too scared to be starved," I said.

"I'm just cold," Sandra said.

"Then get in the middle," Rachel said. "We should take turns being on the inside, staying warm."

"We need to try to sleep," Pia said.

"Not very likely," I said, trying to rub some warmth into my arms.

"I'm serious. We take turns. Sandra, go to sleep. You too, Wini. Me and Rachel will watch out for a few hours."

Sandra got up and tucked herself between me and Pia. I could barely feel her with her extra vest, but her bony shoulders poked into me and she folded her legs under mine. I thought I was freezing, but I shuddered at her meat-locker-cold calves and thighs. Pia, her arm practically around both of us, felt like a warm room in comparison, though every now and then an involuntary shiver passed through her.

"We have just one job," Pia whispered. "To get through the night. Don't think past that, okay? Just go a little at a time, minute by minute if you have to."

Maybe because someone had told me it was my job to go to sleep, I felt my eyelids grow heavy and—unbelievably—found myself with my chin resting on the collar of my vest. To keep my mind off where we were, I pictured us in our seventies and eighties, and what each of our old-lady bodies might look like. Sandra and I would stay in pear mode no doubt, butts getting bigger and top halves tending toward scrawny, especially in the neck and shoulders. Rachel would shrink all over, just get tinier, while Pia would morph into a walking stick, frail and long, in danger of breaking a hip just crossing the kitchen floor. Nested in the overheated comforts of our assisted-living facility, we'd invite each other over for decaf and blond brownies, laughing as we recalled that silly trip to Maine when our guide drowned and we lost the raft but ultimately found our way to safety. . . .

Howling sounds snapped me awake. My heart blood leapt high into my throat. We clutched each other.

"Oh, dear God," Pia said. "Wolves." Her nails dug into the flesh of my arms.

A staccato of yips, followed by long, mournful baying and high-pitched barks. The sound came from everywhere and nowhere. It surrounded us, ricocheted inside our heads, sliced up into the sky; it even silenced the insects.

The yelping stopped. Utter quiet now. The forest held its breath.

Strangled barks broke the stillness, now closer to us and more vicious, in the woods upriver.

"They're over by Rory now," Rachel whispered.

Pia stifled a cry. I pictured her long white hands laying leaves and flat river stones over his eyes.

Sandra's shoulders shook so hard we could all feel it. "Come on, shhh," Rachel breathed. "Don't think, okay? Just don't think."

And so we listened. To the more terrible quiet that came next. In the black land behind my squeezed-shut eyes I saw teeth and bone and blood. How many were there? Impossible to tell. Why couldn't we have gotten farther from him before night fell? Another impossibility.

Time passed in its ruthless way. The normal noise of the forest returned. And suddenly the most pressing of my bodily concerns was a full-to-bursting bladder. I considered going right where I sat,

I was so terrified. I don't know if anyone would have noticed, or cared.

"I have to pee," I whispered.

A bullfrog at the riverbank answered me with a wet croak.

"I'll go with you," Pia said. "I have to go too."

We crawled on hands and knees out of our nest of branches and stiffly got to our feet. Shivering, I pulled my still-damp shirt and shorts away from my skin, nostalgic for that vile latrine back at the lodge, chemicals, whining overhead lights, beetles, and all. I squatted next to a rock shaped like a slumbering bear while Pia relieved herself on the other side of it. As I looked up into the blackness, I concentrated on relaxing enough to do what I had come for. The release of peeing felt almost sexual, the hot stream coming out of me a reminder that there was still heat, still life in me. The rain had passed, leaving a cold mist that cast a ghostly pallor over the trees and water.

"Wini!" Pia whispered hoarsely from the darkness. I heard her zip her shorts, the jangle of her belt buckle. "Do you smell that?"

I did. A whiff of home, of comfort. My shattered mind finally came around to naming it. Woodsmoke.

I heard splashing behind me. Muffled swearing. Then: "Get over here."

My eyes fully adjusted to the dark now, I turned toward her voice. Pia crouched on a slab of stone a few yards out into the river. "Win, you have to—"

"I'm coming, give me a sec." I was loath to get into the water again, but I had to do it, at least up to my thighs, to climb up to where she was. Even then, she had to lean down and give me a hand.

Rachel's voice came from the bank. "What are you doing?"

"I see something!"

High up in the belly of the dark mountain, a smudge of bone-colored smoke gathered, twisting up into the night sky.

"What do you see?" Sandra called out.

"A fire!" Pia dropped back into the water. "Guys—someone's up there! I think we're going to be okay."

I waded behind her toward the shore, teeth chattering.

"How far away is it, do you think?" Rachel rushed to meet us at the narrow bank.

"It's hard to say. Maybe half a mile?" I strained to see back up the mountain, but nothing was visible from the bank. "Who's camping way out here?"

I surveyed our exhausted, grimy faces and remembered someone telling me that hope is always the last thing to die.

"They could be anyone," I said, fear audible in my voice.

"That's who we need," Rachel said. "Anyone."

"Should we yell up to them?" Sandra ventured a few steps toward the inky-black woods. Before we could stop her, she opened her mouth and screamed, "Help! Help us, please! We're down by the river!"

Her words echoed back at us. A stillness before the chorus of insects charged up again.

"I wonder who they are," Pia said quietly. "What they're doing out here."

"Well, they couldn't have come from the lodge. It's just too far," Rachel said.

"Maybe there's another lodge around here," Pia said.

"I don't know, Pia." I thought of Rory's map, as well as his comment that the closest town was thirty miles away.

"Maybe they're lost too, whoever they are," Sandra said.

"I vote we go up there in the morning," I said, a sick worry in my gut.

"I vote we go up there now," Rachel said. "What if they're gone by morning?"

"I'm with you, Rachel," Pia said. "This could be our only chance."

26

My foreboding only grew as we climbed toward the smell of the fire, which had begun to mix with the smoky tang of cooking meat—what kind, I had no idea. We fumbled blindly and painfully over rocks, roots, and fallen trees, wearing the soft-soled water shoes that never seemed to dry. Branches whipped at us. Blackflies hummed in our ears and hung at our eyes and mouths. Partially blind, Rachel gripped the waist strap of my vest to guide her, keeping us both at a crawl. Sandra kept pace with Pia, whose white T-shirt glowed in the darkness. Their silver helmets bobbed ahead of us like beacons as we made our way ever higher; the light on the mountain growing brighter with every step.

Pia stopped short at the lip of a rain-swollen stream that flowed down to the river. We stumbled up behind her, but she shushed us hard, so we did what she said, then followed with our eyes her pale fingers as they pointed into the forest beyond the stream.

Just yards away, a dark figure crouched over a fire pit in the earth that glowed orange and red. Flames leapt up, licking at the sooty forms of rodent-looking creatures skewered nose to anus on a stick wedged between stacked stones. Fat dripped down, spitting and popping. The smell was gamy, but the heart of it was meat—food—and it reminded me of my animal hunger.

The figure—a small man or a large boy, it was hard to tell—got to his feet and watched the fire. Shoulder-length black hair hung down in mats. Haggard and ropy, almost Neanderthal in the slope of his shoulders, he paced alongside his catch, stopping now and then to lift his chin, to listen. To what, us?

We stood motionless, watching. A tortured energy came from him, something bottled and ferocious. Dark rags—the memory of a shirt—hung off his wasted frame; a whip of a belt cinched what might once have been pants but were now shreds of fabric turned leathery with filth. His face always in shadow, he reached over and turned the stick that held the trussed game, releasing more juices that smoked and rose to the stars, then grabbed the body of one of the things cooking over the fire with a bare hand—somehow impervious to its heat—and ripped off a scrawny leg with the other. He devoured it in seconds, throwing the small, clawlike bones into the fire.

Seemingly sated for the moment, he picked up a long, straight stick and something shining—a piece of metal?—a knife?—I couldn't make it out—and began to whittle at the stick, shaving one end to a point.

Our eyes flashed at each other across the gloom. Sandra had been taking a giant step across the stream when Pia halted us and she balanced there still, straddling it awkwardly. Pia put her finger against her lips for silence. We obeyed. My breath roared in my ears. We had no plan. Still the creature huddled over his stick, slicing away at it, stopping only to stroke its smoothness with sensual appreciation, as if he were petting a cat.

I saw it all too late: Sandra beginning to teeter before reaching back for me with a wild look in her eye, but I couldn't grab her in time. Her balance gone, she toppled over sideways, crashing down into the stream, and with a cry of pain landed on her shoulder and knee, up to her waist in rushing water. We threw ourselves over her and pulled her to her feet before staggering back into the clutter of trees and branches.

But we were too late. Like an agile shadow, the man leapt up and came at us, the stick in his hand a weapon held high.

27

I smelled him—sweat, rotted cloth, putrid breath—before I saw him. He seized my upper arm, then whipped me around to face him. Brown eyes, bloodshot and fierce, bored into mine. We stared at each other like two wildly different animals that had crossed paths in the forest and simply couldn't comprehend the other, whether to fight or fuck or flee, deadlocked in some bizarre pas de deux. Finally I tore my eyes from his face—blackened and lined with filth, knotted hair hanging down—to his other hand, which gripped the sharp stick.

His eyes followed mine. He opened his hand; the stick fell to the ground. We locked eyes again. I realized the others had turned to run but had stopped and were staring back at us. With my entire being, I yearned to turn and face them, but I could sense that was a bad idea. He grasped my arm with inhumanly strong fingers but gazed at us one by one with a wild joy in his eyes before turning back to me.

Pia's voice came from the shadows. "Let her go."

"Don't hurt her," Sandra said.

His grip tightened. A scream bloomed in my throat; I suppressed it. The woods hummed with night song as we five stood in thrall.

"Dean? Where are you? Dean!" A female voice from near the fire, low and growling.

No one moved. The voice rose to a frantic pitch, cutting the night. "Get back here, young man!"

He let me go as if my flesh singed his fingers. His face contorted; his mouth moving as if he were trying to force something out.

Finally, he let out a "Gah!" The effort seemed to drain him. He turned me around and shoved me roughly into the woods. I staggered a few yards, looked back. He made a motion as if to wave us away. "Gah!" he blurted once more.

The voice came again, closer, a strong French accent curling the words. "Now you be a good boy, Dean, do you hear me?" A fleshy hand slashed across the dense greenery and a woman appeared. Thickets of brown hair sprouted from under an orange ski cap pulled down to eyes that glittered with feral intelligence. Bits of bone and feathers swung from tangled mats that hung down to her waist. Something like a skirt was tied around her thick middle with a leather strap, while a dung-colored knit top, impossibly stretched out, drooped down past her knees. On her grimy feet, the essence of shoes, strapped on with strips of rubber. Toenails curled like claws over their sooty edges. She was as tall as a man, broad in the shoulders and hips.

"Don't be afraid." She smiled at us with a movie-star set of gleaming white teeth. "My son gets a bit excited when he sees new people. Don't you, Dean?"

Dean looked down and away, shaking his head with a whimpering sound.

"We were rafting, and there was an accident, and—" Pia choked out. "We're lost and we need help. We saw the fire—"

"So," the woman said, with an almost coquettish turn of her head, "you've come to the right place."

"Who are you?" Rachel said from the shadows, her one lens glinting in the moonlight.

"Manners!" The woman huffed and took a step toward us. We shrank back. "Forgive me." Her smell too was overpowering, but mixed with something mustier, a disturbing odor I couldn't place. I held my breath so as not to breathe her in. "I am Simone, and this is my son, Dean." She swept out her arms with a dramatic flourish as if presenting him to us, as if we had not yet noticed him.

Dean looked down, into the woods, anywhere but at us. He snatched up his sharp stick again before bounding back into the woods.

"You will have to forgive him. Bit of an odd duck. And don't expect a lot of chitter-chatter. The boy is mute. Born with no tongue." She grew thoughtful a moment, twirling a rope of knotted hair; now I saw that the woven-in pieces of bone were the skulls of birds or something equally tiny, chipmunk maybe. I was terrified, mesmerized. "It's a shame, if you ask me. But he handles it well."

We introduced ourselves, and she nodded at each of us in turn, seeming to look through us with her direct stare, as if she knew things about us we'd long forgotten and would rather not remember. Without further comment, she turned, and the forest engulfed her.

We followed her—or the scent of her—toward the fire that still burned in the clearing on the mountainside. As I stepped into the ring of light, I felt something above me. A presence. A few yards over our heads, a pitch-dark object hung from the arm of a tree. The head of a black bear swayed and turned in the night wind, its bulbous pink tongue lolling out, close-set eyes glassy and almost surprised-looking above its dusky snout. Other objects twisted from sinewy ropes, staring down at us from the dome of trees, creaking and swaying in the night breeze. A moose head gaped down, its massive antlers framing a starry section of sky. The head of a deer gazed plaintively toward the river. Some kind of catlike creature I couldn't name, caught in a perpetual snarl, faced the brutish gray head of a coyote. The necks were more torn than cut; gristly pieces of flesh hung down in ghastly curtains. Most heads had dried and visibly shrunken from the time they had walked the earth attached to their bodies, but the bear's head looked fresh; a dark liquid oozed from it, puddling on the ground. The heads faced out, forming a kind of lookout around the beaten earth of the clearing. Sandra issued a brief cry as she looked up, but Pia clapped her hand over her mouth and hissed at her to keep going. Rachel caught a whiff of Sandra's fear and whitened, but stayed silent. I was flattened with terror and had pretty much left my body; like one of the animal heads, I looked down on myself as I feigned all sorts of calm.

We stumbled toward the fire, Rachel still holding on to me. From the shadowy recesses of the camp a baby goat came bleating on spindly legs. It bumped up against my knees. My instinct was to reach down and pet it like a puppy, but the mother goat followed, fat with milk. Crying in an eerily human voice, it butted up so hard against my thighs I nearly fell backward. The animal glowered at me with its sideways pupils as it chewed, devil horns twisting back. Two more young goats ran up to us, white ones, braying, busily smelling us out.

"Get away now, Rose," Simone admonished. She slapped the big one on its flank and led it by a curled horn back to what looked like a waist-high jumble of twisted bones. "Dean, how'd these girls get out?"

Dean dashed around us, gathering the animals and guiding them to the enclosure, made entirely of entwined antlers, including the gate, which vanished into the structure once he hooked one antler over another. It was the strangest-looking pen I'd ever seen.

"I could swear they have hands, those goats," Simone said with a prissy annoyance. She stepped behind a log cabin that leaned hard toward the woods as if trying to escape into them. Oblong windows bulged out from three sides of it; it took me a few seconds to realize these were car windows, and the door of the cabin was a car door, caked with rust and dirt.

Simone emerged from behind the shelter carrying a plastic jug and metal cups and set them on a tree stump. A joined section of green and orange leather seats that looked scavenged from a VW bus—springs and stuffing busted through—huddled close to the fire. I moved toward it, holding my hands up to the flames as if to warm them, when what I was really doing was trying to stop quaking with fear.

"Would you ladies care for a drink?"

We all looked at each other. Rachel stood by me, still gripping my belt, her face unreadable. I didn't think she'd seen the animal heads. Sandra's face was utterly drained of color. I gripped her hand, her flesh clammy and cold, her breath coming in shallow bites.

Pia took one of the metal cups offered to her and said defiantly, "What is it?"

Simone barked out a laugh. "Just water, I'm afraid."

"I would love some," Rachel said, stepping forward. With no inquiry as to its origin, she accepted the metal cup of water, spilling it over herself in her haste to drink.

"What's with the heads in the trees?" Pia asked, arms folded. I shrank at the tone of her question.

Simone gazed up at them. "They're rather beautiful, don't you agree? My now-silent friends . . ." She shrugged. "I suppose it's my way of telling the forest who's boss."

Above us, the moon glowed like a piece of plate. Dean busied himself by the fire. He took down the carcasses, now charcoal black, and laid them on a flat piece of river slate. I flashed on the presents Ziggy had left at my doorstep when he was an outdoor cat: mice, a baby raccoon, bunnies, even a garden snake; all headless.

Dean wiped his hands on his pants and approached his mother.

Then he signed, his movements fast and precise, "Women, eat? Women, hungry?"

I looked at Pia. She'd seen it—the words flying from the boy's hands—we all had. He signed again, more slowly this time, "Women, eat?"

"It seems that Dean is wondering if you ladies are interested in dinner," Simone said with a strange annoyance.

"What . . . is it?" Sandra asked.

"Porcupine, mostly. A couple of grouse, maybe a squirrel. Quite delicious."

28

Simone ate her food with a delicate clicking sound; finally it occurred to me that her teeth might be fake. Grubby pinkies extended fastidiously, she nibbled at a leg of something before tiring of it and tossing it into the flames. It shocked me that I was eating what I was told was a vole. The meat came off the bone in long, gristly shreds that I forced myself to swallow. Pia and Rachel sat on the blown-out car seats, turned toward each other as they peeled porcupine meat from a small rib cage. They ate quickly and with an odd shame. Sandra huddled on a stump stool by the fire, warming her hands. She said she wasn't hungry, but no one believed her.

Dean spread out a freshly skinned deer hide in the dirt near us. Its head—four hooves laid neatly next to it—sat staring at us on a nearby stump, nose still glistening wet.

"Such a tragic story about your guide," Simone said as she peeled some kind of root with a short-handled knife. "I imagine you marked his grave?"

"We made a cairn in the river," I said.

"I see. So people will be coming to retrieve him."

We were quiet, imagining this.

"Why do you live out here?" Pia asked.

Simone worked something out of her hair and threw it into the shadows. "We grew tired of people, Dean and me. We're better off without them. We make our own paradise here, as you can see. No phones, no taxes, no noise, no pollution. None of the insanity civilization has to offer, thank you very much. Besides"—she skewered the root and rested it on glowing coals—"they were threatening to take my dear boy, and I couldn't have that."

"Is Dean . . . all right?" Rachel asked.

"Dean is not like everybody else. You can see that. He marches to the tune of a different drummer, I believe the saying goes." She pulled a short twig from a pocket in her voluminous skirt, used it to remove something from between her front teeth. "This world can't handle anybody different. It's like some sort of sin. They want to put you in an institution and shoot you up with drugs and try to make you like everybody else. So we disappeared ourselves. Simple."

An owl hooted, haunting a nearby tree. Sandra shivered and said, "What do you do in winter?"

"Cut a lot of wood. Don't think we'll ever run out of that." Simone smirked, glaring out at the trees that hung over us with what I could have sworn was a touch of disgust.

"Does anyone know you live out here?" Pia asked.

Simone considered Pia, her size and strength. "You four do. I believe that's it."

I shifted uncomfortably in my seat, struggling to keep my expression neutral.

"You see, the secret," Simone said, puffing up with pride, "is in how you burn your wood. That is the key to everything. On flyover days in summer, when rangers patrol by air—bunch of overpaid fatheads if you want to know the truth—you don't hunt, because

you cannot smoke your game. They'll see you. Make a note of you.
Pay a visit. Tell you to leave. If you need a fire, burn clean, dry
wood. It doesn't smoke up. It burns clear, and you are safe. That's
my tip of the day. You're welcome." She snorted out a braying sort
of laugh at her joke—clearly she was out of practice with mirth—
and tossed her homemade toothpick into the flames.

With his hands, Dean scooped a whitish paste from a can and
rubbed it into the deer's skin.

"What's he doing?" Sandra asked.

"He's braining the hide. Using the brains of a moose we killed
the other day. They're full of lecithin, which as you may know is a
fat. Wonderful for curing hides. You see, we use everything here:
fur, sinew, flesh, and bone. We never waste."

"Can you help us get back to town?" Sandra said, unable to
mask a touch of hysteria in her voice. "Can you tell us where we
are? We won't tell anyone about you."

"Of course." Simone speared the cooked root from the hot
ashes and took a cautious bite. "Dean will accompany you in the
morning." Dean looked up at his mother, a flash of alarm in his
eyes. "It's pretty simple where we are. By river, we're thirty-five
miles or so to Grindstone, with lots of rapids between here and
there. Very difficult. Don't recommend it. Over land, we're about
the same distance west of Portage. But the woods are very dense.
You'll be lost without a compass or Dean to show you the way."

Dean's tools—a palm-size rock and shard of bone—dropped
from his hands. He signed, "No, I will not kill women. No, no, no
bad Dean."

With all my will I kept my face blank. My heart slammed so
hard against my chest that for several moments I couldn't hear—a
muffled roar filled my ears. A cry escaped my lungs as a cough
and I feigned the need for a sip of water. My friends looked at me,

questioning, but I kept my eyes on the flames that still sizzled with the fat of the vermin we had just eaten. I clenched my fists, finger-nails digging bloody half-moons into my palms.

Simone pushed herself from her knees to her full height and approached her son. Looming, she looked half again as big as he was. She signed down at him, her hands moving in big, clear ges-tures. "You started the fire."

He stared at her, hands still.

With a hiss of disgust, she coyly flipped her hair back from her face. "You know that brings them," she signed. "Now, we have no choice! I don't know what's going on with you. I can't trust you anymore."

Dean shook his head, picked up his tools, and bent down to his work.

Simone smacked her hands together, a shockingly loud sound. Dean looked up, his mouth a grim line, his eyes full of fright. She signed quickly, close to his sweating face, "You kill them or we lose everything. Do you understand?"

His hands shook as the rock and bone dropped once more to the blood-soaked ground. "Nice ladies," he signed. "Nice ladies. Never seen nice ladies." He rocked on his haunches, pulled at his hair. "I like them, the women. Pretty. Listen to them talk."

Simone took a wide-hipped lunge toward him. She raised her hand over his head, but brought it down gently and patted his back. "Dean is a bit shy, I think," she said over her shoulder. "But he's happy to take you. He says he's looking forward to it."

29

So . . ." Simone said, looking me up and down, chilling me, "you are interested in seeing the inside of my home?" A night bird cried out as it flew above our heads and dropped down toward the river.

"Looks like a work of art to me," I said.

Her eyes glimmered under the rim of her filthy orange hat as she tried to parse what I was up to, which was trying to find out what sort of weapons she had, or any other secrets that might save us, but in the end she shrugged her assent. I guess everyone is house-proud, even those who live surrounded by the heads of animals dripping gore onto their yard.

We all ducked through the hobbit-size car door and stood up inside the twelve-by-twelve-foot space, instantly leaning sideways in sympathy with walls that tilted toward the forest. It took a moment to adjust to the smudgy semidarkness. A pus-colored knot of tallow that looked as if a child had molded it nestled on a ledge of bark by the window, yellow flame sputtering. A tattered black book, perhaps a Bible, lay open on the rough wood floor. The place reeked of wet wool, pine sap, and animal urine. A clay oven sat lumpen in the center of the place; ringed metal tubing, possibly an old dryer vent, looped out of the top of it and disappeared through a hole in the ceiling. Shelves—some made of wood, some of stretched animal skin—lined one wall from floor to ceiling. Jars packed with nuts and seeds, dried berries, all manner of twisted and agonized-looking tubers, crowded the shelves, all thoughtfully organized. The car windows, set into the building with some kind of a dark clay substance, fish-eyed the view of the trees outside and reflected the flame from the little candle, filling the place with an almost cozy glow. Against the wall near the door leaned a longbow, a saw, an ax, and at least a dozen arrows fitted out with feathers at the nock.

"Some fixing up still needs to be done," Simone said, "but, it's home to us." She busied herself straightening two tattered sleeping bags on the floor.

Sandra coughed. Pinched the back of my thigh. When I turned to her, she raised her eyebrows and head-gestured sideways. Something hot pink protruded slightly from between the jars of berries. Her cell phone case.

"It's nice," Sandra said. "Very homey."

From her hands-and-knees position on the floor, Simone turned and cast Sandra a sharp glance before returning to her work. She pushed herself to her knees and appraised us, eyes gleaming in the candlelight. "You four will sleep outside by the fire. Dean can give you some hides to keep you warm." She groaned as she got to her feet, bent down double, and pushed open the door to leave. "Coming?"

"Right behind you," Rachel said.

Sandra snatched the phone from between the jars and zipped it into the front pocket of her vest. We ducked down and stepped outside, the night air a tonic after the fetid stink of the cabin.

Simone loaded her arms with logs from a pile of wood stacked up against the cabin and dropped them near the fire before stoking the coals back to healthy flames. "We're early to bed here," she said, "so this will be good-night for me. Sweet dreams, ladies." She slapped the bark and dirt off her hands and disappeared into the cabin.

A rustling came from a hulking metal structure behind the camp, toward the wall of woods. Shrouded by darkness and undergrowth, the cab of an antique truck sagged in the dirt, its bed and engine and the rest of it gone, melted into the earth with the years. Deflated tires rested against it, engulfed by vines and new growth. Dean emerged from the thing, burdened with what looked like a stack of rugs. Never meeting our eyes, he set out around the fire four animal skins sewn together with gristly thread into rough blankets. We stood spellbound, unable to look away.

He turned on his heel toward the cabin.

I forced myself out of my shocked stupor. This was my last and only chance.

I whispered, "Dean."

His shoulders slumped as if he'd been caught at something bad. With visible effort, he turned toward us, lifting his head as if resisting a great weight, to meet my eyes. Profound sadness rested in his.

Slowly, deliberately, I signed, "Thank you for the blankets." I was rusty at this and the gestures felt awkward. Twice I stumbled on *blankets*, finally spelling out the word to be clear.

There was only the crackling of the fire and the night sounds that breathed in and out all around us. Dean gazed at my hands with new attention, then at my face, his eyes slowly lighting from the inside. He looked younger all of a sudden, and I realized I hadn't thought about his age at all.

He signed, "You sign?"

"Yes," I signed. "I understand you."

"Them?"

"No," my hands said. "Just me."

He ran up to me. I wasn't ready for it. I gasped, stumbling backward as he grabbed my hands with his filthy ones and yanked me toward him as if I were nothing. He turned my hands over, opened them, and placed my palms flat against his cheeks, holding me there. I didn't try to move. His face felt clammy, gritty. I felt his incipient beard and realized he was young, maybe just a teenager. His eyes searched mine with a desperation I'd never seen before or since. I stopped breathing. I felt like I'd fallen into a wild animal's cage. His face contorted as a deep-rooted sob erupted from him, and he lifted my hands from his cheeks, encased them with his own, and held them against his closed eyes. They felt hot and wet as he cried soundlessly, his back heaving.

"Hey," Pia whispered. "What in hell is going on?"

"Dean!" Simone bellowed from inside the cabin. "Quit bothering those women and get in here and go to sleep. They've had quite enough of you for one night."

Dean stiffened, gathered himself, lifted his head. He released my hands and signed, "I sleep. You—"

"Dean, get in here this instant!" Simone roared.

He turned and ran toward the flickering light of the cabin.

30

We lay shivering under the stinking, heavy skins in full moonlight. It had to be midnight, maybe later. For long minutes we listened to the creak and whine of the animal heads as they turned above us, casting black cutout shapes against a spray of stars. Beyond them stood the living forest, unimaginably dense and shadow filled, where for miles around creatures with eyes built for darkness stared, with paws made for silence crept, smelling us in all our fear and soft humanity.

Rachel rustled under the patchwork pelts, whispered, "She actually *told* him to kill us?"

"Keep your voice down, for Christ's sake," Pia breathed.

"Would I make up a thing like that?" I said as quietly as I could. As disgusting as the skins felt—stiff, raw, and damp—I was finally starting to get warm. "He refused to do it," I added. I closed my eyes, replaying in my mind his hands' quick movements, straining to make sure I understood correctly every word he had signed.

Sandra said, "I can't feel my feet."

"Rub them," Pia whispered. "Come on, scooch over here. I'll do it."

As Sandra struggled to turn her body around on the dirt, Rachel said, "We have to get out of here. Now. No fucking around. These people are psychos."

"Where are we going to go?" Pia breathed as she worked on Sandra's feet. Sandra whimpered softly.

"Back to the river," Rachel whispered hotly. "We have to find the raft."

"Looks like they already did," Pia said.

Rachel turned under the crackling skins. "So maybe they pulled it up onshore somewhere."

"Probably hid it."

"So we look for it," Rachel said.

"I say we wait awhile here," Pia said. "Get some rest, and then—"

"*Get some rest?* Yes, I like to be well rested when I'm slaughtered," Rachel hissed. "She doesn't want to be found. Get it? She's not going to let us out of here, she told her freakazoid son to kill us."

"What about the phone?" I whispered.

With agonizing slowness, Sandra unzipped her vest pocket. In my life I'd never heard anything make so much noise.

"What if it rings, Jesus," Rachel breathed.

"Just let her . . ."

She held it out in the middle of our circle, a black rectangle outlined in taffy pink. No cheery, bright screen. "It's dead, I think, I'm—I'm turning it on and off and nothing's happening."

"For fuck's sake, can't we do this later?" Rachel said.

"She's right." Sandra stashed the phone back in her pocket.

We sat up, the skins releasing poofs of musk and earth as they crinkled and buckled. As we stood, they slid off as if we were shedding them. I can't remember ever feeling so naked and cold. On impulse I grabbed the sharp stick Dean had used to skewer the meat and tucked it under my belt. I caught Pia's eye and pointed at a rusted stump of an ax that leaned up against the cabin next to the neat pile of firewood.

"No," she whispered harshly. *"Too close."*

I nodded. She was right. They would hear us.

We crept back into the woods that bordered the stream, Pia leading, Sandra next, then me, Rachel clutching my belt. We were nomads, an island of four. As bound in our lostness as we ever were as friends, we blundered through the living darkness as soundlessly as we could, but it was hard to believe that every footfall, every unintentional snap of branch or rustle of leaf didn't wake the world and call the hounds of hell down upon us. Why weren't we being pursued? Were we being that stealthy? It frightened me more to hear nothing, as if they had heard us but were taking their sweet time to come after us. This forest was their domain, not ours. Quite possibly they had a more efficient plan than we could ever dream of.

We followed the stream toward the river, much of the time wading in it past our knees, lunging at branches and roots that crowded the bank. The water flowed biting cold down from the mountainside, but even sloshing through it we made blessedly less noise than we did on land, or at least that's how it felt. But the chill seeped back into all of us like an old enemy.

For over an hour we battled our way downstream, until we reached the river that had carried us to this lost world. We bushwhacked our way along the bank, often detouring into the woods to forge any progress at all, always keeping the river in earshot. There was no place open enough in the forest to rest together even if that had occurred to us. Trees stood rooted mere feet apart, their branches intertwining at waist height, so we found ourselves crawling like beasts on our hands and knees on the ground, our palms sticky with pine sap and pocked with small stones. Pain, hunger, and cold became secondary to the primal, animal compulsion that propelled us.

As I navigated by feel of root and branch, stepping blindly into rushing water, only part of my consciousness heeded the fact that the outlines of rocks and trees against the sky had grown clearer. Form and mass emerged from a palette of stygian blackness, while color returned to leaf and stone. The river, once meshed with the night, clearly separated itself from its bank. The sky had begun to lighten. The morning, like an unexpected kindness, had arrived.

Sunday

June 24

31

Still moving like one four-hinged creature as dawn came, we fought our way through thick, dark spruce. Several yards ahead an area of the forest seemed brighter, an opening of some kind. With no discussion, we headed toward it.

We burst out of the woods, freed from a prison of green. We found ourselves in a field of rotted cornstalks, once taller than houses but now slumped over in tortured shapes, their moldering leaves grazing the soil as if anxious to return to it. I tried to imagine how the crop came to be, if it had once been part of someone's prized farm. Now abandoned, the corn grew wildly and on its own every summer, only to sink back on itself, a ghost harvest. The field was roughly square, bordered by woods that seemed bent on taking over. Waist-height pines and alders encroached on the putrid stalks.

Stupid with fatigue, we stood gaping around, our clothes torn and black with mud. Though it was a relief to see beyond three feet in front of me, the reality of being out in the open raised the hair on the back of my neck. Sandra hugged herself and wandered off to a sunny spot, lifting her face to the light. The field droned with insects. Grasshoppers whirred by at eye height to land on the drooping stalks, grooming one hairpin leg with the other. Clouds of mosquitoes and no-see-ums swarmed and dined on us, but none of us had the energy to fight them off.

"Hey, Sandra," Rachel said hoarsely, approaching her. "Let's see the phone."

Hands on hips, she peered through her one lens at Sandra as she unzipped her vest pocket and reached her hand down and right through a vicious-looking rip in its side. Her fingers wiggled. She lifted her head, face pale as death.

Rachel squinted at Sandra's pocket with her good eye. "So where's the phone?"

"I don't know, it's gone, it—"

"Where's the *fucking phone*?" Rachel slapped Sandra hard across the face.

I stiffened. Pia took a step back as if she were the one hit.

"I don't know, I don't know. . . ." Sandra looked all around her on the ground, as if she would find it there. As if the world worked like that.

"Oh my God, she actually fucking lost it," Rachel moaned. "She lost the fucking phone. . . ."

"Keep your voice down!" Pia hissed. "She lost the phone. There's not a goddamned thing we can do about it. It could be anywhere."

Sandra began to sob.

I took a step toward Rachel, my arms rigid with rage by my sides. "I can't believe you hit her. What the fuck is wrong with you?"

Rachel sank down to her knees onto the rotted corn. "We are so fucked, oh my God. . . ."

"The phone was dead anyway!" Sandra cried. "I *showed* you—"

"What were you going to do, Rachel, plug it into a tree or something?" I said.

"Maybe it wasn't dead! Maybe it just wasn't on or something!"

Rachel choked a little with laughter or tears, I couldn't tell which. Her shoulders sagged. "I can't believe this." She took off her wrecked glasses and wiped the one good lens on her filthy shirt. "I'm going to die sober after all. What a shame."

"I must have torn my vest in the stream," Sandra said, tearing up again. "We could go back and look. . . ."

Exhaustion rolled through me hard, and for a few seconds I felt as if I were going to pass out. Nausea rippled up from deep in my gut, but passed, with nothing to retch. My field of vision narrowed, and all I heard was the sound of Sandra weeping, the buzz of insects, and the ever-present rumble of the river. I couldn't seem to get enough air to my brain. But the sensation didn't last. An odd fizzing energy and determination replaced it. We were alive. Probably fucked big-time, but unlike Rory, still walking around, still breathing.

"You guys need to stop crying and slapping each other and screwing around," I said. "It's time to think, okay? Figure out what to do next."

Pia started to walk away.

"Where are you going?" I asked.

"To take a freaking piss." She disappeared among the hulking stalks.

Rachel stayed in a lump on the ground. "I'm sorry I slapped you, Sandra," she mumbled. "That was fucked-up of me."

Sandra wiped her eyes with the back of her hand and blinked. "It was *dead*."

"I believe you. It doesn't matter. I'm sorry."

Pia burst back through the corn. "Guys, you have to come see this. I found the raft."

32

We barreled through the rotted crop, stalks flying back and slapping us as we sank deeper into a quicksandlike muck. Each step released a reptilian perfume, the rich black carbon of decay. We arrived at a flattened section where the corn had been trampled over by something or someone. Just yards away the river rumbled by, wider now, calmer.

"Oh, God," Sandra said as she approached the raft, which was barely recognizable as such. "Look what they did to it."

Stripped of all our gear—dry bags, tents, sleeping bags, food, even oars—our salvation lay flat and sad in the mud. Like a desecrated body, it had been repeatedly slashed: only long, angry ribbons of bright canvas and black rubber remained. Even the cheerful blue handles had been sliced off, an obscene touch. I recalled what Simone had said about wasting nothing.

Pia picked up a few lengths of rubber and let them drop back into the mire.

"What are you doing?" Rachel said derisively, confounded.

"Just . . . wondering if there's something we can use, I don't know."

Rachel shook her head and trudged toward the river, past the wreckage of rubber and canvas, the ground sucking at her shoes as she went. I paused at the raft, stunned and struck by the violence that had been hazarded upon it, before hurrying to catch up with her.

Her glasses stored on a neighboring rock, Rachel stretched out belly down on a sheet of slate suspended over a bubbling eddy, head and arms invisible as she splashed water on herself and drank out of cupped palms. We all followed suit; I felt marginally better afterward.

I looked at the river. Here it stretched close to fifty feet across, flowing tamely and with a serenity we had not yet witnessed. I could almost picture barges making their way down it; certainly there was enough room. I remembered Rory's words and sat up. "We're at the Mississippi!"

Pia looked up at me, her face and hair dripping.

"Don't you remember what Rory said about what would happen after the Flush?"

She shook her head, blanching at the sound of Rory's name.

"He said there'd be five or six miles when we'd swear we were on the Mississippi, and then—"

"Satan's Staircase. *That* I remember," Rachel said.

I got to my feet, excited. "But then that's it! That's the last big water. Don't you remember? He said there'd be some small stuff, then the takeout at the Willows. That's *tomorrow*. We just need to keep going!"

"We must have walked a couple of miles last night, who knows . . ." Sandra trailed off.

"So . . . twenty more miles of walking?" Rachel said.

"I can't," Pia said. "I mean, I have to rest a little. Sleep for an hour. I just have to."

The day was heating up fast and the sun beat down on us.

Under a coating of mud and grass stains, Pia looked a sickly white. Her face shone with sweat.

"Be serious," Rachel started. "You know they were here." She glanced around at the buzzing woods, the putrefied crop. "Where's it safe to—"

"There's a place I saw back there—close by—that looks kind of hidden," Pia said. "Come on, I'll show you."

She turned, and we gathered our corpselike selves, shuffling along behind her across the rock and back up the bank, Rachel grumbling. It struck me that we were still following this woman no matter where she led us. But I too felt about to drop with fatigue. Even more than food, the idea of sleep called like a sweet siren to every fiber of my being. Pia paused at the raft to collect several long strips of canvas and rubber, which we carried to the edge of the field. Behind a screen of scrubby pines, a ruined fieldstone foundation bordered a ten-foot square of sunken ground. We gathered a few branches to cover ourselves before Pia climbed down into the depression. She arranged the pitiful remnants of the raft near an old chimney that sat crumbling at the center of the pit, as if there she would find at least the memory of comfort.

Like sheep, we did as she did, half falling down next to each other in speckled sunshine. She took off her helmet and tossed it on the ground in disgust, her hair matted so close to her head she looked as if she were wearing a cloche. The rest of us followed suit.

"You look totally psycho," Rachel said, smiling weakly as she looked at my head.

I reached up, touching corners, hard wings, strange bumps. "Let's ditch these helmets," I said, suddenly noticing how CMYK we looked in all our absurdly bright clothing and orange vests. How very findable.

"Mine keeps my head warm," Sandra said, taking hers off and laying it gently next to her.

"We need everything we have," Rachel said. "I don't give a shit how uncomfortable it is." Her helmet was barely a helmet any-more, it was so bent and cracked, but she removed it respectfully and placed it alongside her. She might have gotten more comfort from hers than we did from ours, as she was hardly able to see three feet in front of her.

Pia curled up on the cool earth and dragged the branches over her. I stored my sharp stick alongside me as we settled under the pine boughs. It felt like a grave, as if we were giving up. Some-how the thought didn't much bother me. My limbs shuddered with exhaustion, muscles twitching and spasming, while my head pounded with hunger, since my stomach was beyond feeling it. I breathed in the urinous tang of the pine branches that rested on us, trying to release my fear with every exhale, but I could still taste it on my tongue. The others were asleep in seconds. Sandra snored softly next to me.

I closed my eyes and saw six-year-old Marcus standing over me, his floppy black hair covering one eye, fists jammed on narrow boy hips. He leaned over and tapped me on my shoulder. I signed to please leave me alone, I was trying to sleep.

He signed, "But it's time to play."

In my dream I got up and pointed to the others, signed, "Don't wake them, they're exhausted."

He scrambled to the top of the fieldstone wall, where he turned and plopped down cross-legged on the stones. "Come here," he signed, looking down at me. "Surprise for you."

I gazed at him. Loved him. Signed slowly, with stiff fingers, "Marcus, I can't take care of you anymore."

He signed, "It's okay." Shrugged.

I climbed up to sit by him, the fieldstones cold under my thin shorts. He reached in his mouth, pulled out a purple LEGO piece, and set it down on a flat section of stone. He smiled with pride. After a pause, he reached back in and withdrew a dozen more—blue, yellow, red, and orange—and lined them up in a row. In dreamworld, this made sense. Marcus helping out in his way. One last time he reached in and extracted bits of colored paper, which he carefully arranged on the rock in front of him. Studiously, he bent over his work and jockeyed the pieces around, like a puzzle. I looked down. It was Rory's map.

A branch snapped. My eyes flew open, and Marcus vanished. I stared into Sandra's face, her eyes bright with fear. Slow as death, I turned my head to look through the branches that covered my face.

Longbow slung across his shoulders, Dean towered over us from where he stood on the lip of the stony foundation, his dark form blocking the sun.

33

His breath came ragged and heavy as if he'd been running, and I could smell the tang of his body under the strips of cloth that covered him. With aching slowness, I lifted a pine bough off my face. Leaves rustled as Pia turned in her sleep, then stopped, nudged awake by Rachel, whose own breathing had quickened from the depths of slumber to shallow gasps.

Dean gazed down on us, his expression ravaged and sad as if he already regretted what he had to do. "Hello, Dean," I said and signed.

He didn't sign back.

"Wini!" Pia whispered harshly. "What are you doing, don't—"

In one fluid motion, never taking his eyes off me, he reached behind his shoulder into a leather quiver of arrows, drew one ablaze with cardinal feathers, and nocked it to the string of his bow. He pulled back to full draw and aimed all that power and savage accuracy at my pounding heart.

"No," I said and signed, forcing my fingers to move. "Please, no, please." The bow squeaked under the strain of his draw, the muscles of his forearm standing out in ropy lines. How could anything so motionless be so full of energy and intent, so alive? I thought of the slaughtered creatures roasting over the fire at his homestead, how they had once been wet nosed and bright eyed, flying or bounding through the forest, armed with the things small creatures are armed with—speed, camouflage, sharp claws, a vicious beak, the talent for impossible stillness—but how even with all that brilliant nature, only a fraction of their numbers survived. How most were lost, tiny throats clamped in the teeth of predators, dead in seconds.

I knew that if I moved or made another sound I was done. I would die in that place, my friends as witness. He had made a promise and he meant to keep it. Our death meant that the only life he knew would go on.

I visualized myself brilliantly alive, sprinting through the forest to safety.

Prayed.

He jerked his upper body a fraction to the left and let the arrow go. The movement was so small it could have been a hiccup or twitch that saved me. A flash of crimson, the arrow sliced the air over my head and shot past me. I heard a *thwump* and turned to look. It had plunged—just inches from my neck—into the soft old mortar between the stones, fully halfway up its shaft, as if it would have preferred to go all the way through.

I exhaled.

Rachel threw off the pine boughs that covered her and sat up, grimacing, a rock clenched in one hand. Sandra lay frozen in place, eyes locked on the arrow that still shuddered between the stones.

"Don't, Rachel," I whispered to her.

Dean turned his fierce gaze to Rachel, dark eyes burning. There was nothing he couldn't do to us. She dropped the stone in the dirt.

"Jesus, talk to him, Wini," Pia said.

"You found us," I said and signed, for those moments unable to think of anything else.

But he had dropped his eyes. Wouldn't look at me, at anyone. Shoulders slumped, he seemed defeated somehow, almost embarrassed. A complete change in affect, though we tensed when he laid down the bow and reached across his shoulders to lift the tube of arrows off his back. He dropped it on the damp ground near where we lay, then dug inside a slender leather bag tied around his waist.

He held out something brown and withered. Nobody moved. He squatted and placed it on the stones.

Finally meeting my eye, he signed to me, "Are you hungry?"

I got to my feet, watching him every second. "What is it?"

He signed, "Squirrel." Then: "Dry."

I gestured at all of us. "Is there enough for my friends?"

He nodded and withdrew more meat from the whip-sewn sack. I picked up a small piece and ate it, my mouth almost too dry to chew, hunger the farthest thing from my mind. It tasted like some gamy old meat that had been left out in the sun, or the horribly overcooked pork chops my father used to force down our throats every Sunday.

"Thank you," I signed and said. "Delicious."

Pia got to her feet and approached Dean. He shrank back a bit, maybe because of her size—she had a good five inches on him. She chose a piece of meat and, watching me, tore off a few shreds and ate it. "Thank you," she said. "This is very good. We haven't eaten since the last time you gave us food."

Dean nodded. The tension in his face seemed to ease. He held out some meat to Rachel, who shook her head, then Sandra, who accepted his offering. She took a tentative bite, nodded, and thanked him.

He seemed fascinated with Sandra. He couldn't stop staring at her. Like a man looks at a woman but more with wonder than lust. With feral grace, he jumped down into our warren of hoary stones and approached her. She leaned backward as he reached down and touched her hair. We all froze. Sandra struggled to swallow the meat.

"Pretty," he signed.

I translated. We all breathed.

He made the sign for "eyes," then "leaf."

"Leaf eyes?" I signed.

"Eyes shape like leaf," he signed. "Pretty girl."

I translated the best I could.

"Sick fuck better stay away from her," Rachel said.

Dean recoiled, took a step back. His face darkened, and he looked to me, questioning. I noticed the glint of a knife under his belt.

"Good one," I said under my breath.

"But he's—" Rachel started.

"He's getting to know us," Pia said, injecting her voice with syrupy calm.

I said, "Apologize to him, Rache."

"I didn't—"

"Do it."

She cleared her throat, sniffed, adjusted her pitiful glasses on her face. "Sorry, Dean."

He ignored her and glared at me. "Why don't they sign?" His hands flew. "What is wrong with them?"

"They never learned," I signed and said. "I know how because my brother signed."

"Where is your brother?"

"He's dead."

"Who killed him?" Dean gestured at the women.

"No one. It was an accident."

"What is 'accident'?" he signed, making the sign for the word several times—a turning of the hand near the face, pinkie and thumb out—seemingly anxious to learn it.

I felt my wound opening. Sick at heart. "It's like a mistake," I said. "When a really bad thing happens, but it's nobody's fault."

Dean looked down at the earth, then back at each of us. Our filthy, scratched, and bloodied faces. "All of you," he signed. "Come with me."

34

We had slept longer than I realized. It felt hours past noon. The worst of the day's heat had come and gone, and the earth beneath us seemed to exhale, cooling our sweating bodies. For a good half mile we followed Dean, tramping through a pathless forest that possessed a logic known only to him. I began to panic that he was leading us back to Simone, but in my gut I didn't quite buy my own theory. Pia and the others trudged along in silence, too frightened to say a word. Finally, we found ourselves in a small clearing.

A roughly square plot had been cleared of brush and trees. An intricate mosaic of gray, green, and white pebble-size river stones described the shape and size of a man lying on the ground. Black stones defined eyes, eyebrows, and hair, his lips a grim line across his face.

Dean squatted at the head of the grave, rocking back and forth on his tire-wrapped feet. He brought the thumb and fingers of his right hand together and touched them to his forehead, then dropped his hand to his waist, as if removing an imaginary cap. The sign for "man." He made the sign again and again, seemingly lost in his memories.

"What man is here?" I said, signed.

He tapped his forehead with an open hand. The sign for "father."
"I'm sorry."

"How did he die?" Pia asked. Good lord. The directness of her.
At least she said it softly.

Dean cast her an agonized glance. Agitated, he jumped to his
feet and paced the perimeter of the grave, arrows rattling in his
hard leather quiver. After two trips around, he signed to me, "Father bad. Bad man." He pulled at his hair, slapped his own face
once, twice, took another turn around the stone man. Then he
stood trembling, as if listening to a voice none of us could hear. I
thought of Marcus and those dark days when I couldn't reach him.

"What happened to him?" I signed.

"He hit my mother. She blood. I saw."

"What did he say?" Pia said.

I kept my eyes on Dean and spoke as evenly as I could. "He
said his dad wasn't a good guy. Beat up his mother."

Dean walked purposefully over to Pia; looked up and met her
eye. "Tall woman," he signed. He cupped one hand to his ear, the
sign for "listen." His hands carved the air around us: "Mother shot
father. He die. I watch. After, she cut my tongue." He opened his
mouth wide and again made the sign for "cut." Pia struggled to keep
the terror off her face. He turned to show me, so I forced myself to
look inside his mouth. The remainder of his tongue, an eggplant-
colored stump of flesh, protruded from the back of his mouth, just
under drop-shaped tonsils and surrounded by blackened and missing teeth. The stench of his breath nearly overwhelmed me.

I translated. Pia made a strangled sound.

"Oh, dear God," Sandra said.

Dean closed his mouth and looked at me, as if for my thoughts
on the matter.

"Does it hurt?" I asked.

He signed that it didn't.

"How old are you?" I asked, signed.

"Twenty-three summer," he signed without hesitation.

"How long have you lived here, in the forest?"

"Eighteen summer."

"Where were you born?"

His face lit up. He pointed to the trees swaying in the wind above us. "Sky."

"The sky?"

"Mom says sky. Sun, stars, moon. I am present for her from sky."

"Before the forest," I signed slowly, "where did you live?"

"I live with bad people. Mom says all bad people in town. Mom says, bad Dean in town. Scared of town."

"Ask him if he knows the way out of here," Rachel said.

"You can ask him," I said. "He's not deaf."

She gave me a look, as much as she could with her one good eye. "Dean, can you take us to a town? Do you know the way, besides the river, I mean?"

"No," he signed.

"That's hard to believe." Rachel snorted. "That the kid's never been out of here."

"Why?" Sandra said. She crouched over the pointillist grave, admiring its exquisite detail. It occurred to me just how young Dean was, close to the same age we'd been when we met—Sandra untouched by cancer and a nightmare marriage, Pia before her Wonder Woman years, Rachel when she was falling-down drunk every weekend, back when we still thought that was funny.

"He was five when he came to this place, sounds like," Sandra said as she got to her feet. "Who remembers when they're five? I don't. Not much, anyway."

Dean had stopped paying attention to us. Squirreling around in a greasy leather satchel, he withdrew an envelope fashioned from a beaten piece of plastic. He peeled back layer after layer, revealing a half-inch-thick stack of photographs.

"Secret," he signed to me.

He shyly handed me the photos. Pia, Sandra, and Rachel crowded around me as we scrutinized each one. The photos had wide white frames, the kind produced by instant cameras popular ten or fifteen years ago. Most of the pictures were so badly water- and mud-stained that only pieces of the images were clear. A laughing young woman in a print dress held a baby, while a grim-faced older woman trussed in black stood nearby, clutching her purse high up under her armpit. A red tractor loomed behind them; beyond it a modest-looking farmhouse and rolling green hills. Other photos: children cannonballed off a dock into a shimmering lake as a chubby girl in a flowered bikini watched from the shore. A man with a rifle slung over his shoulder stood next to an enormous dead bear. The last few were old postcards: the Statue of Liberty raising her light above the New York harbor; a grinning cartoon lobster and the words *Welcome to Boothbay Harbor!* superimposed over a photo of a shoreline.

"Who are these people?" I said and signed.

"Mom says fairy tales."

"They're real people," I said. "Or they were."

"Do you know the nice people?" He pointed to the woman in the photograph, the smiling baby.

"No, but there are lots of people I don't know."

"Do they live in town? All the people?"

"Most people live in towns."

A branch snapped in the forest. We jumped toward each other, a force four strong facing out, while Dean spun around and leapt in front of us, bow and arrow drawn. He turned, scanning the boundless green. Long moments later he relaxed, replaced the arrow in the quiver at his back. He gathered the photos, wrapped them with care, and tucked them in his sack.

"She said kill you this morning," he signed. "Then come home." He gazed up at the sky, at the long afternoon shadows the trees cast across us. "So now she comes for me. And you."

35

Follow me," Dean signed. "Another secret."

I translated. Rachel took a step toward him. Assumed a wide stance, slightly pigeon-toed, arms crossed hard. "No more secrets, Dean. This is bullshit. This is *not working*. We need to get out of here."

Pia grabbed Rachel by the arm. She glared down at Pia's hand, said, *"Excuse me?"*

"You need to chill out," Pia hissed. "This kid is helping us."

"You know what I think?" She wrenched herself free of Pia's grip. "I think Dean has his own ideas about what's best for Dean."

"Good secret," he signed, looking at me.

"Shouldn't we find out what he's trying to tell—" Sandra started.

"Hey, jungle boy. Listen to me—"

"Jesus, Rache," Pia said.

"You need to go back to your mother," Rachel said, her finger in his face. "Tell her what you need to tell her, we don't care. You were late because you had to bury us all. It took time. No one's ever gonna hear a thing about you or her. You will be safe. Understand?"

Rachel shook her head and turned away from us, fuming at

the hovering woods that would kill her, given the chance. Dean listened intently, eyes on our every move as he puzzled out the calculus of our friendship.

"Okay, Rachel," I said. "We ask him to go and then what? Suddenly we know our way out of here?"

Rachel spun back around to face us. "At least we'll be alive and lost. Which beats dead and lost."

Dean uttered a whimpering sound, which made us all jump, so seldom had we heard him make any noise, but he had already turned away from us and plummeted back into the woods. With no further discussion, we arranged ourselves into our pitiful queue and stumbled after him into the choking green. Muttering, Rachel grabbed on to my belt and tripped along behind me, while I followed Sandra, who trailed Pia. By what divination Dean found his way, none of us knew. It was just tree, tree, tree, and more trees, all sickeningly the same.

He picked up his pace. While we did our best to keep up, it felt like we were starting to lose him. I moved as in a dream where the more I tried to push forward, the more sluggish my pace. Thirst was catching up with me, with all of us, I could see it; hunger a luxury lurking behind thirst and exhaustion, but still I felt it weakening me, gnawing away at my strength, making my steps less sure over bulging roots and rocky outcroppings. Guiltily I recalled my clandestine rendezvous with the tiny Mr. Goodbar, ultimately forgiving myself for being a few calories stronger than the others. Of all things, I missed my painful hiking boots, but even as I tripped and landed on my hands or knees, the hurt was a distant thing, not in the forefront of my mind. Survival my only focus. The next step, and the next and the next. When, how, where would we get out of this place?

After an hour or so we began to climb, carving out detours

around boulders so large they put us in shadow; many had saplings
and other new growth sprouting from the tops of them. Delicate
green lichens carpeted the shaded parts. Every instinct said run
and catch up with Dean, beg him to tell us his big plan, but I
barely had the energy to slog along behind Sandra.

We found ourselves on the dark side of a boulder so large it
blocked what was left of the afternoon sun. Dean squatted on
a soft bed of pine needles, waiting for us. He looked anxious. I
endured a wave of terror that he'd decided to kill us after all, that
this second "secret" was an elaborate ruse for this purpose. I kept
my face calm. Lesser boulders surrounded him, footnotes left by
earth's slow narrative of glaciers and unimaginable time.

Dean offered us water from some sort of gourd. As we all took
small sips, he signed, "Need help. All of you."

He walked around the boulder, and then disappeared—
somehow—inside it. We followed him. The rock had cracked
open at its center, forced apart a good three feet by a handsome,
vigorous poplar that sprouted from the top while clutching the two
halves of the stone with thick, intertwined roots.

We crept down into the dark cavity, squinting into dappled
shadow. A flat, square structure made of logs lashed together
leaned against one wall of the split rock face. Dean reached up,
grabbed one corner of the thing, and heaved it toward him. The
mattress-shaped block came tumbling toward me and somehow I
caught the edge. Together we turned it, side over side, until it was
free of its narrow cave. We rested it against the mossy face of the
boulder and stared.

A raft.

Pia went up and touched it with a kind of reverence. Leather
straps and sinew braided into rope bound a dozen pine logs of
roughly uniform size and shape. At both ends, a single log crossed

the parallel ones, binding the raft snugly. Shreds of colored plastic, flattened soda bottles, strips of tire, bright patches of canvas had been woven into it. It looked as cheerful as a bright quilt, but also terrifically strong.

"You made this?" Pia asked.

"Yes," he signed.

Sandra walked around it. "You did a good job. Really good."

I think Dean may have blushed.

"When did you make this?" I asked.

"Two summers," he signed. "Secret."

Rachel plopped down wearily on a hollow log. "I don't get it. You made a raft. Why didn't you use it?"

He looked at her an extra second, as if parts of her were coming clearer to him. "Scared," he signed. "World hurts, Mom says."

"He says he's too afraid, basically," I said. His face in a certain light, especially evening light, looked like that of an old man. Deeply furrowed cheeks, a worried brow.

"So why now? Why bring us along?" Rachel asked.

Dean reached into his satchel and unwrapped the package of photos, shuffled through them. Gazed down at the waterlogged faces. "Family," he signed, and handed the photos to her.

Rachel made no move to take the pictures. "Are they your family, Dean?"

He signed, "Yes," and then, "I don't know."

"When was the last time you saw them?" I asked.

"Eighteen summer," he signed.

I translated the little I knew for my friends.

"I think we're the first people besides his parents he's seen in eighteen years," Sandra said.

Dean reached down and yanked Rachel up by one arm. She squealed in protest—grumbling about how the raft seemed too heavy to stay afloat—but no one else moved as he led her to one side of it. He motioned to Pia to pick up the opposite side. He didn't have to tell Sandra to take the position at the front, next to me.

"No time," he signed. "Go to river now."

Dean grabbed the raft by one corner and hauled it up with a grunt, resting most of its weight on his strong, wiry back. Even though he bore the bulk of it, we stopped a few times to rest and switch positions. But we were polite with each other, our spirits beginning to brighten even as we labored under the heavy load. We rolled the raft end over end, half dragged it, half carried it, banging it into trees and each other, the bark scraping our shoulders and the palms of our hands, but we made progress, dropping down steadily toward the sound of the river.

36

Dean waded waist-deep into calmly moving water and stood staring down at the amber flow. Water striders skated across the surface dragging silvery threads of light. Utterly spent, we sat or lay down on the brief pebbly beach. The raft leaned against the encroaching woods.

When I replayed the scene in my mind a few seconds later, I still couldn't recall seeing Dean's arm move. First he held nothing, then a brown trout wriggled in his hand, as if magically placed there. I stood and looked down into the water. Three brook trout held their own in a row in the current, their white gills fluttering tenderly in the flow. Dean gripped his fish by the tail and slapped its head down hard on a rock face, just once. It lay glassy-eyed and still.

He slipped a knife from his belt and gutted the fish, sliced off the gills, sawed off its head, and scaled it. Glittering silver coins floated swiftly downstream. He split the fish open on the rock, cut it into four pieces, and handed us each a section.

"Eat," he signed, which we all pretty much understood. He made the signs for "no," "fire," and "time."

None of us complained. We each ate our share and thanked

him—including Rachel—then rinsed our hands in the drift. Mine tasted like wet rocks and moss, barely like fish at all. I realized I felt marginally stronger not from the size of my portion—couldn't have been that—but because I had eaten something so recently alive.

Dean secured the raft to a tree with one of its braided leather ropes. Grunting, we all manhandled the awkward thing to the water, where it fell with a colossal splash. It was so heavy part of me never believed it would float—that Rachel was right—but it bounced to the surface and bobbed there like the sweetest salvation we had ever seen.

I'm sure it was the sight of the raft in the water that lifted our spirits to the point where we could actually make fun of each other for a few minutes. The mood lightened the most it had since Rory died.

"Hey, Pia," Rachel said.

"Yeah?"

"Remember the time we all went parasailing off the Keys in Florida because you said it would be a great thing to do, and you told the guy it was all right to let us all out to—what was the maximum? Two hundred and fifty feet?"

Pia rolled her eyes. "Here we go."

"And then," Rachel went on, "the next day we learn that the guy got shut down because the ropes and gear he was using were flawed and not up to regulation or whatever, and that the day before we went up, two people died and he never told us? Remember that?"

"Yup."

"Well, that was pretty fucking stupid too."

We all laughed even though it hurt physically to do so; my ribs and back felt beat-up and sore. Dean watched us intently. He wore a look of confused delight when he saw us laugh, but lost no time in getting us on the raft. He motioned for me to climb aboard first. I waded out to where it rested in hip-high water, jigged and jagged by the mild current, and jimmied myself onto the thing, finally rolling onto it. Because it barely sank under my weight, I stupidly tried to stand, but lost my balance immediately and dropped to my knees, where I stayed until everybody else got on. Rachel, Pia, and Sandra climbed on more cautiously and settled, grinning like idiots as though we were already saved.

From the shore, Dean loosened the rope. Gripping the line, he freed the raft from the waist of the tree, dropped back into the water, and waded out toward us. Here the river flowed as if asleep, like something that only dreamed of violence and churning waters and death. He pushed himself up and lifted his slim body aboard.

We floated. The river bulged out in gentle turns like a fat snake dozing in the sun. Evening had begun to smoke up the air, and I put it at something like seven by the plush feel of the river and orange-lit water. I took off my life jacket, bunched it up for a pillow, and lay down. Smiling, Pia and Sandra joked about what a good idea I had and lay down to either side of me. Some kind of flower graced the breeze, so sweet I tried to breathe in more than out—a wild honeysuckle or clematis or phlox, I'll never know. I just know that for a time I forgot to be afraid.

Dean knelt at one end of the raft, busy untying something, and I realized a flat section of wood had been lashed to the main body, and that it was a crudely hewn oar. He got to his feet, keeping us on course like a gondolier. I turned onto my stomach on the rough bark, letting my fingers trail into the current, and thought about how this easy, mild water was the same water that had killed Rory and nearly drowned us all.

Sandra lay next to me, her head resting on her arms, half-asleep. She blinked slowly and with a little half smile said, "I feel like Huck Finn."

The last words she would ever say.

A small, bloodless hole appeared above her right eye. Her face went slack, but her eyes stayed open, watching me, her mouth finishing the word *Finn*. Then she lay motionless. A popping sound ricocheted from across the river, then another, and another, like distant fireworks. High-pitched whistling sounds. Water dimpled to the right of the raft, as if it were raining. I still hadn't put it together until, viscerally, I did. Bullets.

I heard screaming. It was me.

I knew Loo was dead but rolled her on her back and shook her and screamed her name anyway. I shoved my hands in her armpits and tried to lift her. No idea why. I was out of my mind. I had no plan. Pia cowered by me, her mouth open in horror as Rachel scrambled to her feet and began shouting something, but there was only a rushing quiet in my ears; I couldn't understand the words. Sandra's head lolled back and to one side, and I felt her body absorb the almost soft, sickening impact of two more bullets before I let her go.

37

A vise-strong arm hooked around my waist and wrenched me from Sandra—jerked me up so hard I saw white stars of pain burst in the deep blue sky moments before I crashed into freezing water. For the first few moments of shocking cold, I could not orient myself, I only knew I had to swim underwater as far and as fast as possible. Turning, I gazed up at the black square that was the raft, sunlight glinting down around it through tea-colored water, and at the skittering lines the bullets made as they rammed into the surface then slowed and sank, twirling harmlessly down into the depths. But where was the shore? Which way should I swim?

I felt a rush of water behind my head. Rachel's feet frog-kicked as she swam, her shorts and tank top billowing out underwater, black hair waving. She began to surface but fought it. Rolling, bubbles silvering out of her mouth, she struggled to unsnap and free herself from her life vest, which floated up like an orange balloon. She kicked off into the dark water, and I followed her bright blue water shoes.

Because I'd been thrown in the water and hadn't taken a proper breath—only a shallow gasp—my lungs quickly cried out for air. A copper bullet stuttered down into the water inches from my face as I forced myself farther down into the depths, stroking my way along the silty bottom. I swam like some enormous cat-fish, the curtains of my vision closing on either side as my brain started to die.

Some animal hunger for life took over. I drew my knees to my chest and thrust my legs down, hoping to launch myself to the surface that way. Instead I sank to my shins in sludge and roots, trapping myself. I waved my arms like seaweed, my head a knot of pain, air gone. I blinked up at the light, my will fading. Would this be how it would end? Entombed in river quicksand, dead forever standing up? A visceral memory pushed panic aside for unreal seconds. When was the last time I was trapped this way, airless, gazing skyward through blue space, reaching up and grabbing at water to pull myself up?

I flashed on the moment my father, with his signature casual cruelty, "taught me to swim" one afternoon at the community pool when I was eleven. Marcus by his side, he threw me—without warning—into the deep end. Terror turned to fury as I sank like something weighted, Marcus's shocked face squiggly above the water, his mouth an O, his hands reaching down for me. In a cyclone of bubbles, I kicked and punched at the water, willing myself to rise up. Rage taught me how to swim; fierce love brought me to the surface, back to my brother.

Dimly I realized one foot was wedged in deeper than the other, but if I pointed my toes down like a ballerina, I could wriggle both feet. Kicking hard as if I were doing some frantic dance, I felt one foot come free, then the other, deplorably free of both water shoes. I exploded up and out into sunlight with too much noise, gulping at the air while fully expecting to be shot in the neck and die instantly. In fact, the old me—the part that was good buddies with giving up—wanted it badly, the oblivion, relief from the responsibility of staying alive any longer.

But no bullet came. In the seconds it took to fill my lungs with air and submerge again, I glimpsed Rachel and Pia huddled close several yards away near the bank, their heads barely above water as they took cover under a nest of fallen branches. Doubled over with the strain, the rope scarring his back, Dean clambered ashore dragging the raft behind him. Sandra's body lay spread-eagled on it as if she were making a snow angel.

I swam toward the memory of Rachel's and Pia's ghostly faces bobbing by the shore, and with two or three hard sweeps of my arms I reached them, popping out of the water. They yanked me under the cluster of branches where we herded together, arms around each other, crying. Dean stepped out onto the raft, now resting on the bank. He lifted Sandra's limp body over his shoulder and carried her into the forest.

We knelt in a circle around our friend, weeping but as unaware of our weeping as young people are unaware of time, and I remember trying to clean her face with whatever we had, leaves or pieces of our own tattered clothes, and combing her hair with our hands. The last time I'd done so had been right before her wedding, because the stylist she hired to do her hair had made her look ridiculous, all poofy and fake. Minutes before she walked down the aisle, in the back of the church in a dim bathroom with a greasy mirror, the three of us—giddy with nerves—deconstructed the silly updo. We set aside the waxy white flowers pinned there as we restyled her hair, then clipped the flowers to the side of her head. It was one of the most intimate things we had ever done for her, and she had never looked more beautiful than she did smiling back at us in that badly lit restroom. This was her real, about-to-get-married self. Still our Sandra, but about to change that too. We all knew she wasn't 100 percent sure about this man waiting for her a room away, but we also knew she saw enough good in him for a marriage. I felt her trepidation as well as her passionate love, and it had worried me, but what could I do? We could already feel her moving forward, swept by relentless time into her own future with her own children (one already nestled in her and growing), so really, who were we to stop her?

What had remained of Rachel's glasses was gone. Washed away. She knelt down, her face close to Sandra's as she caressed her cheek.

"I slapped her," Rachel said hoarsely. The rest I couldn't understand because of her crying.

Pia fell on her knees beside her. "It's okay," she sobbed. "She knew you loved her."

"Did she?" Rachel breathed, and was again lost in a paroxysm of grief.

I picked up Sandra's hand, so cold, white, and small, fingernails black with dirt. Really not in my right mind, I tried to warm it pressed between my palms. Rachel dropped into a little ball next to her, rocking back and forth on her heels, moaning.

As if wrenching herself from the earth, Pia pushed herself to her feet, eyes red with sorrow. With rough movements, she wiped her face with her hands, only making it grimier as she striped the dirt across her cheeks and forehead till she resembled some sort of warrior, frightening to look at. "All right." She glanced around the glowering woods. "We have to move."

Dean squatted nearby. He held his head in his hands, mouth agape, with such a look of sadness in his eyes I thought of comforting him somehow, but didn't. He rubbed his closed fist in circles around his heart, again and again, the sign for "sorry."

"I know," I said to him.

He signed, "Tell them sorry."

"Dean is saying how sorry he is," I said quietly.

"What are we going to do?" Rachel wailed from her puddle on the forest floor.

A colossal squawking erupted from the mesh of leaves over our heads. A half dozen black crows dropped down all around us. Screeching and cawing, they battled out some crow feud, then took off and flew downriver. We watched with weary detachment.

"Wini, Rachel, get up. Come on," Pia said.

"And do what, Pia? What's the big plan now?" Rachel said, blue eyes naked without her glasses.

"We run."

"We bury our friend," Rachel said. "Or we take her with us. Or I die here."

38

In the end we did for Sandra what we had for Rory: we covered her with stones, branches, anything we could find to protect her body. Two of the life vests and the oar had washed onto shore several yards downstream, and Dean sprinted off to retrieve them. Cutting off one of the bright orange straps, he climbed a tree with branches that hung over the river and tied it there, so we could come back for her. The more I tried to shut out of my mind the idea of wolves and other animals, the more I saw them, snarling and hungry, waiting for the night.

"We leave now," Pia said. "We have an hour of sunlight."

"I'm staying here," Rachel said. She sat cross-legged near the pile of stones that covered Sandra, staring at nothing. "I'm done."

"Don't be ridiculous." Pia bent over and grabbed her under the shoulders. "Come on, Rachel, get up." Like a rag doll, Rachel let herself be lifted to a slouchy standing position.

Dean signed to me with quick hands. "Bullets from other side river, but she comes. Little time we have, only. We leave now."

Pia watched Dean sign. "I don't know what he said, and I don't care. He needs to go."

"Yes," Rachel said, coming to life. She took a few steps toward

Dean and stopped, marionette-like. "He needs to go back to his mother. This is fucking crazy. She's going to kill us all."

"No," he signed. "We take raft and go. Everybody."

I translated, adding, "We should do it now, because she's crossing the river."

"How does he know that?" Rachel sputtered. I have to think it was easier not making eye contact with him—her glasses gone—when she added, "Look, Dean, this is over. You need to go back. Stop her. Kill her."

He glared at her.

"If you care about us at all, you can't stay with us. Do you understand?"

Dean shook his head, rooted around in his pouch, and pulled out the plastic packet of photos.

Rachel swatted them out of his hands. He dove down, frantically gathered them, jumped to his feet. Seething, he seized her by the shoulders and rammed her up against a tree, her helmet cracking against the bark. Her round blue eyes focused on his, inches away.

"Whoa, Dean, calm down," I said.

They stared venom into each other. Nobody moved. A full minute passed. "Take your hands off me," Rachel said evenly.

He glanced over at me, a question. I shook my head. Still he held her there.

"I can't fucking believe you did that, Rachel," Pia hissed. She took a few cautious steps toward them. "Come on, Dean, you don't want to do this, really you don't."

"Maybe say you're sorry, Rachel," I said. "Maybe mean it this time."

"I'm not—"

"*Say it.*"

"Sorry about the photos."

Dean shook Rachel by the shoulders, teeth-rattlingly hard, then shoved her away from the tree.

She fell off her feet, nearly losing her balance, but ended up stumbling off a few steps down toward the river. In a vain attempt to regain her pride she squared her shoulders and recalibrated her cockeyed helmet.

"Look, I don't care about your goddamned family or whoever they are. This is my family, my friends here. The only family I have left, and we are down one. We are not going anywhere with you, so you may as well leave, got it? Go back. Your mother is your family, your home."

I gazed at the pile of stones that covered Sandra, picturing not just her serene, lovely face, but her body, which had beaten back cancer, which had borne two remarkable children, one who'd arrived as easily as breathing, the other a torture to bring into the world but who became her biggest joy on earth: her boy, Ethan. All that fighting only to die in this useless, meaningless way; even the scars on her body—marks of grace—to disappear forever.

"No," Dean signed, his face hard and unreadable. "We go to town. All of you. Safe. Come."

I didn't translate.

"Win, you have to tell him," Pia said. "He'll listen to you."

"Dean." I held him with my voice and my gaze, while I was seeing Marcus the day I had to tell him I was going to abandon him to the home, and in his eyes I saw how unimaginable this was for him, how I may as well have been pushing him over a cliff. "You have to go back. I'll come for you, after we get some people to help. Do you understand?"

He shook his head; his stringy hair flew around his shoulders. He signed, "No," over and over, but after some time he slumped and signed, "She kill me too."

"No, she won't," I said. "You are her son. She won't hurt you."
But I had no idea what this woods creature would do to her son.
Look at what she had already done to him.

"You my family," he signed, tearful. "Sandra, family."

I felt myself crying again and said, "Okay. We are your family."

"Happy," he signed, though his eyes stayed sad, and I could see
that in his mind he was already racing through the forest.

"But, Dean, go. Now, all right?"

I watched his face working, hatching a plan. "Wait for me by
the raft here," he signed. "Wait overnight. I make you all safe. Wait
sunrise."

Pia and Rachel stood talking in low voices, glancing back at us
every now and then.

"Make promise?" he signed.

"Okay. Promise. We wait here till first light. If you're not here,
we go, do you understand? We take the raft and go."

He nodded, turned, and vanished into the forest.

39

I ran down to the bank, barefoot. Pia and Rachel, ropes slung over their shoulders, were already hauling the raft back down toward the muddy bank. The river ran silvery green where it wasn't darkened by evening shadows. I stood watching them, hands in rock-hard fists at my sides.

"What are you doing?"

They ignored me. As if I were already dead, a ghost. I closed my eyes and tried to conjure Sandra, but I couldn't even feel her spirit anymore. Was she already gone from this earth? I watched Pia and Rachel as they positioned the raft at an opening in a tangle of brush near the bank, chatting together easily as they had since they were children. I had never felt so alone.

Finally Rachel looked up, squinted in my direction. "Is he gone?"

Pia glanced back at me and said nothing while something like guilt flickered across her face.

"Yes, but he's coming back in the morning."

Pia snorted, yanking the raft so hard over the mossy embankment that one corner dipped down, tasting the water. "We're leaving, Win."

A cavity opened in the depths of my gut. My head seemed to vibrate slightly. "What do you mean 'we'?"

Rachel faced the river, away from me, legs planted wide apart in the dirt. With a grunt, she bent down and heaved the raft a few feet forward. It landed half in, half out of the water, resting at a forty-five degree angle to the bank. Already the river wanted it; one more solid shove would set it free. "All of us," she said, staring at the lagoon-dark water.

"Listen to me," I said.

No one made a sound. The current sang its burbling song and tugged at the raft, inching it farther from the shore.

"He says he's going to get us out of here."

Rachel stepped into the water up to her knees, splashed over to the far side of the raft that bobbed and flirted with the waves. Pia stood at the shoreline, arms folded, watching her.

"Did you hear me? He says he's going to make us safe."

"What does that mean?" Rachel turned in my direction. Her curly hair had begun to dry; it stood out in a crazy halo around her head. She looked walleyed and unstoppable. The water rumbled past her waist, yanking at her shirt. "Is he going to kill her?"

Our ragged breathing filled the air. The green pressed in on us as long-legged mosquitoes swarmed our foul, sweating bodies. I watched one bloat to twice its size with my own blood before I smacked it, reddening my thigh. I felt, viscerally, Sandra's body lying yards away, already starting to become not Sandra, but a part of the earth we stood on. We owed her something, a large and complex debt I was too depleted to face or even comprehend.

"Is he?" Rachel repeated, hate in her voice.

I took a few steps down the bank, my feet stinging and aching on the sharp stones, before I clambered onto the raft, anchoring it to the shore with my weight. "I promised him we'd wait till dawn. He'll help us."

They eyed my every move but stayed where they were. Pia's bare feet were bruised, scratched, and bloody.

"We don't care what you promised him," Rachel said. I couldn't tell which stung me more: this *we* business again or their refusal to listen; all the time the loss of Sandra stabbed me like shards of glass in my spine.

Rachel rested her arms lightly on the raft, her eyes aimed vaguely skyward toward a point somewhere over the wall of black spruces that crowded the bank. It occurred to me she needed at least one of us to even think of getting out of here. "And honestly, Win?" she continued. "Between you and me and Pia and the trees and shit? I'm not even sure you're telling us everything Dean is saying. Or not saying."

Anger rippled through me. "Rachel—*seriously*? You're accusing me of—"

"Wini," Pia said, stepping gingerly toward the water, "don't take this the wrong way, but Dean is not your brother."

I planted myself on the raft, glared at her. Still she wouldn't meet my eye. "So what the fuck does that mean?"

"It means we can't save him too, okay, Win? We have to choose."

"But I *am* choosing! Without him with us she *will* kill us if she finds us, don't you get that? Either of you?"

Suddenly Pia landed with animal grace next to me, eyes blood-shot, hair wild. "You don't think she'll be ripping mad if she finds him still with us?" she hissed, her face inches from mine. "What do you think she'll do then? Write us love letters?"

I recoiled into myself but stayed where I was, rooted to my seat on the raft.

"She shot at the raft with him on it, for Christ's sake!" Pia blustered. "He's no protection at all!"

"What I get," Rachel said, "is that they're both out there in those woods that they know—you can't tell me that kid doesn't know these woods, where we are and how to get out of here—and they both have weapons, and we're sitting here with nothing. No food, no warm clothes, zippo. And I will not just sit on my ass waiting to be killed."

"Weren't your parents off-the-gridders?" I asked, feeling ganged up on, so—stupidly—making things worse.

"What the hell does that have to do with—"

"Nothing, I just—"

"We grew up in the sticks. There were nine of us, and we were too poor to pay the electric bill. There's a fucking difference between growing up on government cheese and ripping the heads off wild animals and decorating your yard with them."

Pia snickered at Rachel's retort but stayed uncomfortably close to me. I gazed at the tight, complex weave of leather straps that bound the logs beneath me, suddenly queasy as I pictured Dean returning at dawn to no raft, to no one. His disappointment, his rage, and, frankly, what that might turn into. Would he join his mother in a murderous rampage against us? What had he meant by *make you safe*? What were his plans for her, anyway? Still—maybe because I could communicate with him—I felt safer with Dean at our side than not. Crossing him seemed like the last, fatal thing to do.

Pia stood up but did not back away. "So, Wini," she uttered in a low voice I barely recognized as hers, "are you going to get off the raft or not?"

Rachel waded closer to me and gave the raft a shove. With my weight she could only nudge it an inch or two deeper into the pulling drift. She wouldn't look at me. I recalled her ceaseless devotion to Sandra when she was so frail and debilitated after her chemo, and now I couldn't shake the thought that she might leave me here.

"You guys aren't thinking this through," I said. "We haven't even hit the worst of these rapids. Don't you remember the map? The roughest part is just ahead! Satan's Staircase."

Rachel and Pia exchanged glances, sharing information I was not privy to. Face flushed with the strain, Rachel leaned down and put her shoulder into another push. The raft scraped a foot more down the bank.

"Stop it!" I was screaming now. Violence buzzed in my hands.

"Wini, you have to calm down," Pia said.

Both of them bent down toward the raft as if gathering their strength for one last assault, a terrifying emptiness in their faces.

"Stop it or I'll fucking kill you!" I slammed my hands down on the raft. "How long do you think this thing is going to last in rough water? Have either of you taken two seconds to think about that?"

"What's that got to do with—" Pia started.

"We have no choice," Rachel said.

"Of course we have a choice. Dean's coming back and he's going to—"

"Wini," Pia said darkly. "Get off the raft." She put her hands on her rangy hips and glowered at me. I pictured them pushing off into the river, their faces receding into darkness and me alone in those hellish woods. I thought, *If this is my real family—the people*

I choose to be with—then how much more devastating to be abandoned by them?

I looked up at Pia, considered for the first time her size and strength as something to possibly fend off. She loomed over me, expression unreadable, eyes cloaked by the shadow of the trees, the lowering sun. Rachel, though weakened as we all were, looked sturdy and capable. As purblind as she was, she glared with a fury I'd never before witnessed into the vicinity of where I had installed myself. A light-headedness came over me—hunger, numbing fatigue, shock—for a few seconds I closed my eyes.

At the same moment I sensed the two of them about to collect themselves to move toward me: Pia from behind, Rachel from the water. My eyes snapped open to find them a few steps closer to me, Rachel fully out of the water now, dripping onto the sandy bank. I could feel the heat of Pia's body as she came toward me.

I couldn't stop a flash of Marcus breaking into the pills at the group home and swallowing them all down with the ginger ale he loved. It was three o'clock in the morning, night's most desolate hour, only days after we'd moved him in. Was he thinking about his sister, asleep in her comfortable bed a town away? Was he drowning in a sea of loneliness, since no one at the home understood his pidgin mash of "real" sign language and his made-up signs? They told me he must have been asleep in minutes, dead within the hour. As I looked out at the water, the surface purling midstream, I was overcome by the idea that maybe Pia was right, perhaps Dean was just another brother I couldn't save, and it was foolhardy and dangerous to try.

I pushed myself to my feet and stepped off the raft with slow deliberation. Pia and Rachel regarded me for a few seconds, unsure what I might do next. But I had deflated. My rage had deserted me, and I felt weak in every way. Wordlessly, sweat pouring off their faces, they bent down and deadlifted the raft. At the last second, perversely, I lent a hand, and together we sledded the thing down and out into the waiting current.

40

The river took us faster than it ever had. We seemed to ride higher up somehow, ferried along with a brusque efficiency for half a mile or so of what turned out to be the final easy stretch. We sat on the raft like ticks on a horse, just clinging, no plan at all, until I felt the water surge as the walls of the forest moved in. The river narrowed, and we were swept around a turn.

We could feel the river changing underneath us; I read it in our faces, the effort to ready ourselves for whatever was coming next. Rachel crawled to the center of the raft and sat tight, clutching the leather straps that trussed the logs, while I struggled to get to my feet with the oar, hoping to control the thing as Dean had, but that plan turned futile right away. The river wheeled us completely around as if some laughing devil were spinning the raft for sport, and we tumbled back on our asses and stayed there, cursing and shaking. We dug our bleeding heels into the splintering logs, and it was all we could do to jockey the oar to ward us away from fallen trees and islands of river detritus clumped in nightmarish shapes, all hurtling at us fast.

The air freshened. We didn't speak. I missed terribly the relative softness and give of our rubber raft, which slid over obstacles or bounced off them. Nothing gave with this primitive bitch of a craft we clung to like animals. There was no bend or ability to coast over the steep drops we'd bested before; it was as if we were caught in a flood and riding on a rooftop, something never meant to float down a river. We were the wrong shape—an awkward square—made of the wrong substance. And we couldn't stop ourselves. The insanity of what we were doing felt fluttery in my throat. My own death loomed in front of me. I saw Sandra's face. Her mouth as she spoke her last words.

But really, as fast as we were moving, we hadn't seen anything yet. We hit another bend, swung around sharp, dropped down. The river began to seethe and boil with newfound energy. It felt malevolent, like it knew all our private terrors, like it relished just what a raw hand it was about to deal us. Rachel's eyes grew wild; I knew her dread was even worse than ours—we could at least see what was barreling toward us. Rory had told us to always head into the rapids, but the idea seemed nuts. The mineral taste of water filled my mouth.

An island sprang up before us, this angry knot of crags and nested sticks like spears sticking out, and the river—we could feel it—wanted to impale us there. We moved toward it as if notched into a groove and shot forward by unseen hands. Pia scrambled to her knees and held out the oar. It hit me that she had some shit-crazy idea of knocking us away from the thing.

"Pia, *stay down!*" I yelled, but she didn't listen or hear. The oar caught in the fist of rock, and the butt of it slammed back into her chest. She screamed, fell back, and rolled to the edge, one leg fully in the water, spray flying up at us. We spun around and hurtled on past the island.

"Wini!" she shrieked, her eyes sick with fear as I caught her arm and held on with nothing to brace me. Rachel grabbed my

waistband with one hand, a rope with the other, heels jammed
into the wood as I wrestled gravity and centrifugal force to drag
Pia back onto the raft. My shoulders nearly wrenched from their
sockets, but by God I had her, pulled her up hand over hand till
I caught at her belt and heaved her toward me with a strength
foreign to me. Pia tucked her legs up to her chest, rolled over to
Rachel, and curled in a ball, shaking.

"Are you hurt?"

"I don't know," she cried as she struggled to get back up. She
said something else, but the river erased her words.

"Get down!" I screamed. "Forget the oar!"

We huddled together as the raft spun again and nausea flooded
me. I vomited hot bile between my knees while Pia moaned next
to me. Dense forest receded from either side of the river as walls
of pocked, chalky stone rose to replace it. The water lightened as
the remaining sun reflected off the now-rocky bottom. The river
quickened over it, as if encouraged by the smoothness to race
even faster. Our view of the sky became a narrow cerulean corridor as the walls of the canyon continued to rise.

In minutes, the vertical bluffs cast their shadows across us
and our sunlight vanished. As if fed by gloom, the water rumbled
under the raft, foaming even between its logs, which had begun
to loosen in their ties. Sound meshed together and echoed from
everywhere, louder than our thoughts. We seemed to be sliding
down a ramp over unseen boulders; I had a moment of hope that
the water had become deep enough that we wouldn't hit anything,
that we had somehow seen the worst of it.

We skidded up onto something hard and sharp—a calved,
knife-edged boulder. A terrible screech of stone tearing wood,
louder even than the howling water. The jagged rock ripped out
a section of log just beneath Rachel, who screamed and scuttled

away from the hole under her. We balanced on the apex of the rock for several surreal seconds until the wood groaned as we unimpaled ourselves and dipped down the other side of the edifice and were carried away. Water lathered up through the gash in the middle of the raft, soaking us in one constant spray. The oar was gone.

Unable to utter words, we linked arms in a circle around the hole and turned to look downriver at what was coming. Glassy waves rolled under us. An outraged roar came from up ahead, a deep booming sound that thrummed in my jaw, and I thought, *If these are falls, we are dead for sure.* My limbs felt thick and stiff, and I'd never been so cold. My teeth clacked in my skull, and I pictured my skeleton in all its brittle, pathetic humanity. Rachel's fingers dug welts into my forearms. She made a high, keening sound I don't think she was aware of. I felt sure that Dean had never seen these rapids, because he would have known his raft would never survive them.

"Hold on, everybody!" Pia screamed.

The raft whipsawed around an elbow in the river, and then we saw them. A ladder of rapids descended in orderly horror down and down and out of sight around a turn. Just dropped into nothingness. Satan's Staircase. Of course. No better name possible.

My stomach flew skyward as the raft smashed down on the first rock stair, like a piano dropped out a second-story window. With a wrenching screech, a three-log section at the front tore off and rolled under us, then popped up behind us as we crashed down to the next stair. We all watched the broken piece toss and roll furiously behind our battered raft, visions of Rory's death haunting us, but we were moving faster than the lashed segment, and in seconds it caught between two rocks and hung there, water foaming and spraying out all around it.

"We have to jump!" Pia shouted, her eyes like a madwoman's. I looked where she looked. We were a heartbeat from flying over the next stair, where the raft would dump us for sure.

None of us jumped. We clung to each other, screams stuck in our throats.

We shot over the watery cliff, and I felt the raft drop away beneath me. Rachel, utterly disoriented, pushed away from me even as I grappled to hold on to her. Pia let go of me to lunge for Rachel but lost both of us. For strange, long moments I was airborne in a cloud of hissing spray. Alone and falling.

I heard a crack and boom beneath me. I clattered down on the raft, my body a limp puppet, just a collection of pain and bruises and cuts. Half the raft had broken free. Rachel was gone. Pia fell like a cat next to me, her grace and strength serving her as never before. We clung to what remained of the raft—a section maybe four feet wide and six feet long, barely held together by the straps, like loose teeth in a diseased mouth. Together we looked out and down to the next stair, which dropped and disappeared into the boiling currents of a vast granite basin. A line of frantic water riffled at the base of the drop, endlessly curling back on itself.

Wordlessly, together, we decided that the next drop spent on the raft would kill us, so we jumped.

41

A black vortex of water siphoned me down, then flipped me around so many times and so fast that when I tried to lift my head to breathe, up was not up. I forced my body to turn but was pummeled back in the direction the water wanted me to go. My head bump-bumped along what—the bottom?—as I grappled for light and air. I glimpsed a patch of brightness and kicked off toward it, but something big and heavy and soft fell on me. Dark purple shorts, black tank top, swirling black hair. Rachel. For long, harrowing seconds her body tangled with mine, both of us frantic. Her ass and arms in my face, she blind and kicking. We freed ourselves from each other, and she vanished in a whirl of bubbles. Beaten and scraped, I shot up and ate the air. Huge, greedy gulps of it as hard water smacked me, pasting me like a lover against a rock face of some kind. I could breathe, but water firehosed so mercilessly at my face I could not orient. I thought I heard myself scream, but it could have been any of us; it could have come from inside my own head.

My hands swept across the moss-slicked basin looking for purchase, but the water was alive and sucked me back and down into the seething heart of the bowl. Again I churned around and around like a sneaker in a washing machine, and I knew I would drown unless I could somehow hook on to the lip of the thing and flip myself out and down to the next stair.

As I swept around the belly of the basin, I fixated on the feeble light flickering down from where I'd emerged before. I tried to time it. At the light I flung both arms up to latch onto anything that was there to stop myself. I burst out of that water like a breaching whale. Immediately one arm wedged in a crevasse in the rock wall while the other flailed again and again over the edge of the bowl. I hung there like a puppet, my shoulder slowly dislocating. A corkscrew of water drummed into my back as my arm began to slide out of the crevasse.

Over the rim of the bowl, water sluiced down a chute for several yards to the next stone stair, then dropped out of sight; this next horror my goal. No sign of Pia or Rachel. A sheer rock face next to me shot up fifteen, twenty feet. Below me, the water hauled at my hips and legs and feet; the cauldron wanted me back. I had an impulse to laugh, it was all so insane. Me against this devil, how silly to even go to battle. With a sick sort of strength, I worked one knee up the side of the slippery chamber and, using that leverage, lunged forward to grab a whip-slim sapling growing sideways out of a fissure in the rock wall of the canyon. My other arm slipped from between the wet stones.

The laughing thing was over. Crying and praying, all I asked of the young tree was to hold me until I could free myself from the churning waters that yearned to suck me down. Hand over hand I hauled my body up. With sickening dread, I felt the tree begin to detach from the rock. For every inch I gained, a root would loosen and break free from its mooring, scattering the mulch and moss it clung to. Screaming, I pulled myself up and over the lip of the bowl, the sapling in my arms as I tumbled forward down the stone chute.

Arms out straight, I cascaded steeply down and landed hard onto a plate of stone where I felt something important in my arm go before I was dumped back into the river proper. A crazy braiding kind of water shot me along. It pounded me in places on my body I never knew existed, and I fought to swing my feet forward as Rory had said to do, but where was forward here? I tried to touch along the bottom, but the water whooshed me up. Finally I got my feet out and up, but Satan had more stairs—smaller ones now, drops of two and three feet—for which I was weirdly grateful. At least by now I had learned to keep my head up and out and curl forward when I slid over rocks.

I dropped down the last stair and was ushered along over smaller boulders and between them, just helpless fleshy flotsam tumbling along. I knew my arm was broken but I couldn't look at it. Just held it close to me, a white flame of pain clutched to my chest.

Pia screamed my name. Thank God, she was alive! I glanced a few yards to my left, saw her spread-eagled against a boulder trying to climb up and out. Her shoulder was covered with blood, pulsed with blood. She reached out for me, but I faced the wrong way to grab her hand with my good arm so I swept by her.

I floated along now with a purpose: *get myself out*. I slapped at the water with my right arm, trying to aim myself the least bit toward the bank, and with some dread, dropped my legs and feet a bit to push off whatever was coming at me so I could start to control my route. Arctic-cold currents mixed with just cold ones now, and oddly warmish ones, all of them running along my body with an eerie knowledge of it. Every now and then, my feet hit bottom and scooted along it as if I were in some watery wheelchair, and in that way I scuttled closer and closer to the bank.

I looked up. To my left, Pia sprinted along a sloping ridge of stone that flattened into overlapping sheets of shale. She was keeping pace with me.

I kicked myself into an eddy, working my body into an area of shallows where the water felt unrecognizably kind. It sparkled in a waist-deep pool the green of old bottles. I realized I could stop fighting and had to redefine myself as something not under the river's command. I was a pitiful ball of pain.

Pia scrambled over the shallow rock steps. She ran splashing into the water toward me while I was still summoning the strength to stand. Blood coursed from a long, ugly cut across her shoulder, running down her arm and hand and pinking up the water near me.

"Are you okay?" She bent down to help me, comfort me, lift me, I don't know.

"Don't touch me!" I wailed. I blinked away the river water and let myself look down at my left forearm, which had a bend in it now, halfway between elbow and wrist. It floated fish-belly white in the water in front of me.

"Shit, Wini, that's definitely broken." She glanced up at the barren rocks. "Come on, you have to get out of the water. Put your good hand on my back."

"Your shoulder—"

"It just looks bad. It's just messy. Let's go."

"Where's Rachel?" I said, crying. I almost missed the river doing my moving for me. I couldn't imagine standing.

"I don't know. Up ahead."

"I can't . . ." I started to bawl.

Pia splashed water on her cut. It bled unabated. "Yes, you can. You have to get up. Do I have to carry you?"

I blew snot out my nose, laughing at that. "Even you can't do that, Pia."

"Of course I can," she said, as I realized she could. "But I don't fucking want to, so let's go."

Blubbering, I got to my feet and draped myself over her back, my right arm gripping her shoulder as she half lifted me up the bank and onto the flat stones.

42

I sat gasping and shuddering on the shale. My legs and feet were laced with scratches and small cuts and bled in places, but I couldn't stop staring at my arm. I held it out, slightly away from me. It looked like someone else's arm, a broken doll's arm. I moaned something about Rachel, something about dying.

"Shut up, Wini. Don't move." Pia whipped her T-shirt over her head, blood pumping out of her left shoulder. I saw the mouth of the wound, a good four inches long and deep too. I saw the meat of her. She grabbed a torn end of the shirt and ripped it in half.

She glanced at her shoulder, at me, eyes bright with urgency. "Help me with this."

"What do I do?"

"I want you to hold the skin together before I wrap it."

She dropped down into the eddy and dunked once before she climbed back out and sat in front of me, facing the water. "Hurry up and do it," she said.

I reached across her back and gripped her shoulder, already slippery with blood, and tried to draw together the lips of the wound with my one good hand. The iron taste of blood mixed with the cool evening air. Now wearing only her black sports bra and shorts—her helmet tossed aside—Pia slipped the armhole of one of the T-shirt halves over her bad arm and slid the remnant up to my hand that still clenched her wound. I could feel her heart pulsing in her arm.

We stiffened as a sound floated over the boom of the river. "Where are you?" came Rachel's voice, part scream, part moan.

Fifty yards downstream, helmet askew on her head, Rachel hugged a boulder near the bank. She pushed herself to her feet, her footing bad on the tilted rock. We screamed her name and she waved both arms in our direction, then ducked down and dropped out of sight behind the rock.

"What the fuck is she doing?" I said. "Where did she go?"

"Hurry up with this, will you?" I finally got that Pia wanted my good hand to act as her other hand, so together we tied a feeble knot over the cut and she stood up. In seconds, the improvised bandage was heavy with blood and sagging. "Keep this," she said, tossing the other half of the shirt in my direction. "I'm going to get her."

Through a haze of pain, I watched as Pia, clutching the bandage, blundered off into the woods near the river. For long minutes I sat slowly closing and opening my eyes, praying each time that I would spot my friends in the distance. Finally, Pia emerged dragging Rachel up the bank. I shut my eyes and whispered my thanks, opening them to watch Rachel as she tripped along behind Pia, anchored to the back of her shorts.

Rachel collapsed down next to me, panting and shivering. "Pia says your arm is broken."

I nodded. "How did you get past me in the river?"

"Fuck knows."

"Are you all right?"

"Still blind, but compared to you guys I'm really good." Her bare feet were scraped and blotchy with bruises. It hurt to look at them. She tossed aside her mangled helmet and repositioned herself, squatting on a ledge just below me. "Let me see your arm," she said as she moved in close, her head inches from my arm as she first scanned it with her eyes, then fluttered her fingers over it. Pia stood over us, a bleeding sentinel.

"You don't have to break it again or any of that shit, do you?" I said, realizing I was still crying, and that it had become almost perpetual.

Again her mop of drenched hair tracked up and down my forearm, dripping on my gooseflesh. I tried to leave my body for a bit, but, no. Even though I could feel the wisdom in her fingers, I shuddered with pain at any touch, including her hot breath on me. As she uttered the words "This'll just take a sec," she gripped my wrist and elbow, leaned in with her shoulder at the break, and with her body weight snapped my arm back into place.

I screamed. Partly from surprise, but mostly from agony. Pia slapped her hand over my mouth. "Quiet, Win, come on, you have to . . ."

I wailed into her palm.

Cradling my arm, I rolled over onto my good side and stuffed my screams back into my throat and down into my body. My cheek pressed against the cold stone. A balm. I floated in and out of consciousness, maybe to grab a few seconds away from detonating pain. From far away, I heard Pia and Rachel shuffling around me, talking in low tones.

Consciousness returned with the feel of Pia's hand cupping river water to my mouth. "Come on," she whispered. "You have to get up. We have to hide."

I pushed myself up to a sitting position with my good arm. It had grown dark enough so the colors of things had leaked away, and the trees behind us reached up like wraiths against an azure evening. A few yards beyond us the river rumbled blackly, intent on its night business.

Rachel squatted next to me.

"Sorry, but I have to do this." She laid a stick along my forearm and looped Pia's belt around it several times, finally buckling it in place. I struggled to not cry out. Patiently she held open the other half of Pia's T-shirt as I slipped my injured arm through it, then jury-rigged it into a primitive sling.

"You are one slick asshole with that arm-breaking thing," I said.

"You'll thank me later, hon," Rachel said, "when your arm isn't shaped like a horseshoe."

"Hey, you guys," Pia stage-whispered from somewhere behind us in the gloom where the forest met the rocks we sat on. "Get over here. You're too out in the open over there."

Rachel helped me to my feet, and we made our way to the sound of Pia's voice, which came from the base of a massive beech. Impossibly heavy branches encircled the trunk, extending several yards at waist height before curving skyward as if reaching up to grasp something. Rachel got down on her hands and knees and crawled to the base of the tree to join Pia. I crouched down, my head and arm pounding. Inhaled the peaty smell of moss and damp wood. Soon we sat butted up against the tree, peering out at the descending shelves of granite and shale and the river beyond. Pia was right. No doubt we'd been practically glowing in the moonlight on those rocks. Still, no tree was going to save us. The air rose up chilled from the river, full of the smell of wet stones.

"I'm going to get some rocks together," Pia said. "In case someone comes."

Rachel and I watched her silhouette hunt along the river. Though she treated her bad arm gingerly, still she used both to forage. She gathered sharp sticks and fist-size stones, every now and then dropping a bundle of forest weaponry next to our tree. I watched the pile grow, too blown out to comment on the futility of the thing, trying to picture how stones would defend us against bullets and arrows. I wondered why none of us had had the presence of mind to stash a knife, matches, anything of use into the many fancy pockets of our vests or clothing at the beginning of this trip. Idiotic. But I also thought about Pia's harping about living in the present and realized I had been present more than ever these last few days, and maybe that was the only reason I was still alive.

Pia tossed one last armful on the pile and crawled in with us, shivering. "We have to be ready," she said hoarsely.

"How can we be ready?" I said.

"We have to be ready to kill them. Do you know what I'm saying?"

"Jesus Christ, Pia," Rachel said.

"Well, are you?"

We didn't answer her. A lusty chorus of night insects started up, cued by some unknowable agreement. Full dark dropped down over us along with the reality of spending another night outside. I wanted to fragment into one giant panic but forced myself to pull back from that. There was an energy to being outside in the woods at night, I had learned. I thought, *Maybe I can use it*. A fizzing sort of calm came over me.

But my arm would not settle. Pain mushroomed in fantastic colors in my head. For a moment I closed my eyes to watch my agonized fireworks, but I snapped them open right away. Something buzzed around my ear. Another creature—segmented and much larger, winged—hummed against my cheek. I held my breath, then made myself exhale. Only insects, flying past.

"Maybe they're done with us," I said. "Maybe he's gotten her to stop. Convinced her to let us go." But even as I said it, I didn't buy it. It felt silly hiding under a tree in the dark. Three wounded sitting ducks. Three children playing hide-and-seek with killers.

"You can't think that way, Win," Pia said. "You'll make yourself helpless. We don't know what's happened. All we know is Sandra is dead and they're both still out there."

The mention of Sandra made me ache. I couldn't even look at her with my mind's eye, as if all that had happened was too large to take in just by looking or it would be too damaging to do so, like staring at an eclipse.

"Who knows what happens in these woods?" Rachel said. "People must disappear all the time, right? We can't be the first. Just look at this godforsaken place."

Whimpering, we moved closer together and tried to warm each other, avoiding our various wounds. Lit by the moon, the river flowed like pearly lava around the big rocks that divided it. The one Rachel had clung to an hour ago rose up like a ghost rock. I wondered if I could kill someone. Could I kill Dean? I pictured the tide of intelligence in his hands as they spoke to me, the photos he rubbed between his fingers like talismans, the way his face broke open with joy the first time I signed to him. I remembered his swift fingers nocking the arrow on the string, heard the creak of the bow as he aimed at my heart.

43

Pia and Rachel fell asleep like beaten, sleep-deprived dogs next to me. Pia looked as if she had conked out on her way to finding a comfortable position but was too tired to actually make it there. She slept sitting up with arms folded, chin on her chest, long legs stretched out in front of her, leaning away from Rachel and against me. Her head weighed heavy on my shoulder and I ached to move but didn't. She'd stopped bleeding, but in the darkness the dried blood showed black on her arm and hand and covered a fair amount of her left leg. Rachel slept curled up in a ball on the ground next to her. She snored softly, steadily, as if she were someplace safe.

The plan was to take turns on watch every couple of hours, but since I was first up and my throbbing arm kept me awake anyway, I just let them sleep. As long as I was awake and on the lookout, it seemed the best thing for us. The night turned mild, and I was thankful for it. My eyes adjusted completely; if I had a book, I could easily have read it in the moonlight. The river became a bright coil of energy I drew from to keep going.

But the rush of the water was loud enough for me to fear I

wouldn't hear the softer things, like footsteps, like the breathing of someone other than Pia or Rachel. The ache in my arm vibrated with its own noise I struggled to listen over. How much warning would we have, anyway? Would there be a thunderous crashing through the woods? A puff of air as an arrow flew past? Or just a hole appearing in one of our chests? I pictured the animal heads swinging in the night breeze over the camp—the bear, coyote, deer, moose—wondered if any had seen their own death coming before they were snuffed out.

Only a yard from me, a branch dipped and swayed with the weight of a magnificent bird, an owl by the contour of its round head and broad body. It fanned out speckled brown-and-white wings and fluffed its wedge-shaped tail, then arranged itself, tucking back all its parts in proper order. It faced the river, its tufted ears cupped toward the surging current. I was close enough to watch its bony talons unclench, then resettle, clarifying their perch on the bough.

As the creature moved, the branch swayed over the rock ledge that bordered the river, a coercion of grace. Pia shifted in her sleep. The owl's head swiveled until it looked at us or past us with glowing yellow eyes. Unimpressed, it turned away, lifted its mantle of wings, and flew. It vanished among the branches, then reappeared as a black silhouette that skimmed across soft night clouds. I felt myself flying with it, and for those moments I was free of pain, free of my past, free of any fear. We were going to make it out of this place, I felt sure of it. The sweetness of the night informed me, the owl told me in its way; even the drumming pain in my arm declared that my living blood still pulsed through me.

I don't recall falling asleep. I only remember being up with the bird, soaring and hunting, until—with all the logic of dreams—I was back in art school. Massachusetts College of Art, Boston, 1995. It was late at night and I was alone in one of the fine arts studios. Dressed in paint-stained jeans and a T-shirt and stupidly high on too much coffee, I slathered oils on a canvas as tall as myself. I was deep in that stop-time thing when nothing else mattered but painting. The delirium of youth informed me that the parade of beautiful paintings I would create stretched out forever and without end. No death. Just this. I was joyous. I inhaled the turpentine fumes as I worked, a smell that forever became inseparable from elation.

But even in dream logic something felt off. The smell wasn't quite right. What I detected was something ranker, less chemical based.

More human.

The insides of my eyelids glowed a roseate pink. By degrees I came to understand that morning had arrived, as much as my beautiful dream wanted me back. I allowed into my reverie a sensation of being observed. The hair lifted up on the back of my neck.

I let my eyes open to slits. My mouth and throat were parched; my lips cracked apart slowly. I had fallen asleep propped on my good elbow, head and back against the tree, legs splayed out. A foot below my eyes, hundreds of tiny red ants swarmed around a neat cone of sandy dirt near the coiled, stiff fingers of my broken arm. Pia's pile of rocks sat several feet away, utterly out of reach.

I heard a cracking noise. A sound my dad used to make as he crushed two walnuts in one strong hand. Someone chewed something; crunched, openmouthed. A sniffle. Rachel stuttered awake, but I watched her settle down, feigning sleep. Her eyeballs jerked under her closed eyes. Pia slept on, her flat, muscled belly rising and falling, her bandage slipping off her ghastly wound. I closed my eyes again.

I inhaled a rancid smell of sweat and rotted cloth.

Heard a rustling sound.

A click.

"Rise and shine, little ladies." Simone's gristly voice. "Day's wasting away."

Monday

June 25

44

Simone squatted on a rock ledge behind and just over us, her gnarled feet spilling out of tire-rubber shoes, her dirty leather skirt tucked up under her. Nests of hair twined with bits of bone and tiny pinecones snarled from under the orange ski cap. Pendulous breasts swung free under her stretched-out sweater. Eyebrows working, she peered down at some sort of nutmeat in her palm that she picked at delicately with grimed fingers, some of the nails so long they curved down and in, wedged with triangles of dirt. A tidy pile of shells was arranged in front of her, next to Rory's gun, which lay pointing in our direction, so close I could smell the cold copper, the snap of gunpowder. She didn't look at us.

"Here's a question for you, my friends: Do you have any idea how many times I could have killed you in the past twenty-four hours? Anybody?"

Rachel pushed herself to a sitting position. Pulling up her sagging bandage, Pia winced as she turned toward Simone. I jimmied myself up with my working arm, in the process trying to edge myself closer to the pile of stones. Ridiculous.

Coyly, she shook back her hair. It rattled with forest detritus. "Yes, it is a rhetorical question, which means, of course, no, you don't have to answer it. Granted. But let's look at the facts. I do have a gun pointed at you, which—well, *I* think—demands a higher level of politeness." She lifted her eyes from her snack and lasered them into me. "Winifred, what are your calculations? How many times could I have blown you to bits, say, or cut you all to ribbons like your pitiful raft?" She nibbled a morsel of nutmeat, white teeth flashing in her weather-beaten face. "Thoughts?"

"I don't know."

"My opportunities were limitless, dear ladies. On your stupid log raft. All night long by the light of the moon. Early this morning. But I am discreet. Everything has its time and place, especially death." She picked up the gun and stood to her full height, shells tumbling from her tattered skirt. Good God, I'd forgotten how big she was, all over but especially through the shoulders and chest. "The fact is, I thought the river would do me the honor, but no. Here you are, so, I still have homework to do." Her arms hung by her sides, one stretched-out sleeve obscuring the gun.

"We never did anything to you," Rachel said. "Just let us go."

Simone's mouth dropped open. *"Never did anything to me?"* She raised the gun and trained it at Rachel's head. Eyes wide, Rachel scuttled backward on the dirt. Simone tilted her wrist skyward and fired.

Birds flew off, chirping and screeching as the sound ricocheted through the forest. Watching them scatter, I noticed what looked like a mummy's head hanging from a branch not far from the one where the owl had landed the night before. A hornets' nest. It shuddered and droned as insects circled it, entering and exiting the ragged gray holes.

"You ruined my life," Simone declared. "That's all you did. Took everything from me. Stole my only son from me. My family. You think this is *nothing*?"

"We didn't steal—" Pia started.

"Then where is he?" Simone roared. "What have you done with him?"

"We sent him back to you," Rachel cried. "That's what he wanted. To be with you."

"Bullshit," Simone snarled. "I really should shoot you for that. If he wanted to be with me, he would be with me. But you changed him. You changed all that." She took a step closer to us, her hair clacking together, her stench wafting over us. "Where is he?"

"We're telling the truth," I heard myself say. "He ran off after we buried Sandra—"

"If you've hurt him—"

"He was fine when he left us," I said. "He was going back to you. Where else could he go? Maybe he's at your camp, waiting for—"

"I think I would know if he was there," she said with disgust. She waved the gun in our direction as she spoke, like it were part of her hand, like they were one organism. She seemed so aggrieved, so distracted by her thoughts, that I'm not sure she remembered the gun was even in her hand. "He's got something in his head now, all because of you. Lies, fairy tales, all manner of claptrap. His mind has been poisoned with the fantasy of civilization. Of society," she said sarcastically. "What a joke. There is more barbarism in one city block than in all these woods." She squared her shoulders. "It's simple. You've destroyed us. Our beautiful life. Nothing matters anymore." She gesticulated at me with the gun. "You. Get up."

I began to tremble uncontrollably.

"Now. On your feet. All of you."

Rachel and I exchanged glances. As she pushed herself up, she put her hand over mine and squeezed it briefly. I knew she felt me shaking. Her eyes said, *I love you, but get your shit together. This is bad.* I reached my good arm down to help Pia, who was struggling for leverage against the tree in order to stand. I smelled warm urine and dirt and felt desperately ashamed—even in my terror— that I had peed myself.

"Get down by the river," Simone grunted. "Hurry up."

A fine drizzle had begun, misting the air over the river into a bluish smoke. It buzzed with ozone and I could taste the rain. Simone followed close behind me as we stepped down the cantile-vered rocks in silence.

We stood at the river's edge, three lost souls. It raced by under the rocks we stood on, brown and dark and full of trout. Simone's humid breath steamed at my neck.

"You," she said to me. She shoved the gun into my spine, as if she thought I'd forgotten she had it. "You're first. You started this whole thing. Signing to him and whatnot."

I looked into the water, stricken; in it swollen clouds moved across a blue expanse.

"Turn around."

I did as I was told. Stared at the top of her worm-eaten hat thinking, *I am going to die here by this lunatic's hand, my life wasted on fear and worrying about the wrong things and not enough love in it at all.* Followed by an odd flash of embarrassment, of all things, to be slaughtered in front of my friends.

"Get down on your knees."

"I'm sorry," I blubbered. "I didn't mean to—"

"Get down on your knees."

I actually began to do it. Brace myself for my own execution.

It was like standing on a precipice, preparing to fall from a great height. So easy; seductive even. Shuddering, I resisted the image of a bullet tunneling through my brain and lodging deep inside. Willed myself to lift my head and find some way to live. Any fucking way I could. Simone ground the barrel of the gun into my forehead, a cold, lewd circle.

The hornets' nest hovered like a full moon just to the right of Simone's head. I caught Pia's eye. With a flicker of my own I glanced up at the nest, praying Pia understood what I needed her to do. *Good God, please, Pia, you've done it before—you need to do it now: read my mind.*

With a basketball player's grace Pia sprang from the rocks. Airborne, bellowing like an animal, she arced her long arm through space as her fist crashed down on the thing. It disintegrated in a hellfire of raging insects, of parchment-colored scraps, dust, and ash. Hornets screamed out everywhere, a black cloud that spared no one. Shrieking, Simone threw her arms skyward—never letting go of the gun—as the insects swarmed her. She ran a short ways into the woods but they followed her there, seething and humming. The three of us spun in circles, flailing and bleating.

"Go to the river!" Rachel shrieked as she flew toward the water, dropping onto the bank mud and rolling in it as she howled. Pia jumped into the current, but like Rachel I never made it that far: stabs of pain on my face, arms, legs, and back sent me tossing myself down into the muck, skidding and flipping over and over to coat myself with slimy black grit, insects crunching under my flesh—my arm screaming but what could I do?—anything, *anything* to get them off me. Mad minutes later, the hornets lifted up from us as if by some sudden instinctual decision, leaving us twisting and writhing in the filth as they dispersed and rose up in a cone shape together, swirling in a black tornado downriver.

I crawled toward Rachel and pulled her to me with my good arm—her pale blue eyes blinking in a black mask—hugged her as I brushed the last remaining hornets from her, her heart slamming against mine.

"Are you okay?" I said. Clearly I had been stung a dozen times or more, but it was just pain, and I was getting used to it.

She nodded, too terrified to speak. I'm not sure she'd even seen the nest, only felt the onslaught of enraged insects from nowhere.

Simone staggered from the woods, cursing, tears running down her face. Welts bloomed on her forehead and chest. She shook her hair like a dog; spittle shot from her mouth. "You bitches!" she screamed, then, weirdly, seemed to calm. She pulled the odd hornet out of her hair, tossed it behind her. "The indignity of it all."

Pia stood to her waist in the river, splashing her face and body, brushing off the remaining insects that clung to her.

"Well, there you are," Simone purred. "The alpha female. Of course I should have killed you first."

Wild-eyed, Pia dove into the river and let it take her. She bobbed up once in a channel of vigorously moving water, glanced back at us, then disappeared.

"*Pia!*" Rachel shrieked, her voice raw as meat. She stumbled forward toward the water's edge but I grabbed her shirt and dragged her back.

Simone raised her arm, the baggy sleeve of her sweater swinging down low like a pelican's pouch. She aimed the gun with a steady hand and fired at the last place we'd all seen our friend alive.

45

A brightly colored object—azure blue and finch yellow—whistled by my face. Simone's hand jerked up and away, the gun arcing up into the sky. It took me a second or two to understand that an arrow had torn off the sleeve of her sweater and sent her tumbling onto the rocks.

Hugging the bank, Dean climbed up and over a pile of boulders downstream, bow slung over his shoulder. Simone lay on her back propped on her elbows, sputtering, one filthy arm exposed. She watched him till her shock wore off, then scrambled to her feet, ignoring us.

"Dean!" she cried with genuine longing and pain. "Dean, what are you doing?" She hazarded a few steps toward him. "Why did you do that? I wasn't going to hurt them."

He signed something to her I couldn't catch; he was still too far from me and her body partially blocked my line of sight.

"Get *away* from you?" Simone shifted from a position of supplication—arms outspread, one foot forward—to one of caution and circumspection. She huffed to her full height, shaking out her hair under her ski hat with an odd vanity. "Why should

I get away from you? You're my son. I love you." Her voice thickened with cloying sweetness.

Rachel grabbed my arm, whispered, "The gun . . ."

I mentally replayed the image of Simone, her body and arms
flying back, the gun jettisoning skyward. I'd heard no splash, no
clanging of metal on rock. Had it landed as far back as the trees?

I stumbled forward, pretending to still be favoring my arm, to
get a better view of Dean. He signed to his mother, "You kill girl
with smooth black hair. I love her."

Simone rolled her eyes and spat. "You stupid boy. You didn't
love her. You didn't even know her. She was nothing to you—a
fantasy. Come on, come to me." She walked toward him with arms
open wide, as if to engulf him.

He flipped the bow in his arms and came at her hard with
it, cracking her forearms with an ugly sound. She cried out in
surprise and pain. Balance lost, she windmilled her arms backward, stumbling, then landed on her ass on the rocks for the
second time in as many minutes. Stunned more by this than the
business of the arrow tearing off her sleeve, she lifted her arms
and turned them. Two lines of blood oozed from sharp cuts. She
examined the wounds in disbelief before turning to Dean with
narrowed eyes.

"Why, you little shit." She got to her feet quicker than I thought
she could, like all big animals that move faster than you can imagine. But Dean was faster. He'd nocked an arrow and leveled it at
her before she could rush him. His face ran with sweat, his eyes
red and tortured.

"Now you listen to me, Dean. These women here—including
that coward in the river . . ." She gestured in our direction. Blood
dripped from her arms and stained her skirt. "They don't care
about you. They don't love you. They haven't taken care of you

your whole life, fed you, kept you safe from your own father, from all the animals out there, and I don't mean just the ones in the forest. You know the animals I'm talking about, don't you? You remember. You were young, but I know you do."

Dean shook his head, kept the arrow trained on her heart.

Her voice lowered to an intimacy that bordered on obscene. "You know there's nothing out there for you. There is no family for you beyond these woods. Only savages who would tear you up. Oh, yes, my son, they would have you for breakfast. But here"— she opened her arms to the sky, did a girlish twirl toward the forest and back—"this is ours, Dean. And I've told you, it's not good to meet the people who get lost here. It's not good to trust them with our story. Because not everyone understands. We've seen that, haven't we? This is our world, Dean. Yours and mine, not theirs."

His arm trembled at the bow; the arrow shook in its notch.

She moved closer to him; one more step and she could have reached out and touched the bow. "We have all God's creation to ourselves. We have paradise, and you want to throw that away? Have you lost your mind?"

The forest hushed in anticipation of blood.

"Come on now, Dean," Simone said, a catch in her voice. "Where is the boy I knew? Where is my beloved son? Put the bow down. Do as I say."

I didn't see his hands move. Only saw the big black bird—a cormorant—as it thumped onto the rocks next to Simone, an arrow piercing it through, oily blue-black wings splayed as if it were still trying to fly, long neck twisted backward. We stared as if we'd never seen a bird before. Dean nocked another arrow into his bow and aimed it at the center of his mother's broad chest.

"So, this is it," Simone said, her voice softer, chastened. "I understand. You've made up your mind to leave me." She tossed up her arms and shrugged her shoulders, a parody of defeat. "Fine. There's nothing else to talk about. You're free to go. God knows, you've always been free." She gestured a beefy hand at him. "Look at you. You're a grown man. I've never put you in chains, have I? I've never locked you up."

As she spoke Dean lowered his weapon bit by bit; tension draining from his shoulders and arms that held the arrow straight in its notch and the bow forward in perfect readiness.

He blinked.

She dropped her head like a bull and charged him, ramming her bulk into his midsection, felling him onto the rocks closest to the surging river. He disappeared under her mess of rotten clothes and hair. With a wild cry, Rachel leapt on her back. Simone flung her away as if she were nothing, but she jumped right back on as if possessed.

The three bodies rolled and churned a foot from the water's edge. The river roared all around us, orchestral, magnificent. I breathed in its white energy as I snatched up the biggest rock I could lift with one hand, picturing myself smashing Simone's skull through her ski hat and viperous hair, but nothing stayed still long enough for me to take good aim—would I kill Rachel instead? Or Dean? Gasping, crying, I raised the rock.

Pia, drenched, almost inhuman looking, burst out of the water near the bank, sprinted past me and threw herself on the mass of writhing bodies. She locked her arms around Simone—who lost precious seconds in her surprise—and grappled her away from Rachel, who still clung to her. Dean found his chance and rolled away, instantly on his feet. Pia spun Simone facedown in the dirt, smacking her head down into it as Dean seized her wrists and lashed them together. Rachel rolled away, moaning, "Pia, Pia, you're alive."

With some roughness Dean spun Simone onto her back. She snarled, kicking and jerking. We all stood back and out of range.

She wriggled herself to a seated position, hat half-cocked on her head, hair more chaotic than ever. "Fuck you all. It doesn't matter," she hissed. "Do you really think you're going to find your way out of here? You're all going to die, one way or the other."

46

A fine, steady rain patted at the leaves on the trees, on our bodies as we worked in determined silence; it flattened Simone's mane until it hung down in long strings nearly grazing the ground where she sat. Using every bit of Dean's sinewy rope, we lashed her to a tree facing the river. Every so often she'd burst forth with a vicious rant, then go quiet and sullen, a dull seething. Dean ignored her, his eyes glazed as he cinched her wrists tighter together.

With a nod, Pia motioned for us to step a few yards away, toward the river, and we obliged, gathering in a huddle. Bruised, barefoot, she breathed hard, ribs showing with every exhale. Her shoulder wound had reopened and bled profusely; her eyes flashed with something new and terrible. "I'm going to kill her," she said.

Rachel grabbed her by her elbows and shook her, gazing up at her. "Pia, you have to calm your shit down."

"She's got the gun."

"No, she doesn't."

"We looked everywhere," I said. "It's gone." I thought of the hunter back at the store; that rapturous flush from his recent kill. Pia looked like that now. Bloodthirsty. Crazy.

"She must have hidden it or something. Fucking bitch. We have to find it."

"When could she have done that?" Rachel said, her face inches from Pia's. "She hasn't been out of our sight."

Pia wrenched herself from Rachel's grasp. "We could drown her. Or I could strangle her. It will be on me, okay? *On me,*" she whispered hotly. "Or I could bash her fucking brains in." She paced in a tight circle, unable to contain herself.

"So then you're a murderer," Rachel said.

"Fuck yeah. But we're fucking alive."

I began to taste it. What it would be like to obliterate Simone. Rage came alive in my hands and sent them quaking; my scratched and bloody fingers shuddered by my sides. I saw Sandra in her grave of river stones, so terribly still, so terribly cold.

Rachel read my face. "Wini, seriously? Dean would slaughter us."

"Win? Are you with me?" Pia said.

I thought of my hands around that mottled, filthy neck as I watched the light dim from her deranged face, how it would feel to choke the life out of her. How it wouldn't bring Sandra back. Pia's eyes bored into mine. I could smell her: the salt and copper of her blood, her sweat, the taste of the river fresh on her.

Dean had begun to take notice of us.

"Jesus Christ, Pia, snap out of it," Rachel said, her face blanched with terror. "Wini? Help me out here!"

She was right. I exhaled all that ugliness. "Let it go, Pia."

Pia nodded, but kept her eyes on the ground.

"Look at me, Pia."

"I could do it, you know." She stared at Simone, a writhing pile of hair and stink.

"We work as a team. Rory said that, remember? That's how we survive."

Eyes still downcast, Pia shook her head and wandered to the bank.

Dean finished with the ropes and stood back from his mother. Her fury seemed to leave her. She dropped her head and rested her chin on her chest, big shoulders sagging. Phlegmy sobs bubbled out of her as crocodile tears bloomed on her cheeks and ran down her face in impressive volume.

"You women—well, I don't think I'd put anything past you," she said, voice clogged with tears. "But, Dean . . . *you*? You would leave your own mother out here to die? To—to freeze to death? Die of exposure? Thirst? You want me to *starve* to death?" She tried to wipe her eyes against her bare shoulder. "Look, I know I've made some bad choices, but I don't think I deserve this."

Dean looked at me, panic in his eyes.

"We'll send someone for you," I said.

Simone ignored me. "Dean, son, it's not too late to let this whole thing drop. You made a mistake. It's over. Forgiven. History! Come on, honey, untie me. I won't be angry." Her neck corded as she strained at the ropes.

"She'll be okay, Dean," I said, my eye on Pia's rangy profile. She stood a few yards away by the river, watching the water sort itself out midstream.

"You're doing the right thing," Rachel said to Dean with uncommon softness. "You're being brave."

Disgusted, Simone let her head drop back against the tree and gazed up into the branches above her head. A subtle change washed over her face. A widening of the eyes, lips ever so slightly pulled back. She had seen something. I should have known what it was—so obvious later!—but my concern at the time was Dean and his wavering.

"Are you hungry?" he signed to her.

"Starving!" she whimpered.

Dean loosened his leather sack and pulled out a handful of long, stringy objects, each with a webbed foot on the end. He approached her with them, but she turned her head away in a pout.

"That's all you have? Dried frog?" She spat into the dirt. "You know that's not Mom's favorite. Go catch me a fresh trout. Won't take you a minute. They'll be jumping in this rain."

Dean stuffed the pieces of frog back in his pouch, his face ashen, concentrated. "Let's go," he signed to me.

"But, Dean," she wailed. "Your mama's starving! You're killing her!" She lunged at her ropes, shook her head, kicked like a tantrumming child.

He turned to leave but just as quickly swung back around and approached her, just out of range of her thrashing limbs, and sank to his knees. He fell forward onto his hands like a penitent, head down, sobbing silently, his body shuddering. She grew quiet, watching him with an expression between a snarl and hope. Fog hung in ghostly shrouds around us as we watched them, transfixed.

He signed, "I will come back for you."

She stopped kicking at the dirt, quieted, then lifted her head. For just one moment, her face softened and the insane glint left her eyes. I could almost picture her as a normal mother speaking to her son. She whispered, "In my dreams, I never laid a hand on you. In my dreams, we could go home."

Dean pushed himself to his feet, wiped his wet eyes, and gazed off into the thick woods. He seemed done with her, with all of us.

"Dean, please—" she cried out to him.

But he had already turned, vanishing into the green. The forest settled around the place he'd stood as if he had never been there.

"Pia!" Rachel yelled. "Let's go!"

Without a backward glance, Rachel and I took off after Dean, Pia at our heels. Soon she ran past us, calling for him. I clutched my broken arm to my chest with my good one as I stumbled down a densely wooded hillside, finally descending into a copse of dwarfish pines, all but their sad drooping tops obscured by fog and mist. Inhuman sounds—Simone's unearthly caterwauls—echoed from the river behind us. I could just make out Rachel's form only a yard from me as she clung to Pia's waistband.

We slogged along for a good half hour that way, dropping down and down through the hemlock forest, the hush of the river to the right our only constant.

"Dean!" Pia cried, exhaustion in her voice. "Where are you?"

We stopped and listened to our ragged breathing and Simone's wordless howling. Rain banged down on us. We looked like savages. I remembered something Richard had shot back to me one day as I complained about something stupid like a parking ticket: *Pain and suffering is simply the human condition, didn't you know that, Wini?*

I yelled Dean's name. Nothing.

Pia bent over to catch her breath, pale and shivering in just her athletic bra and shorts. "We are so royally motherfucking fucked." Her wound did not look good, the edges whitish and swollen as the rain diluted the blood into orangey rivulets down her arm and legs. Rachel gazed blankly into Pia's back, hair hanging in her face like a lunatic.

Dean's shape came into view, a fierce apparition out of the fog. Deep furrows darkened his cheeks, his hooded eyes sunken in their sockets.

"Slow down, Dean, please! We can't go so fast," I said. "We're hurt. All of us."

He stared at me too long. I couldn't read him, and my heart sped up. He took a wide stance in the mud, and though he was slight, I considered his bestial strength; every muscle tensed and full of unknowable resolve. One hand clutched the bow to his chest as the other reached up toward the quiver, his fingers grazing the arrows as if to count them. Three remained.

"You took raft," he signed in clipped, slicing gestures.

I didn't like the look of his face. A wave of nausea hit me, and I steadied myself against a branch. "He's asking why we took the raft."

"Jesus," Pia whispered hoarsely.

How could I have forgotten my promise to him? "We had to," I breathed.

"*My* raft," he signed, pounding himself in the chest with the sign for "my."

Rachel stared at nothing: the seething rain, the haunted woods. "I made her do it, Dean. I was the one who—"

"No glass circles," he signed, close to her face. "Dangerous."

"He says he knows you can't see," I said.

Rachel breathed heavily in the humid air. A big welt had risen up close to her right eye and festered there. "The thing is, Dean, Pia and me, we got scared. Haven't you ever been scared? Really terrified?"

Pia had begun to weep, her warrior-woman persona in abeyance. "We're sorry we took your raft, and that it got wrecked."

Expressionless, he watched her cry. "Scared is weak," he signed. "No help in scared."

With a look of disgust, he turned away from us and pushed into the gloom, but we saw that he had begun to pick his way more carefully, so we were able to track him through the phantom pines. Often his body would vanish in the fog, so we followed the bow he wore strapped to his back, which bobbed ahead of us, until we passed through the scrub pines and found ourselves in scummy water up to our shins. The fog settled thigh-deep, and we saw we were walking in some kind of bog, one in a series of sumps plugged up by beaver dams bristling with thatches of sticks chewed into points.

"Hold on, everybody," I said. Rachel bumped into Pia, who stopped and turned to me. Dean's face floated in the mist. "Dean, where are we going? Do you know?"

"Quiet," he signed. "Listen."

I did so. Only the hum of insects, the trill of an occasional bird. Something plopped into the water nearby. Nothing from Simone. We were either too far away to hear her, which didn't seem possible, or she had given up. Also unlikely.

"But, Win, he doesn't know—" Pia started.

I shushed her and we women huddled together, heads nearly touching. Dean stood apart from us, listening so hard he appeared to vibrate. The trees, the air, sky, the thrum of the insects— everything that seemed hellishly the same to us told him some sort of story. At the surface of the water a snake wriggled by, a long striped muscle.

Dean pointed excitedly to our right and with no discussion splashed through the muck in that direction. We could only follow.

47

Pine trees rose straight and strong around us, spaced at such gentlemanly intervals that we could see our way to the clearing where the river tumbled by, genies of fog swirling up from it. The forest gave off an air of cultivation, as if someone had planted these trees just so, but I couldn't be sure. We slowed our pace for several minutes on the bank, drinking from the river as we gazed across it at what looked like a field of Christmas trees.

Downriver on our side, the stretch of red pine marched up a steep embankment. We slogged up the slope in worn-out silence while Dean sprinted past us to the top. In minutes, he came crashing back down to where we'd stopped to rest, nearly plowing into us.

"Cow," he signed excitedly. "Field."

I translated for Pia and Rachel. We ran on bloodied feet to the top of the hillock and looked out and down.

"Holy shit," Pia said. "Thank you, God."

Fifty yards away, a cow stood in a meadow banked by the river, which now ambled tamely and lushly by. Wide brushstrokes of goldenrod and purple loosestrife colored the tall grasses. Along the bank, pussy willows waved in a brisk wind, their plum-size sacs ripe to bursting. The rain had quit for the moment, perhaps gathering itself for another round.

But—the cow. That simple domesticated beast. The sight of it filled me with joy. Rooted in the undulating grass, vast black-and-white nethers toward us, it swung its anvil-shaped head around and gazed our way as it chewed. A crumbling stone wall ran along behind it, disappearing over the hillside.

"Can you see the cow?" I asked Rachel, who squinted toward where I was pointing.

Her eyes teared up, and she managed a smile. "No, but I believe you."

Pia unstrapped her helmet and let it drop with a thud to the hard ground. Rachel did the same, and I followed suit. They looked like a pile of skulls.

Over the next hill, the pasture unspooled before us as the river widened and mellowed. We staggered through meadow weeds and sedge that raked at our bare legs. Twenty or thirty cows, black-and-white, or brown-and-white, standing or lying down, watched with little interest as we passed. Steam rose off their big warm bodies into the cool morning air, and we smelled their wet coats and dung. I could have kissed every one of their sweet, endlessly stupid faces.

The field crested once more at a cluster of shimmering yellow trees. Long slender branches hung mournfully down.

"Look," Pia whispered. "We're at the Willows." Soundlessly, she began to cry.

I looked up. Blue sky, windswept. Bruised-looking clouds scuttled across the horizon in full retreat, their shadows racing across the field. We wandered among several dozen willows that grew in stands of five or six, as if they favored small groups, the long tresses of those near the bank cascading into the river. Rainwater soaked us as we stepped through golden curtains. It felt as if the trees were there to comfort us; it was like a place seen in dreams, lit by otherworldly light.

Thunder rumbled around us. We squinted up into sunlight, wondering. Another round; this time the earth shuddered beneath our feet.

Beyond the grove of willows, a sparkling gray ribbon spanned the river at what looked like its widest section before disappearing into an expanse of green.

"Wini!" Pia shouted from a few yards ahead of me on the bank. "It's a road!"

A truck laden with logs barreled over the bridge with the booming roar we'd thought was thunder moments ago.

Rachel took a few tentative steps forward. She lunged at Pia's belt, hooking herself on with both hands. "Pia, what are we waiting for, come on!"

I stood next to Dean, watching him. He'd stopped short and squatted in the tall grass, one fist jammed into his open hand.

Pia turned back to me, patience gone. "Let's go!"

"Come on, Dean," I whispered. "Get up." His forehead creased with worry. I could feel the fear pulsing off him as he stared glassy-eyed at the road.

"Go ahead," I called out to Pia and Rachel. "I'll catch up with you."

Another truck, equally burdened with its unthinkable tonnage of logs, burst into view and rumbled across the bridge. This time I caught a whiff of exhaust, delectable as perfume.

Pia's face pinched with stress and fatigue. "Jesus, Win, what are you doing?"

Dean sat motionless, eyes locked on the road.

"Leave him!"

With some kind of curse I didn't catch, Rachel and Pia took off straight for the bridge at full trot. Dean squeezed his eyes shut, opened them, and we both watched the women make their way through the field toward the road. Every cell in my body screamed, *Run,* but something chained me to that spot. To leave him at that moment would have compounded an age-old grief in a way I simply could not bear.

As I crouched down next to him, some part of me noticed I barely minded his smell anymore; that or I was beginning to smell just as bad. "Dean. Look at me."

He didn't.

"What's the matter?" I glanced back anxiously at the field we'd just crossed, at the cows watching us with dull-eyed stares.

"I am afraid. Weak," he signed in small, tight gestures.

"I can understand that. It's all so different for you," I said, my eye on Pia and Rachel as they closed in on the road. I thought, *What am I doing here with this feral boy when my friends—the ones left still alive—are running toward salvation and freedom? Have I lost my fucking mind?* I forced myself to focus on him, think how in hell I could get him to move. "Have you seen trucks before?"

"I don't know," he signed. "Too big. Too loud."

"They're big, and they seem scary, but the drivers are nice. These people will help us, okay? But we have to go. . . ." I was desperate to not care about him but sat there frozen. Exhaustion and despair rolled over me. I couldn't leave him. I had to leave him.

"What is in the world?" he signed, finally meeting my eye with great interest.

I racked my brains. My God, what a question. Cable TV? Mortgages? Parties? Meaningless jobs? Bad marriages? Fifty thousand unanswered emails? Wine?

"People who will love you and take care of you, Dean. Beautiful things. Things that are hard to imagine right now, for me to explain. But good things, like delicious food, and books you can learn to read, and—"

He rocked back and forth on his heels. I felt like a zookeeper coaxing some beautiful wild thing into a cage. "I don't believe you," he signed with an air of embarrassment.

I scanned the field for Pia and Rachel. Limping, clinging to each other, they climbed up an embankment to the road. Another behemoth truck burst forth from the willows, not slowing for a second as it charged over the bridge. Dean rocked harder, faster, uttering odd, guttural sounds I'd never heard from him before.

I knelt in front of him and took his hands in mine, held them fast. He watched my white fingers holding his dark, gnarled ones, too shocked to move, I think. He became still and silent. I tried to imagine what Sandra would do, here, now, my calm and patient friend, the one who had understood better than any of the rest of us that friendship is more than the funny and the flash; it's also for bearing witness, for life's requisite doggedness, for never giving up on each other.

"Look, Dean, I can't say everything is perfect out there, okay? I'm not going to lie to you. But there's really great stuff waiting for you that I don't even know how to describe—music, movies, friends, school—you're going to love it all so much. And you have those pictures, and they don't lie, right? Those are real people, you know it in your heart. We'll try to find them. People like me and

Sandra are out there, lots of them, people who can sign with you, much better than I can, okay?"

He smiled a little, and I thought, what *did* I really know about what was good in this world? How could I call myself an authority on that? Who knew, maybe the forest was a better place for him . . . at least here, all around us, was beauty and certainly bounty if you knew how to find it—he'd shown me that—and I thought, *Why not let him be wild? What if it's wrong to sell him on the greedy, dirty, moneygrubbing, backstabbing, brutal place we call the civilized world?*

A change in the air; a quickening. My body tensed.

I looked up.

A dot. On the far side of the field, just past the trees that guarded it. The dot moved with dispatch down the hill. Grew. I turned to the road where Pia and Rachel stood like two rag dolls, waiting.

Dean signed in my hands that still held his. It felt intimate, like Marcus when he was little and sharing a secret with me or telling a joke. "I remember chocolate," Dean signed in my sweating palms. "Do you have chocolate in town?"

I watched the dot take shape terrifyingly fast, grow arms and a head as it disappeared and reappeared among the tall grasses. "That's the first thing we'll do when we can get to a store, okay? Get you some chocolate."

He looked up at me finally. Signed, "You stay with me?"

"Yes, I will stay with you." I got to my feet, pulling him up with me. "But let's go. Right now, okay?"

He gave me a long look, as if holding me to my words with the force of it, then picked himself up and began running toward the road, much faster than I could. I held my arm in a vise grip to my chest, choking back a yelp with every jarring footfall through clumps of waist-high grass, my blood pounding in my ears.

Fifty yards from the road, I glanced behind me. An orange ski cap bounced up and down among the cattails and goldenrod. Simone was catching up.

48

Pia jumped up and down waving her good arm as the monster truck plowed hell-bent—horn blaring—straight at her.

"Get the fuck out of the road!" I leapt out onto the blacktop to pull her aside, but the trucker had seen her and began to steer to the shoulder where we stood huddled together.

The immense grill snarled headlong toward us. Rows of steel rods on either side of the truck bed cinched logs stacked two stories high, rear tires flattening with the cargo. Just the scale of the thing was mythic. I wasn't convinced it would be able to stop, but it began to slow as if an unseen force were yoking it back. It screeched to a halt on the thin spit of gravel, dust billowing up all around the ten giant wheels.

Charged silence. The smoke lifted, leaving the smell of pine sap, singed wood, and diesel.

All around us—a series of dull popping sounds.

"She's coming!" I screamed. "Get in the truck!"

Pia hurdled up onto the running board, lunged for the door, and opened it. A smallish man with greasy hair and a bushy mustache glared down at us from high up on his cracked leather seat.

Given the size of the truck, I had expected a bigger man. He was none too happy looking.

A bullet pinged off the huge side mirror, yanking it to a crazy angle.

"What the motherfuck do you think you're doing? Are you trying to kill me?" He scowled, rat-colored teeth showing under thick lips, followed by a look of incomprehension, probably because of how barbaric we looked, Pia half-naked too. Her arm had caked over, but as a whole she looked pretty terrifying. We all must have.

The road felt foreign under me, damp from the rain but having nothing to do with dirt or rocks or roots, the sun heating it up under my bare feet. In my nightmare, Simone ran toward us. In reality, she did the same. Fifty feet away now, she paused, crouching in the grass to take aim. Dean couldn't take his eyes off her. I looked back at the river with something like longing. Time slowed down, then sped up twice as fast.

Pia grabbed Rachel around the waist and shoved her up into the cab of the truck. "Someone's trying to kill us!" she screamed at the driver. "You have to help us!"

I thought, *Please, God, understand this, and understand it fast. Or, hell, just believe it.* A bullet sank with a thud into a log, rang off the hood of the cab.

"Somebody *shootin'* at you?" the man said, his face screwing up, then growing pale and slack with fear.

Pia climbed up into the cab, knocking Rachel nearly on top of the driver before reaching down for me. The floor was littered with fast-food trash and the air stank of rancid oil and wet tobacco; the seats were desiccated with age and wear. It felt as if we had crawled into the giant dusty rib cage of some extinct beast.

I clambered in. "Dean! Get in the truck!" I called out through the still-agape door.

He ignored me. He stood on the road facing the field where his mother had stopped shooting long enough to scramble up the berm the road was built on. There was something so pitiful about her yet something so worthy of our terror—her riveting presence, her daunting will. No one could look away. Even the clouds stopped moving across the sky, as if to frame her. With a growl she wrenched herself free of the last tangle of buckthorn bushes that lined the road. Now just a dozen yards away, she stood swaying, her body buzzing with rage, grotesque skirts rustling. Unsteady, she hazarded a few steps forward, toenails curling over her rubber shoes and scraping on the asphalt.

"Dean," she cried liltingly, "my darling boy." She raised the gun, aiming at her son's head. Heat tricks shivered on the blacktop as beads of sweat rolled down her forehead. She blinked and shook her nest of hair and, in that moment, seemed to lose her purpose. Her body slackened. A cry burst out of her, followed by sobs that left her breathless. She lowered the gun.

"I would never hurt you. You know that. But listen to me, son, you get on that truck, your mother will never see you again, do you understand? These women, this world"—she gestured at the road, the truck, its cargo—"it's all an illusion."

Dean dropped his eyes to the road. His shoulders slumped with a familiar sort of shame. As if moving through cold mud, he took a step toward her, then another, and I thought, *My God, he's going to do it. He's going to go back to her.*

Pia huddled against Rachel, who was doing her best not to crush up against the trucker, who revved the engine hard and loud.

I leaned out the open door and screamed, *"Dean, get in the truck!"*

Crushed by his impossible choice, he turned his head toward us, his face a map of sorrow. His chest and shoulders caved, all defeat and gloom.

"Come with me, Dean," Simone cooed. A flash of fire had come back into her eyes. "It will be as it has always been, we can forget this ever happened—"

"Dean, no!" I cried to him. "This is your only chance!" The trucker gunned the engine, and we lurched forward. I screamed at him to stop, and he looked at me as if I had lost my mind.

Dean signed, "Family," and took out the packet of photos. With badly shaking hands he peeled back the plastic layers and fanned the snapshots out toward his mother. Tears streamed down his face.

She lifted the gun and fired. The photos scattered like white birds. He watched the scraps of Polaroids falling down all around him, uncomprehending, till his face hardened and he signed something to her I couldn't catch. She began to raise the gun again toward Dean, or the truck, it was hard to tell.

Dean spun around and bolted toward us, vaulting up onto the running board and catapulting himself into the cab, bow and arrows clattering. He slammed into me, kinetic, an animal pursued, all muscle and intent. The pain in my arm was incomprehensible.

"How dare you leave me!" Simone shrieked, sprinting toward us at a stunning pace. "I'll kill you all!" She lowered the gun toward one of the tires. Fired. A popping sound, a hiss.

"Go!" Pia shrieked, and slammed her foot down on the accelerator. The truck roared to life and leapt with fury against its multiton load. Cursing us, the driver wrestled the wheel back from Pia and slammed the engine into gear. Suddenly we had traction. We all pitched backward as the truck surged forward, overcoming the loss of the tire with sheer horsepower and momentum. Grimacing, the trucker ground the gears higher and higher as the rest of us stared into the oversize rearview mirror. Simone ran at us, firing until she appeared motionless in the center of the road, growing smaller with each second that passed.

Just the sense of motion, of being carried by something with a motor, and by no physical effort, was enough to make me weep with relief. And to be borne aloft by this enormously strong machine, by someone who knew how to harness it, felt almost supernatural, a blessing beyond comprehension.

Pia and Rachel sank back into the decaying seats of the cab, crying softly and mumbling all kinds of thanks to gods none of us believed in, or maybe we believed in them lately. Dean sat up rigidly, gripping his bony knees with trembling hands. He gazed into the rearview mirror long after Simone was out of sight.

Pia's shoulder had begun bleeding again, and pretty badly. The trucker glanced at her as we thundered down the pitted road.

"I'm going to take you to the Regional Hospital down Millinocket, okay?"

We each nodded or grunted our assent.

"But, hell, who's chasing you back there? The way you come at me, like a bunch of crazy people, I never seen anything like it."

No one said a word. The effort to tell the story was beyond anyone's capacity, yet I wanted to tell it, needed someone to believe us, some act of recognition for what we had been through—the death of Rory, Sandra's murder. But at the time, just the fact that someone wanted to hear it was good enough.

Soon we turned off the logging road onto a real highway, one with lines down the middle, the occasional streetlight glowing an eerie green even in daylight. Telephone poles looped by as we entered the complex machinery of the world, the McDonald's and the Subways, the Exxons and Burpees, the Laundromats and strip malls. Dean had given up on the rearview and sat up staring at everything man-made that went by until after an hour or so he collapsed back in his seat and watched the woods, the endless parade of green in all its variety and all its sameness.

After

September 27

49

It's been just over three months. My arm still aches now and then, but thanks to Rachel, you can't tell by looking at it that it was ever broken. The thing is, I don't mind the occasional twinge because it takes me back there, to all that happened on that river in those woods, and reminds me that there are things I should never forget. Not that I ever could.

A media circus enveloped us when we first got back to Boston. Endless questions and investigation, not to mention lots of entertaining headlines. Stories about a wild boy leading a group of lost middle-aged women out of the Maine wilderness. Stories we could barely believe were about us. Turns out, Alistair Dipredis, Simone's husband, had been wanted for his brother's murder in the midnineties. But he was one slippery guy. Alistair, along with Simone and five-year-old Dean, disappeared outside Fort Kent in 1997, with no trace of them until now.

Police and detectives in helicopters, locals flying prop planes, professional trackers with dogs—the entire state of Maine, it seemed—ventured out to search for Simone, and to find Rory's and Sandra's bodies. At first they leaned on Dean to lead them, but he refused and they didn't press him. They found the bodies where we had marked them and removed both for a proper burial, but even though they found Simone and Dean's camp—animal heads in the trees, the strangely slanted cabin, goats wandering and hungry—Simone had vanished. Still, the searchers felt they must have been close. They'd found coals glowing red from a recent fire and the bones of a juvenile moose piled neatly next to the makeshift grill.

I visit Dean in the halfway house where they've placed him, a sad suburban ranch house a few miles from me. After much red tape and wringing of bureaucratic hands, I have become his legal advocate. I fought for it, as did he, mainly by refusing to speak to anyone else for the longest time, so there was only me for the first few months to try to settle him. And he is not at all settled. They cut his hair short, taught him how to use a knife and fork, how to tolerate this society's level of cleanliness, all the surface trappings of civilization. Soon he will go to Walmart and Target and be brain-dead like the rest of us, and I dread it.

He's partial to dark khaki pants, plaid flannel shirts, and loafers with no socks when he'll give in to wearing shoes at all, and he loves his Clark Kent glasses. Walking down the street, he looks like a smallish, studious, unhip college student, perhaps with his belt notched in a bit too tight. He does things like escape from the group home at night and walk the four miles to my apartment, barefoot, where he tosses pebbles at my window like a lover until I let him in and we sit and sign or I read to him. Most television shows frighten him; he has an intolerance for violence I've become immune to.

Mostly, we search online for his family. We discovered an uncle who headed up a local chapter of the National Association of the Deaf in Fort Kent, as well as photos of a beautiful chestnut-haired nursing student—Simone as a young woman. I have the feeling Dean knows where she is and won't tell me, won't tell anyone.

When I gently posed the idea that she might be dead, he looked at me as if I were crazy.

We also found aunts, younger cousins, even a grandfather. Dean sat by me, transfixed. He begged me to pick up the phone and call the ones whose numbers we could find. He's learning to read at a startling rate, knows the subways now, and has figured out there are buses and trains that go anywhere and everywhere.

I started worrying about Pia when she stopped updating her bucket list on her website; in fact, it had been radio silence from her since mid-August. She'd taken herself off Facebook, Twitter, even LinkedIn, as if she were trying to erase herself. Rachel and I agreed we'd better plan a bit of reconnaissance.

We booked a weekend at a small cabin in Provincetown, right on the beach where the land ended and the sea had its turn just yards from our back door. On Saturday we woke to the dregs of a hurricane that had churned north from the Carolinas, rain slamming down so hard we couldn't see the ocean, only hard gray lines outside our rented bay windows.

We gathered our coffee and installed ourselves on a shabby couch in the cozy kitchen nook, panes rattling in the wind. Just outside, on a stone patio that bordered the beach, four pastel deck chairs sat facing the sea. In my mind's eye, Sandra perched in the turquoise one, waving and smiling as her black hair whipped in the wind. Even as I tried to acclimate to our new world of three, it was no use: four still seemed the best number.

"Do you guys dream about her too?" Rachel asked, gazing out at the churning sea.

"Simone?" Pia shuddered as she popped her bagel out of the toaster. "Not me."

"I have nightmares, absolutely." I did. I'd lie awake those early-autumn evenings listening to the leaves rustle outside my window, a trace of smoke in the air, Simone's face emerging from the darkness each time I closed my eyes. Every sound I couldn't explain, every late-night footfall on the apartment stairwell, made my heart slam against my chest. How could she find me? Impossible. But how could she disappear so completely? Anything is possible.

"I dream about the river, mostly," Rachel said. "I wake up and I'm coughing, my lungs are filled with water." A shiver went through her and she concentrated on blowing the steam off her coffee. "It takes me an hour just to calm the fuck down and go back to sleep."

Pia and I gave her a questioning glance.

"No, no, I've been good." She laughed. "Are you kidding? I feel like I've looked into the face of something even more monstrous than my own disease. Trust me, that'll sober you right up."

Between bites of her bagel, Pia fidgeted with a bracelet looped a few times around her wrist. It looked pretty ratty, whatever it was, not like the hip jewelry she usually wore. And then I recognized it.

"Is that Rory's bracelet?"

She nodded.

"When did you—"

"When you guys went to look for the raft that first time, I just wanted something . . ." She cleared her throat, then added more softly, "He's the last guy I've been with, you know. I can't bring myself to . . . Well, I know you guys didn't think much of him."

Rachel gave her a look. "Earlier, when I asked if you dreamed about *her*, I was talking about Sandra. Do you think about her, is what I meant."

Pia whitened, tossed the bagel on her plate. "Do I *think* about her? Jesus, Rachel, did you really just ask me that?" She shook her head, disgusted. "And of course I dream about her. I'm covering her face with those leaves and stones, over and over again. . . ." She launched herself off the couch, snatched her rain slicker off a hook by the door, and threw it on. "I'm going for a walk."

Rachel and I exchanged a glance. "Pia, it's a hurricane. Sixty-mile-an-hour winds."

"So I'll go by myself."

I jumped up and slipped on my coat over my pajamas; Rachel did the same. Oddly, Pia's desire to go for a walk in a storm comforted me. A touch of normalcy; Pia out the door, full steam ahead.

Head down, she marched out onto the patio, where—momentarily knocked off-balance by the wind—she put her shoulders into it and soldiered off into the deluge toward the crashing waves.

Clasping her hood tight to her neck, Rachel called out, "Pia, what the fuck are you doing?" Barefoot, we sprinted after her, the soft sand dragging us back.

I could tell she was crying, even turned away from us, even with all that rain and wind. "I was going to train for this iron-woman thing, but I don't feel like iron," Pia choked out. "I'm a piece of marshmallow shit."

"Well, we all can't be—" I started.

She whipped around to face us. "I can't forgive myself!" she cried. "I keep looking for ways to tell myself it's all right, like it was just chance and shit happens and life is hard like that and tragic, but I can't! I killed her, you guys, you know it, and I'll understand, you know I'll understand if you never want to see me again or hang out or whatever, because things will never be right, never—"

"Hey, Pia, come on." Rachel rested her hand on Pia's shoulder. Pia wrenched herself away.

I blinked in the torrential rain, trying to see my friends' faces, but they were ghostly washed-out ovals. I thought about Pia at Sandra's funeral, how she had kept herself together better than any of us. It worried me more than if she had fallen apart.

"She saw through all of our bullshit, you know," Pia said. "Especially mine. All my jumping out of planes and shit, she knew I was trying to prove I'm Superwoman, when I'm not brave at all. I'm more scared all the time than anyone I know."

"We're all scared, Pia—"

"And Rachel—she knew you were a softy underneath all your tough crap. She saw that. And you were there for her with the cancer thing, and I just wasn't. I was fucking off somewhere in New Zealand or wherever. And Wini? You?" Pia looked at me, stricken. "With Marcus? I don't even *know* where I was. . . ."

"She loved you, Pia," Rachel called out into the wind. "She loved all the adventures you dreamed up and dragged us to. Come on, *you know that*! She was *game*. Always. Especially this time. Nobody wanted to be there with us on that river more than she did."

The rain slammed at us sideways. "Did you see her mother's face at the funeral? When she looked at me?" Pia pushed her sopping-wet bangs away from her eyes. *"Did you see her face?"*

We had. There was no forgiveness. All horror.

"And her kids, now, with no mother . . ." She seemed to crumple before us.

"You inspired her," I shouted, the wind sucking at my words. "She told me she was going to leave Jeff. You inspired her to be brave. She didn't get the chance, but her mind was made up."

"Oh, God." Pia covered her mouth with her hand. "Oh, dear God."

She turned away from us and started to walk toward the

pounding surf, but Rachel and I threw our arms around her and dragged her back, made her stay. We pulled her long, tall self down toward us and locked her in like that, until we became a solid unit of three, the rain drumming so hard on our backs it felt like a blessing.

The next morning, Rachel told us she had decided to become certified in neonatal care. She'd had it with car crashes and heart attacks and wanted to be around "new beginnings." As Pia and I congratulated her, I wondered what my big news was and realized it wasn't anything I could put into words. I had no grand announcements. I hadn't quit my job or found a new one. Couldn't recall the last time someone had winked at me on Match.com. If anything, there was an absence: Richard's ghost. He was simply gone from the apartment when I returned after our trip. The whole place felt lighter and full of air.

But I did have news, something precious and private. Being alone has a whole different flavor for me now. Solitude has turned into someplace I find sustenance instead of despair. No doubt the terrors will return, along with the old version of loneliness, the kind that guts me and sends me tumbling into the void, but for now it's not the case. I know now that more marvels than we can possibly imagine exist on earth—the trick is remembering this every day.

As I listened to my friends talk about their plans that Sunday morning, I couldn't wait to go home and free my paintings from the back corner of my closet where I'd tossed them in a fit of self-loathing the day Richard left; gaze into them—maybe find something beautiful in there to celebrate—maybe tear them all up and start over again. Either would be fine. I couldn't wait to hug my sweet fat Ziggy, feel his hot heart beating close to mine, stroke his cat head full of dreams of a freshly opened tuna can or of the chase and the kill.

Something else too. The fact is, I'm a middle-aged woman who should have middle-aged concerns, but I don't. Fear feels quaint somehow. I just don't have any these days. Now when I swim, I feel powerful and sleek and swift. I delight in my mass, in all that water I displace. I am this joyous creature plunging into my element: water. What difference does it make how old I am or what jeans I can fit into or how fast my roots come in? My aging body, my dull job. I mean, really, who cares?

I'm alive.

Acknowledgments

I would like to thank the entire team at Simon & Schuster for the infinite care taken with *The River at Night,* Jennifer Bergstrom for her encouraging words, and especially my brilliant editor, Kate Dresser at Scout Press, for her singular ability to inspire me to create my best work even when I want to stop at "good enough," for her unerring eye and almost supernatural intuition. To my wonderful and wise agent, Erin Harris at Folio Literary Management, incalculable respect and gratitude.

To everyone in Maine who put me up and answered countless questions, especially Danielle and George at the Eureka Hall Restaurant in Stockholm, I am indebted to you. Thanks also to the brave souls living off the grid who invited me into your buses, teepees, cabins, yurts, and boats to share your insights and inspire me with your impassioned individualism. A big nod to the state of Maine itself, as well as my apologies for the liberties I took with your geography.

To my beta readers who helped me through many a dark night (and day) of the soul, who saved me with your kindness and encouragement, or maybe a much appreciated kick in the ass, or both: Anne McGrail, Ray Bachand, Dona Bolding, Mary E. Mitchell, Glenn Skwerer, Steve Gentile, Lira Kanaan, Mary McGrail, Betsy Fitzgerald, Miranda Loud, Sandra Miller, Linda

Werbner, Marguerite McGrail, Valerie Spain, Matt McGrail, Collette Kellogg, Tasneem Zehra, and Jeffrey Steinberg. Special thanks and gratitude to Jude Roth for your unending support and enthusiasm.

Big nod to all the kind, patient librarians—everywhere!—but especially those at the Goodnow Library in Sudbury, and the Cary Memorial Library in Lexington who put up with my insistence on nabbing the quietest study rooms.

I am forever grateful to my friends and family for your love and encouragement. You make my world brighter in countless sweet ways.

Finally, this book would not have been written without my husband, George, who never allowed me to give up, and who gave me the priceless gift of time.

A Note on the Author

Erica Ferencik is a Massachusetts-based novelist and screenwriter. She holds a Masters in Creative Writing from Boston University and her essays have been featured in *Salon*, the *Boston Globe* and on National Public Radio.

EricaFerencik.com